HANNAH DOYLE is a bestselling author and journalist. She has written for national magazines and newspapers, spent five years working as a celebrity journalist at Reveal magazine in London and has appeared on TV and radio as a showbiz commentator. Hannah now lives in Sheffield with her husband and twin sons. *The A to Z of Us* is her third novel.

@byhannahdoyle
@byHannahDoyle
byHannahDoyle

The A to Z of Us

HANNAH DOYLE

ONE PLACE. MANY STORIES

HQ
An imprint of HarperCollins*Publishers* Ltd
1 London Bridge Street
London SE1 9GF

www.harpercollins.co.uk

HarperCollins*Publishers*
1st Floor, Watermarque Building, Ringsend Road
Dublin 4, Ireland

This paperback edition 2021

1

First published in Great Britain by
HQ, an imprint of HarperCollinsPublishers Ltd 2021

ISBN: 9780008441722

MIX
Paper from
responsible sources
FSC
www.fsc.org   FSC C007454

This book is produced from independently certified FSC™ paper
to ensure responsible forest management.

For more information visit: www.harpercollins.co.uk/green

Printed and bound in Great Britain by
CPI Group (UK) Ltd, Croydon, CR0 4YY

For Love

Art Exhibition

Alice

There's crap *everywhere*. Hair bobbles. Half a Babybel. A lipstick with the lid missing. In the middle of the mess sits my best friend, frantically excavating the contents of her bag. She seems oblivious to the fact that she's just silenced an entire art exhibition by shouting 'YOU ABSOLUTE TOOL' into the room and yet the once noisy venue is now pin-drop quiet, all eyes turned on her as she props up the bar. I suppose art lovers aren't used to being interrupted by angry blonde women like this. The soles of my trainers squeak as I rush over to her from the other side of the room.

Sensing that someone is coming to her aid, the crowd turn back to one another and resume their lofty chat, which is a relief all round because by the time I reach Natalie's side I can hear that she's peppering the air with some choice expletives. Even the unflappable bartender looks a bit nervous.

'Hey, what's wrong?' I puff, regretting the canapés I stuffed into my mouth before making the mad dash over here.

My best friend turns wild eyes to mine and then flicks them back in the direction of her phone, nestled in amongst the mess on the bar.

'Alice, I liked it,' she says, clawing at the sleeves of my dress.

1

'I *liked* it.'

I take a closer look. On Natalie's screen is an Instagram photo of her snuggled up to Jake, a couple of backpacks next to them as they stand at an airport's departures lounge. I note with alarm that it was posted in 2019.

This is not good news.

'You remember when Jake and I went to Venice not long after we got together? Well I just accidentally liked a photo of that trip. I mean, it was literally taken in a different decade. What am I going to do?'

'It's okay,' I soothe. 'Just double tap it.'

'I've been TRYING!' She stabs at her phone so hard I'm worried she's going to poke a hole through it. 'The screen has frozen so now this big red heart is glaring at me. Why did the people of Instagram have to choose a heart? It's so emotional. What's wrong with the good old-fashioned thumbs up of Facebook? Aren't they owned by the same company anyway? I've basically just told my ex-boyfriend that I *love* an old photo of us. So now . . .' Having apparently run out of words, my best friend holds her bag aloft in exasperation.

'Now you're searching for your passport so you can leave the country immediately and be free from the shame of it all?' I suggest.

'Exactly.'

'Right, breathe,' I rally. 'You won't find your passport in there. It's probably in a box back at my house you've labelled "personal" with your label-maker, tucked safely away in a folder called "private docs", subcategory "travel".'

'Now is not the time to mock me for being organised,' she huffs, slightly manic.

'Just trying to lighten the mood. I have never seen you happier than when that label-maker arrived but that's not the point right now. Let me help you fix this.' I give her a squeeze and together we restart Nat's phone, open Instagram back up and finally manage to unlike the pic.

Natalie slumps her head into her hands. 'Sorry, I didn't mean to snap at you. You've been my rock through this split. I'm not sure I'd still be standing without you, let alone have somewhere to live. It just sucks that now Jake knows I've been deep-sea diving through his timeline like a pathetic ex-girlfriend.'

'You are not pathetic,' I say firmly, pulling up a bar stool next to her. 'Look around you, Nat. This entire evening is down to you. You are a brilliant events planner and you should be incredibly proud of yourself for achieving this. I've never seen such a busy art exhibition and even the snooty art crowd here are impressed with it. Also the tiny food you organised is delicious. Only successful people organise tiny food. Have you had a tiny taco yet?'

At this, Natalie starts to cry. Dismayed, I search for a tissue among the contents of her bag which have been tipped onto the bar.

She sniffs. 'Tacos used to be our thing. Jake would make tacos and we'd watch comedies and now . . .'

'And *now* you're living with the current world title holder for Greatest Best Friend. I know it's tough Nat, but it's also a brand new chapter. One where you don't need to check in with Jake, or argue over whose turn it is to buy cereal, or pick up his soggy towels from the bedroom floor. Who needs a man anyway? You're operating on your own schedule!'

She brushes a tear away with a manicured finger and pats me fondly on the cheek. 'Oh you. My breezy, free-spirit of a best friend. So busy living life to the max that the thought of settling down or having kids isn't even on your radar. I know the idea of coupling up is awful for you. But we're all different Al and for me that stuff is important. I want the whole monogamy, marriage, and multiple children thing. Only it turns out that the guy I thought I was going to share it all with has decided that he's scared of commitment. After all this time together! I never thought at thirty I'd be back to sleeping in my best friend's spare room and pity-scrolling through photos of my old life.'

3

Not for the first time lately I find myself harbouring Very Bad Thoughts about Jake. I pull Natalie in for a cuddle. 'Heartbreak is gut-wrenchingly shit, I know, and I'm so sorry you're having to deal with this. But please don't let what Jake did make you give up? You are a strong and brilliant woman and you will be happy again, I promise you. That is not going to happen if all you do is sit at home getting snot on my PJs while we cry at *The Notebook*, though. It's time you started to look forward again. Put your hot damn phone away, stop mooning after the past and start living in the present.'

'Brutal.'

'Brutal but true. Or some may say, truetal,' I grin.

'You're a buffoon,' she says, the tiniest hint of a smile on her face.

'I know. And I love you. You will find what you're looking for, you just need to get through this messy bit first and the good news is, I'm here to help! So put that half-eaten Babybel in the bin, stop hiding at the bar and go be proud of all the hard work you've put into tonight.'

I usually spend my nights drinking with friends, eating with friends, dancing with friends or all of the above. Art exhibitions are a bit off-brand for me, though I rarely say no to a night out because I suffer from clinical FOMO and tonight I'm very much here for Natalie. I cast another glance in her direction to make sure she's doing okay and set about mingling myself. I relish a challenge and I'm determined not to be intimidated by the aloof arty bunch here. It's the first showing of an up-and-coming artist's latest work, apparently, so Natalie and her company have hired out this event space for the occasion. Everyone in attendance is wearing black or grey so I do stand out a bit in my canary yellow dress but I will not let a muted colour palette put me off. Tonight I'm going to transform into a high-brow appreciator of the arts! Take this black square hanging on the wall, for example. So square-like! Just jam-packed with right angles.

4

A woman with gold-rimmed glasses and a severe haircut moves next to me.

'This one is practically unctuous,' she marvels. 'I've never felt closer to the Amalfi Coast. It's as if I'm sat by the sea, eating ragu and drinking an earthy red. What's the piece called?'

I peer at the tag underneath. 'Black Square.'

'Wow. Have you ever seen a less square-like square?'

I try to make informed, appreciative hmming noises but they come out as a splutter. So maybe my transformation into aesthete isn't quite complete. You'd think, as a florist, that I'd have an innate appreciation for all the arts. After all, most of my days are spent arranging bouquets, styling my little flower shop and taking pictures of commissions for social media. Stylish photos, I can do. Abstract art? Not so much. I'm not convinced Gold Glasses and I will have masses in common so I make my excuses and potter off to the loos, stopping at the entrance to take a shot of the beautifully arranged ivy hanging along one wall.

I tinker with the light and sharpness of the picture before uploading it to my flower shop's Instagram account and tapping in a caption.

Prettiest trailing ivy we ever saw! For the less green-fingered among you, there's good news. Ivy makes the perfect houseplant as it's practically unkillable. Want even more good news? Our houseplants are back in stock soon so stay tuned for more!

I add the usual hashtags and it doesn't take long before the likes start coming in, giving me a familiar buzz of pride. I set up an account when the shop opened so that I could share pictures of our displays, the shop itself and anything flower-related, really. It took off and I have a big following now which is amazing. My shop has featured on interiors influencers' blogs and I work on large displays for lots of Sheffield's independent shops, too. Customers can DM with enquiries and whenever I'm not in the shop, I'm usually to be found hunting for social media content.

However, flower inspo is not the main reason I'm here tonight. I'm on very important best friend business and I keep glancing over at Natalie to check she's okay. She's fighting hard to be her professional self, I can tell, but underneath it all she's still so sad. My last check-in confirmed that she's just had a peek at her phone and is now on the verge of tears. I'm so mad at Jake, I hate that he's done this to her. And I can confirm that pretending to be absorbed in the art (the piece I'm standing in front of now is called 'Red Circle') is not easy when you're actually plotting your first murder. Jake, frankly, is going to have to meet a sticky end and soon. When I look across again, Natalie is walking towards me, looking sheepish.

'Don't be cross, but Jake's just asked to meet,' she says.

'I hope you told him where to stick it.'

Natalie coughs. 'Um, no, I've agreed to go. Will you be okay here by yourself?'

'No I will not! You can't meet him now Nat, we're in the middle of an event you organised and you should stay 'til the end. Also, it's just not a good idea. He's made you sad enough, he doesn't deserve any more of your time.'

Natalie sighs. Her bag is already on her shoulder and she looks so lost that I want to bundle her into my arms forevermore. This is *exactly* why you should never fall in love, I remind myself. It opens you up to all kinds of emotional distress.

'I've checked with my boss and he's happy that everything is running smoothly.'

'Of course he is. He just turns up, drinks wine and takes all the credit for your hard work!'

Nat bites her lip. 'He does do that,' she concedes. 'But for once I'm grateful for it. I just need some answers.'

'Let me come with you to make sure you're okay? Maybe push

Jake under a bus as we say our goodbyes? You know, by mistake,' I say, making finger quotes around the last two words.

'I'll be fine,' she smiles. 'Stay, enjoy the art or at least enjoy the free bar. I'll see you later.'

Propping up that makeshift bar an hour later, I realise I'm quite drunk and have abandoned all hopes of "enjoying" the art. I take a sip of my third glass of wine. Or fourth? Can't be sure, the bartender just keeps topping me up now. The good news is that I'm fully invested in the conversation I've struck up with myself.

'And then she said something about ragu and the Amalfi Coast and earthy reds. I mean, talk about pretentious. It was a black square. It was even called 'Black Square'! Want to hear the best bit? It cost four hundred and fifty quid! The artist must be laughing all the way to the bank. I could literally have painted that myself,' I snort.

It dawns on me that the man on the bar stool next to mine has been listening for some time, his deep green eyes looking at me intently.

'That's interesting, because 'Black Square' *was* inspired by the Amalfi Coast. My family are Italian,' he says.

I'm confused. Who is this absolute snack sat next to me?

'I don't think we've met,' he smiles, holding out a hand. 'I'm Zach and this is my exhibition.'

I blink. Surely . . .

'I'm the artist,' he clarifies.

'Oh god. I'm so sorry,' I cringe, taking his hand and shaking it a little too enthusiastically. 'I'm Alice and as you can tell, I really don't know anything about this kind of art. I'm sure your work totally is full of . . . ragu?'

Zach laughs and I find my gaze lingering on the tangle of dark hair framing his handsome, angular face. The intense eyes peering through inky lashes. I beam back, enjoying the way his laugh makes me feel like I've just stepped into the sunshine.

'This is the first time I've displayed my work like this, with a big opening night I mean,' he's saying. 'Or, it *was*. We're the last people here now.'

I peer around us and realise that he's right. 'Well, congratulations! Did tonight go well?'

Can art exhibitions go "well", I wonder.

'I think so . . .' He pauses, looking deep in thought as he drains the last of his drink.

I've upset him. Natalie's going to kill me! She's always telling me off for being bullish and now I've offended the artist who's employed her to plan his first big event.

'I'm clearly a philistine and really didn't mean any offence,' I backtrack. But as he catches my eye I see there's an unmistakable glint in his.

He laughs, pushing his hair back from his face. 'Don't worry about it. I'm going to take heart from the fact that I made a couple of sales tonight, so hopefully not everyone took one look at my work and decided they could do something similar at home with a pot of paint.'

'I'd say a piece of paper and a sharpie would do the trick,' I tease.

'Oh I see,' he grins at me, clutching at his heart and pretending to be wounded. 'Will my tortured soul and bruised ego ever recover?'

'Poor soul,' I wink, enjoying the rush of adrenaline you get when you meet someone new. Chatting to new people is one of my favourite things and I'm not sure I've ever had the pleasure of hanging out with a hot-yet-brooding artist before. 'Perhaps I could help with the recovery process?'

'I'm not sure I can take any more of your searing art critiques, Alice.'

The way he says my name.

'I'll go easy on you. Besides, you made some sales so you should be celebrating. Why don't we nick a bottle of prosecco before the caterers leave? I don't want to brag but I did get an

A for my art A Level and if you're lucky, I might give you some tips for your next exhibition.'

Zach shakes his head, his eyes staying on me the entire time, and I realise that I'm very much here for the way his eyes train on mine. It's incredibly sexy and full of possibility.

Damn the mix of a free bar and tiny food! I must remember to give Natalie some feedback before the next event she plans, that free bars should be accompanied by regular sized food to soak it all up with and stop everyone getting too drunk. I might be a bit tipsy. But at least I'm only still here for selfless purposes, namely cheering up this tortured artist. I'm categorically not still here because I think he's kind of handsome. Nope.

Besides, I think it's working. He seemed lost in thought when we met and that cloud has lifted since we took up residence on the floor in the middle of the venue.

'Papier-mâché truly is an understated art form,' I point out, legs crossed under me, hands covered in gloop. 'Who'd have thought I'd be fashioning a papier-mâché moon at an art exhibition with the artist himself when I left the house earlier. I love how evenings turn out sometimes.'

'That's meant to be a moon? Looks a bit phallic,' Zach says, eyebrow raised.

'How dare you.'

'So Alice, what brought you here tonight if you're not into my work? I noticed you taking pictures of the plants over by the loos earlier and I couldn't quite figure out why.'

Embarrassing. But also nice to know he'd been looking over at me.

'I did not come for the loos, if that's what you were wondering,' I chuckle. 'That was just me taking a picture for Instagram. I actually came along to support my friend Natalie. She works for the events company who organised tonight.'

Zach nods. 'She did a great job, I must email her to say thanks.

9

The venue, the food . . . did you try those tiny tacos?' His soulful eyes widen in appreciation.

'I loved those tiny tacos! She had to leave early for a personal emergency but I'm sure she'd really appreciate your email.'

'Is she ok?'

'Yeah, she's just got some stuff going on. A case of ex-boyfriend dickheaditis.'

'Ah I've heard that's quite common. I'm sure she'll make a full recovery.'

'I hope so. I've prescribed a lot of time wallowing while watching sad films on Netflix. I was hoping tonight might kickstart a new chapter for her but, I don't know . . . Breaking up with people sucks, apparently.'

'Apparently?' He repeats, rubbing his jawline.

'I haven't done much of it myself.'

'Ah, so you're the heartbreaker?'

'Um, I don't think so.'

'So you're one of these smug settled types with a long-term boyfriend and no relationship drama?'

I shake my head. 'No, not smugly settled down.'

'You haven't found The One yet?'

'That's a very personal question, Zach. Can I let you into a secret? I'm not convinced The One exists,' I whisper.

'And why's that?' he whispers back, his brows furrowed as he looks at my quizzically.

'I guess I just feel like my job and my friends are enough. I'm happy, you know? Right now my best friend can't even find the lid to her lipstick, and let me tell you that she is normally incredibly organised, and that's all because she's had her heart broken. I guess that's just a reminder that love is hard.' I pause, realising that if I don't get down from my soapbox soon this handsome man might run off before I've had the chance to enjoy his company a little longer. 'I'm a bit of a cynic when it comes to all that,' I add with a shrug.

'So you've sworn off love because it might cause havoc with your make-up?' When Zach smiles his eyes crease, ramping up that ruggedly handsome thing he's got going on.

I feel the thrill of anticipation shoot through me. 'You know what I mean!'

He'd been sitting with his legs kicked out in front of him, leaning back on his arms, but now he shifts to mirror me.

'Well, I hear what you're saying,' he says thoughtfully. 'But I'm more the "I love love" type. There's nothing like that feeling of connection, of adventure, of finding another person who you can't get enough of. It's . . . it's the whole point, really.'

His eyes light up as he talks and for a split second, the passion and intensity in his voice makes me wonder if he's actually right. Then I remember that he is categorically not. We couldn't be more different and yet for some reason I want to stay right here in his company, all night long. And that's when I remember my trump card.

'I don't think I've met a woman who carries a pack of Uno around with her at all times before,' Zach laughs as I fold my arms in mock-protest. We're five rounds in and I am not winning.

'I can't believe this. I'm usually the champion of all Uno players ever.'

'The score speaks for itself,' Zach grins. 'Four wins for me. Does that make me the champion of all Uno players ever?'

He's a tease *and* he has a competitive streak? I congratulate myself on suggesting a card game before we called it a night. We play some more, me getting increasingly competitive as his winning streak continues.

'Lady luck is shining on you tonight,' I say as he calls out 'Uno' again.

Zach looks up from his cards, his eyes locking onto mine.

'I am very much inclined to agree with you,' he says after a pause. 'How can I say this without it sounding awful? I'm very sorry that your friend is having a hard time but I'm also . . . quite pleased?'

I drop my own cards. 'What? Don't make me add you to my hit list, Zach.'

'You have a hit list?'

'Yes I do. Natalie's ex-boyfriend is the only one on there . . . for now.'

'Okay, I get it. Don't mess with Alice's friends. I'll make a mental note of that for next time. Look, I don't know about you but tonight has been exactly what I needed. I've had a lot of fun.' Our eyes move over to the papier-mâché penis/moon now discarded on the floor next to us and he bites back another laugh. 'Thank you for my art lesson. I will keep it all in mind when I'm back in the studio. As non-dates go, this has been a good one. And, well . . . I'm wondering if you'd like to do it again some time?'

'Are you saying you'd like another art lesson?'

'How about a proper date?' He suggests. 'The things is, I've been thinking about my chance meeting with Alice at the art exhibition tonight. How our names bookend the alphabet. So maybe we should do something beginning with B next time, work our way through the alphabet . . .'

Alice and Zach. He's right. I feel my cheeks flushing as I'm struck by his thoughtfulness. I don't think anybody has asked me out quite like that before. Usually it's the offer of a drink down at the pub, or maybe a dinner, though I generally avoid dinner for a first date because what if I realise my date is awful before I've even made my order and then we have to endure an ENTIRE MEAL of awkwardness.

Zach's watching me, looking adorably expectant and hopeful in equal measure, and it dawns on me that there have been no why-did-I-order-a-starter regrets here, tonight. He's right. As non-dates go, this has been perfect.

'Did you just invite me on twenty-six dates?' I finally manage. 'Because that's quite keen.'

12

'I am keen,' he says, more confidently now.

WOW. This guy is cute. I've had way more fun than I expected tonight and it would be fun to do this again. I mean, there's no way we'll make it to the twenty-sixth date, because of my strict three date maximum policy, but one or two more chances to hang out with Zach could be a *lot* of fun.

'Let's stick with one for now,' I reply, taking a sip of my drink to cool myself down. 'But it will have to be good for us to get to C.'

'I'll take my chances. And if we do get to C then you have to choose a date, so the pressure will be on you.' One side of his mouth is curving into a sexy-as-hell smile.

Right then my phone beeps, forcing me to break eye contact.

Back at yours. Jake's seeing someone else. I hate everything.

I frown. 'It's Natalie. She needs me. I'm going to have to go.'

'I hope she's okay,' he says, the genuine concern in his voice drawing me to him even more.

'Well, it's been a pleasure to meet you, Zach.'

'You too,' he replies, pressing a business card into my hand. Now that we're both standing, I notice that Zach is a good foot taller than me. He leans down, stubble brushing my skin as he drops a goodbye kiss on my cheek.

'See you at B,' he says, voice low, breath hot against my face.

As I walk towards the bus stop, I turn the business card over in my hand.

He's scribbled on the back.

'A-Z. Call me.'

Bookshop

Zach

One wrong move can make the difference between a piece of art I'm proud of and something that gets booted over towards the bin in my studio. One bad stroke of the paintbrush can write off a week or a month's hard work. It's as simple as that. And then there's the opposite, when everything seems to turn on a pinpoint because of one *right* move.

That's exactly how I feel about the day Alice danced into my life.

I'd been incredibly anxious before the exhibition that night, battling imposter syndrome and a whole load of other crap too. And then right when I'd least expected it, along came this beautiful woman dressed in bright yellow. Alice was like a sunbeam breaking through the clouds and I haven't been able to stop thinking about her since.

Now she's walking towards me, the fabric of her blue dress blowing in the light summer breeze. A confident smile spreads across her face and she peers up at the bookshop I'm standing outside.

'So you didn't go for bondage then?' Alice jokes, disarming me with a sentence just like last time.

'Bondage?' I cough, looking apologetically at a couple of shoppers walking past us.

'Our A to Z theme! B for bondage?'

14

'Thought it might be a *bit* much for a second date? Though we can always change our minds?' I suggest, recovering myself with what I hope is a playful wink.

'You've missed your chance now,' she teases, her cheeks going a pretty shade of pink.

'You look really nice,' I say.

Nice? Come on, Zach! You could have chosen something better than *nice*.

'Thank you. It's good to see you again,' Alice stands on her tiptoes to kiss me on the cheek. Her hair's tucked behind a pink hairband and she smells like green apples. 'So, what *are* we doing at a bookshop?'

'I was in here the day after you and I met,' I explain. 'I'd come in to pick up a book on pop art and decided to stop at the bookshop's café to read it. But about half an hour later I realised I spent most of the time ignoring the book and thinking about you.'

'You smooth-talker!'

'I promise it's true. I had a lot of fun that night.' I sneak a look at her and see that she's smiling at me. 'And . . . you said something about fresh chapters which really resonated with me.'

'Oh? You mean when I was telling you about Natalie and her ex-boyfriend issues?'

'It reminded me that even when things aren't necessarily going to plan, you can always turn the page and start a new chapter. So here I was, trying to get some research done and failing spectacularly because I couldn't stop thinking about you, when it dawned on me that this bookshop could be perfect for our first proper date. We could browse the books, pick one for each other to read and . . . maybe start our own new story?'

That sounded cheesy didn't it?

Alice is leaning against the bookshop's window, watching me with her mouth slightly open.

The nerves kick back in and I make a show of shrugging the idea off.

'Yeah, no, it's a lame idea. We could do something else instead? Bowling? Bird-watching? Obviously not bird-watching, that's even worse.'

What the hell? I'm babbling now.

After a painfully long pause, Alice playfully bumps her shoulder into mine then says, 'You can't stop thinking about me, huh?'

Sometimes I worry that I'm too much of an open book. Growing up, all my friends operated on a 'treat them mean, keep them keen' policy but I was never good at playing games in relationships because I will always wear my heart on my sleeve. It's not exactly worked out well for me and maybe I should learn to play it cooler but Alice *has* been on my mind. Although now I've said that out loud I'm feeling embarrassed. 'Also, the cinnamon buns in the café here are ridiculously good,' I add.

She laughs.

'I see your buns and raise you the apricot tarts. Have you tried one? They should be made illegal. I'd actually banned myself from coming here because I was using "flower research" as a shameless cover for my developing pastry habit. You're leading me astray today, Zach.'

Now that I can handle. Grinning, I take her hand and we head inside.

Right, I really need to improve my date chat and just relax. So far I've asked her if she reads much and cringed hard at myself for sounding like I've just googled 'questions to ask on a date'. Seeing Alice again has got me tied up with nerves and I try to remember a technique I've learned through running. It's pretty much just breathing, so perhaps calling it a technique is a bit much, but if I focus on that simple task I might stop talking crap and start being cool again. Or at least just be able to chill out enough to enjoy myself.

Luckily Alice appears to be undaunted by my shit chat. 'Reading is one of my favourite ways to wind down so a bookshop is the perfect date for me.'

'Good to hear. And after such a strong start, it looks like we are on track to make date three, then.' That's better! Flirty. I've got this.

'Well, don't get ahead of yourself, Zach,' she grins, letting me know that she's joking. Or at least I *think* she is. I'm struck with the impression that Alice has got the measure of me already. I do have a tendency to rush into things at a hundred miles an hour.

Alice is still chuckling about the fact that we've gone shopping for books on our second date when I pause by a display of Japanese literature.

'I think I'm choosing this one for you,' I say, handing it to her.

Alice takes the book from my hands and flips it over to read the back page. 'It says it's "a gripping tale of sixteenth century missionaries in Japan" Zach.' She turns to look at me, amusement etched across her face. 'I mean, come on! The word gripping sounds a bit misleading there.'

'It was very good, actually. If a *little* long,' I concede.

Alice flicks through. 'Over six hundred pages! I'd say that was six hundred pages too many on the topic of missionaries in Japan, no? Are you seriously telling me that this is what you read when you want to relax?'

Disarmed once again. At least let me pretend to be deep and interesting, Alice!

'All right,' I laugh. 'I do also read a lot of Scandinavian crime stories. The type of book where someone inevitably ends up dead in a bath in a beautiful fishing village in Sweden.'

She rubs her hands together. 'That's more like it! I was really getting into true crime documentaries before Nat moved in but she's not a fan.'

'Seriously? I'm into true crime too.' We lock eyes and I feel a spark of connection as we find common ground. 'Come with me.' I weave my fingers into hers as we make our way through the shop to the crime section, feeling like a teenager with my first crush all over again.

17

Having established that Alice's preferences lean towards the gorier, the better, I select the most gruesome book I can find while she deliberates what to pick for me. She has this endearing habit of chatting away, making me feel like we're floating along on a cloud of easy conversation. I guess it's a confidence thing. I'm constantly worried that I'll say something ridiculous whereas Alice seems so easy-going and free of insecurities.

'At first my mind went straight to *Sweet Valley High*,' she's saying. 'I devoured those books when I was younger, along with every Point Horror I could get my hands on. But I figured they would not be cool enough for Zach the artist . . .'

Her breezy confidence must be infectious because I find myself leaning in conspiratorially. 'I'm not so sure about that. If you ever tell anyone this, I will strongly deny it because I've a reputation to uphold . . .'

'Oh? Tell me! I'm quite good at keeping secrets.'

'How good?'

'Very good,' she bites her lip. I'm not sure she's telling the truth.

'I used to read Point Romances when I was younger,' I whisper.

Alice has bubbled over with glee. Her whole face radiates amusement and now I know exactly why I felt compelled to tell this beautiful girl one of my most embarrassing facts. Just seeing her laugh makes me feel good.

'*What*?! *You* read Point Romance?'

'Maybe one or two.' (At least a dozen).

'I am shook,' she says. And then, more quietly, almost to herself, 'You really are into love, huh.'

Will that put her off me, I wonder? She's a self-proclaimed cynic when it comes to 'The One' and I'm a closet romance reader. Thankfully I don't get the chance to dwell on it because whirlwind Alice has already moved on, bouncing us along to the contemporary fiction aisle to make her own selection.

* * *

18

Not wanting our date to end, I'd asked Alice if I could persuade her to ditch her pastry ban and now we're sat in the café area chatting away, our new purchases on the table. Alice is busy recounting an ongoing argument she's been having with the pigeon in her garden – 'I call it the Big Shitter because it keeps pooing on the washing line and our tumble dryer has broken . . .' – and I'm trying hard not to smile. Listening to her talk is like watching champagne being poured into a glass. Even a story about a shitting pigeon is made effervescent by Alice who fizzes her way through conversations with a carefree energy.

'It's not funny, Zach! I spent an hour with a new client before I noticed that I had bird poo on my shoulder.'

'Tell me more about being a florist,' I say, watching her eyes light up as she talks about her business.

'I set my own shop up in my twenties and it's been pretty intense ever since. I'm up early every morning and often work after the shop has shut for the day dealing with order enquiries. I just feel really lucky that I've managed to turn a passion into a career.'

'It sounds like you're being incredibly modest. It takes a lot of hard work to start your own successful business. You should be proud of yourself.'

'Thank you,' she beams. 'I am. But look at you, people pay for the artwork you create. That's awesome.'

'What's that? Not teasing me about my art that someone with a piece of A4 paper and sharpie could have done today?' I laugh as she takes a bite of her bun. 'Seriously though, thank you. It's hard to turn creative interests into something to live off but I'm so glad I have a job I love. What got you into flowers?'

For a brief second, a shadow crosses her face but she dismisses it, taking a sip of her coffee. 'When I was a kid, my dad would come home with a new bunch of flowers for my mum every Friday night. Sometimes flowers he'd picked from the garden, sometimes a bouquet from a shop. Then we'd gather in the kitchen, arranging them into jam jars and I'd dot them around the house. It was my favourite part of the week.'

I find myself lost in the image of Alice's childhood. It sounds like everything I didn't have.

'I worked part-time at a florist's while I was at uni and spotted a gap in the market for something more appealing to the younger market. The shop's become a bit of an Instagram hotspot now because it looks really cute, if I say so myself. We have rows of flowers in old wooden crates on display outside, under a green and white-striped awning. Inside there's a neon sign against one wall which customers love to take pictures next to, a mesh wall stuffed with our latest arrangements and a massive oak table at the back which we use to wrap up bouquets. I found it at an antiques shop in town. People come to me from all over Sheffield just to buy a bunch and take photos of the shop floor. We've got a big online following and I get commissions from all around Yorkshire.'

'It's amazing you've built up the business like that.'

She smiles proudly. 'It's been hard work. I bet you can relate to that?'

'God yes,' I laugh. 'When I finished uni I quickly realised that no one was going to pay a total unknown for his art so I took a job in a coffee shop, working as many shifts as I could and spending every spare hour painting in a corner of the bedroom I rented off a friend. The light in there was shocking! I spent a lot of time worrying that I'd never become a real artist, that I'd have to give up the dream and get a "proper job", but I was really lucky because a local art gallery decided to run an exhibition of up and coming talent and that was my big break, really. I started getting commissions and one thing led to another. It felt like a long slog but I'm so happy to be able to rent my own studio space now.'

'And you've just had your own exhibition! I love that,' grins Alice.

'And I'm no longer inflicting my coffee-making skills on the people of Sheffield, so it really is a win win.'

'It's a steep learning curve, isn't it?' she says. 'I mean, I had no idea about the business side of things when I started out, but it's also super rewarding. Sometimes I feel like I have so many ideas of where I'd like to take it next that I'm actually going to burst.'

'Well, please don't burst just yet. I'm having way too much fun.'

'Don't worry, I am strictly off duty for our date.'

'In that case I consider myself extremely lucky. You're right, by the way.'

'Oh?' She says, her fingers curling playfully around her coffee cup.

'The apricot tart *is* a winner.'

She laughs then, taking a bite out of her cinnamon bun.

'Dunno, these are pretty good too. You have excellent taste in pastries, Zach.'

Normally I struggle chatting to new people but not with Alice. We've already spent a couple of easy hours together and I'm keen to carry on but when one of the staff starts clearing our table around us, I have to admit defeat.

'I had fun,' she says, her eyes turning up to me as we leave. 'And I'm excited for this Scandi crime. Though I'm worried it might give me lots of ideas for Nat's ex-boyfriend's brutal demise.'

'Just to be clear, you're not actually a murderer, are you?'

'Just to be clear, you're not actually an avid Point Romance reader, are you?' She bats back and I turn to face her as we wait at the bus stop.

'I can't help being an old romantic.'

Just kiss her! I tell myself.

'I'll let you into a secret,' she whispers. 'I'm not actually a murderer. I do, however, harbour grudges on behalf of the people I love.'

'Well then, I intend to do nothing which could encourage such grudge-harbouring on our next date.'

'You're assuming there's going to be another one?'

21

'I'm hoping there will be.'

There's a very long pause and I feel that familiar sense of dread rising in the pit of my stomach. Maybe I've imagined it and it hasn't gone as well as I thought. Maybe Alice hasn't had a good time and was just waiting until she could leave. Now would be the perfect time to kiss her but what if she's about to friendzone me?

'You'd better leave me to arrange a C date,' she smiles.

Relief washes over me. We're on for another date. What a bloody result! I'm so happy she wants to do this again.

Alice is looking deep into my eyes now and I don't need any further cues.

This is the moment to kiss her. Be confident and go for it, I tell myself. I lean down to do what I've wanted to do since we met, to feel her lips against mine. As my face draws closer I can smell the apples of her shampoo mixing with cinnamon. When our faces are almost touching I pause, wanting to savour the moment, training my eyes back on hers.

But, wait, she's not actually looking at me at all.

She's looking over my shoulder. I follow her gaze and spot the bus pulling up next to us, its doors opening by my side.

Argh.

I'm attempting to style it out when her eyes really do meet mine. 'On time for once,' she says with a tut as I straighten up, trying not to look like I was just about to make out with the side of her face. God.

'Are you getting on or not?' booms the driver.

'I'd better . . .' she says, motioning towards the open doors.

'Yep,' I say, holding my palm up for a high five.

A *high five*. I've gone from a missed kiss to a high five faster than a sports car goes from zero to ninety. As the bus pulls away I give the curb a sullen kick, lamenting the unbelievably not-smooth end to our date.

Comedy Show

Alice

As usual, my stomach is rumbling long before it's acceptable to start eating lunch. Friday mornings are extra busy in the shop as our customers stock up on fresh flowers ahead of the weekend. I love to see their delighted faces when we hand over expertly arranged seasonal bouquets, but even that hasn't stopped me thinking about the halloumi salad I prepped first thing.

EAT ME, ALICE!

Stop talking to me, food!

'Uh oh, is your lunch calling to you again?' Eve asks from her spot by the till. 'You've got that borderline hangry look on your face. I'm more than happy to hold the fort if you want an early lunch break?'

'You're an angel,' I say, so grateful I could kiss her though I'm pretty sure that would be overstepping the employer/employee boundaries. I congratulate myself daily on hiring Eve. She's brilliant with the customers and is much better at maths than me which comes in very handy with things like, you know, running a business. Pottering into our little kitchen to make a cup of herbal tea, I grab my lunchbox from the fridge and head into the courtyard out back. The sun is peeking through the clouds and I'm about to dive head-first into lunch when my phone rudely interrupts me with a message.

ALICE! Very excited to see you tonight. Shall we do drinks after the show?

DYLAN! I tap back. *Yes please. I want to make the most of you while you're back because it doesn't happen very often.*

Pointed as ever, Pickle. But I know. I miss home a lot.

Yes, it must be so very tough being famous and living in London now. Don't forget I've seen the size of your duplex.

And you haven't stopped taking the piss out of my wine fridge since.

Let's not forget the jacuzzi bath, the glass stairway. I could go on . . . I type with a grin. *The fact that one of my closest friends now lives in such luxury will never fail to amaze me.*

Which is exactly why I'm coming home to see you this time. Me and my flat can't take any more criticism.

I'm proud of you really. But also, bullshit! You're coming back for a gig because real people have paid to watch you make jokes. Are you staying with your folks?

Yep, got back earlier and Mum's gone into overdrive.

Give her a squeeze from me? How long are you back for?

Just the weekend. I start filming again on Monday.

FFS.

Sorry Pickle.

Will they be rolling out the red carpet for you tonight?

HAR HAR. I can ask them to roll one out for my special guest though. You want a plus one?

Yes please.

How is Natalie?

She's okay, not great. It's a long story. The ticket's not for Natalie though. I'm bringing a guy. DO NOT BE CRINGE ABOUT IT.

My screen informs me that Dylan is typing, shortly followed by cheesy GIFs of teddy bears holding hands and rabbits shooting carrots through love hearts. I knew this would happen.

😒 *Have you finished?*

A love interest?

Don't mention the "l" word! Bloody hell.

All right! Tell me more . . .

He's called Zach, he's an artist.

Do you want him to paint you like one of his French girls?

Hope the jokes are going to be better tonight. See you later!

I'm about to exit the chat when I panic and hastily add: *Please don't turn it into a big deal. Repeat after me . . . NBD. It's really early days and I'm not sure where we stand.*

Leadmill at 8 p.m., types Dylan. **No Big Deal's on the guest list.**

As I pop my phone away and start munching, I mull over where things do stand with Zach. I'd sworn there were sparks throughout our last date and really thought we'd end it with a kiss, so the awkward high five was kind of a let-down. I'm usually pretty good at reading people but maybe this time I've misread the signs and let's face it, I am no pro in the dating department. Perhaps Zach is just one of those super-hot guys who flirts with everyone? I dip the herbal tea bag in and out of the hot water in my mug absent-mindedly. I guess it would be simpler if Zach just wanted to be mates, though I feel strangely disappointed by the idea.

Throngs of people mill about close to the venue, that familiar hum of anticipation growing louder by the minute as I'm waiting to meet Zach for our third date. Or just-friends hang-out . . . whatever.

'Hi,' Zach says confidently as he appears next to me.

'Hi!' I smile back. I've never known Zach to wear anything other than dark, loose-fitting T-shirts with rolled-up sleeves but tonight he's pulled on a lightweight jumper which falls perfectly on his shoulders. I can see the definition of his lean body underneath. His wild hair's been pushed back and tortoiseshell glasses frame his face. Even if we are just going to end up as friends, there's no harm in him being so handsome. A friend can *definitely* think their friend is good-looking *amiright*?

'It's so busy here tonight, how did you manage to get tickets? I'd heard it sold out within hours.'

'I have a confession, I know the comedian,' I say as we weave our way to pick up our tickets. 'He's my best friend, we grew up together. He's not back that often now but the timing seemed perfect . . . comedy night for our C date and we can all hang out after the show.'

'You're *friends* with Dylan Smith?'

'Yes and he's very lucky to have me.'

'No doubt. Whenever I stay at my brother's house we always end up watching his TV show. My sister-in-law Ellie thinks he's hilarious and, I suspect, has a massive crush on him too.'

I laugh. 'Don't mention that to Dylan, he's got a big enough head already!'

Zach and I are sat close to the stage and he's howling with laughter as Dylan makes jokes about the realities of being a Yorkshireman in London. I'm so proud of him though it's always a bit weird seeing the boy who used to come around to my house to raid the Mini Milks in the freezer on stage as one of the hottest comedians around.

As Zach reaches out to grab his drink I feel his hand accidentally graze mine. My fingers tingle in response and I'm convinced that sparks are flying again, which sends my brain into a sudden tailspin. I think there's chemistry but does he like me back? And why do I want him to when I know that tiny sparks can lead to big fires which hurt people? Oh my god, I need to chill out. It is not like me to overthink things. Turning my attention back to the stage, I focus on watching Dylan's friendly face make people laugh and I stand up along with everyone else as his set draws to a close, the venue filling with applause.

'What did you think?' I ask Zach over the din.

'He's really funny,' he smiles back at me. 'Plus I love live comedy, so that was a good shout for our C date . . .'

'Great!'

'Listen . . . Alice, I was wondering if you fancied . . . grabbing . . . just the—'

I can't hear what he's saying, it's that loud in here, but I feel my phone vibrating so I pull it out of my pocket, smiling apologetically at Zach for having interrupted him. 'I've just got a text from Dylan,' I shout, pointing at my phone and then back to the now-empty stage in a kind of sign language. 'He says do we want to go grab drinks at Public. DRINKS.' I throw back an imaginary shot. Zach frowns so I motion for us to head outside.

'Dylan's suggesting drinks.' I say when it's quieter. 'Is that ok with you? Sorry, what were you saying in there?'

'No, I was just chatting rubbish. Yeah, if you want to go for drinks with Dylan let's do that.'

The streets are full of people spilling out of pubs and bars to make the most of the warm early summer air.

'It feels like I'm on holiday,' I say as we make our way to the bar.

'I was thinking the same thing,' Zach replies.

'It's amazing how Sheffield can do that. I love this city.'

'Ah, it's being in your company that does it for me.'

Oh that's cute. That's definitely not something a guy says to you when he just wants to be mates, right?! We've reached the bar now and I turn to face Zach, the questions ricocheting around my mind coming to a stop when our eyes lock. Slowly, he reaches an arm around my back and I step closer, neither of us losing eye contact as I rest one hand on his chest.

This is *definitely* a kiss moment.

My heart starts to race and warmth pools at my back where Zach's fingers have found a tiny patch of skin between my top and my jeans. The feel of his touch on my bare skin is electric. He leans down ever so slowly and I tip my head up to meet his.

'PICKLE!'

The shout comes from across the street, causing us to pull apart. It's Dylan, striding towards us.

FFS Dylan.

'Oops, sorry, didn't mean to interrupt.' He winks at me as he realises what he's just gate-crashed.

'Pickle?' Zach says, eyebrows raised.

Bloody hell.

'He's called me that forever,' I explain. 'Zach, this is my deeply annoying friend Dylan. Dylan, this is Zach.'

Trust Dylan to suggest a former underground toilet for post-gig drinks, I think, grinning to myself as we wait outside. I'm sure you usually need to reserve a table here because it's pretty small but by some miracle we're sat down and perusing the cocktail menu within minutes.

'Sorry to interrupt,' a gorgeous woman approaches our table. 'I was just wondering if you two are together?' I'm sandwiched between Dylan and Zach on a small sofa and I realise that it's Dylan who has his arm draped behind my back.

'Oh, no,' I reply hastily.

'Just good friends,' Dylan grins, scribbling his number on a piece of paper he finds in his wallet and handing it to her before she walks off. Dylan is one randy doggo.

'Dylan has his own fan club,' I explain, rolling my eyes at Zach. 'The Twitter handle is something like HeckYeahDylanSmith and I occasionally send screengrabs of it over to him. Some of the chat is obscene.'

Zach smiles as he listens but I can sense that Dylan's territorial behaviour has annoyed him. Every now and then his eyes dart towards Dylan's arm around me and I think back to the woman who just came over, inwardly cringing. I guess it's a bit awkward that I got mistaken for Dylan's date, rather than Zach's. I lean back, trying to surreptitiously nudge Dylan's arm out of the way and scoot closer to Zach, but there's not much room for scooting on our little sofa. Plus Dylan has insisted on sitting with his legs spread wide as per usual.

'Never mind my fan club,' Dylan says, ignoring my nudges and reaching his arm even further round my shoulder. He's never been great at reading a scene. 'Tell me what's going on with Natalie?'

'Urgh, Jake is an absolute fool,' I say with a shake of my head. 'Turns out he was seeing someone else behind her back for a while before he ended it and it's all been unravelling over the past few months. I'm trying to take her mind off the split but every time we seem to make progress he gets back in touch and she can't resist. It's like she's deliberately hurting herself by meeting up and listening to him explain every single detail of what happened.'

Zach leans forward, resting his arms on his knees. 'Sometimes break-ups are like that. Sometimes you want answers to questions. And sometimes you surprise yourself by realising that something you thought was huge was actually nothing at all.'

My attention turns straight back to Zach and I have to say, I admire him. Here we are talking about someone he doesn't know and he's still making an effort, joining in with the conversation with his own personal experiences.

'Definitely agree there, mate,' Dylan replies. 'I had a bad break-up once, I didn't want it to end and it was like: "Why am I not good enough for you?" Maybe Nat could do with some time away? I could ask if she wants to come and stay with me for a bit. You're both always welcome and a change of scene might be good. What do you think?'

'That's a great idea,' I reply, deciding it's time to steer us towards a conversation where we can all join in, but Zach gets in there first.

'So you guys are all friends from school?' he asks.

'Alice and I were next-door-neighbours,' explains Dylan. 'We met Natalie at school.'

'You must have got up to all kinds of trouble together?'

Dylan's face lights up. 'Oh me and Pickle got up to all sorts,' he laughs, shooting Zach a look. I feel like there's weird energy between these two tonight, even though it's all jokes and smiles right now.

29

'Tell me more,' Zach says, signalling for another round.

'Okay,' Dylan rubs his hands together gleefully. 'Where shall we start? The time when we "borrowed" a tractor we found in a nearby field and ended up trashing a lot of hay? The farmer was furious.'

'That was your fault!' I say. 'Dylan insisted it would be good practice for when we could drive and we ended up working a *lot* of summer jobs to pay the farmer back.'

'Or the time you really got into tie-dye and decided that you should set up your own clothes range?'

'I made Dylan and Nat model the T-shirts,' I giggle.

'We looked horrendous,' laughs Dylan. 'Remember that summer we went over to France with your folks and I had to rescue you from the kayak instructor who took such a shine to you that he kept turning up at the house your parents rented?'

'I'd forgotten about him!'

'Creepy kayak guy.' We're roaring with laughter at the memories and now Dylan's on a roll, deciding to unleash the majority of his most embarrassing material in one giant dump and practically giddy with amusement. Thankfully Zach doesn't seem too put off by the fact that I spent two solid years insisting that I was a unicorn called Barry. But I give Dylan a short, sharp jab in the ribs to make him stop. Besides throwing me under the bus good and proper, he's also been hogging the limelight and not giving Zach a chance to get a word in.

'Oh and she was always hungry,' Dyl laughs, very much not stopping. 'The kind of kid who'd hoover up a whole roast dinner and still have space for three helpings of pudding. I once caught her eating pickles out of a jar in the fridge as a mid-morning snack, hence the nickname. My mum had to buy twice as much food when Alice was coming over.'

'That is not accurate,' I protest. 'Besides I just like puddings.'

Dylan pulls me in for a hug, laughing. As I playfully push him away, I spot Zach watching Dylan intently, as if he's trying to weigh him up. They are so different, after all. Dylan loves to showboat and Zach seems much happier sitting back.

'Did you go over a lot, then?' Zach asks me.

'Loads. Dylan's mum sort of took me under her wing for a while.'

As always when things get a little too close for comfort, Dylan deftly sweeps in. He's been doing it since I was a teenager and I love him very much for it. Although despite my dig in the ribs, he's also continuing to plough on with his Embarrassing Alice material, which I love him a little bit less for.

'She was bossy, strong-willed, had absolutely no filter whatsoever. She can still be bloody brutal. But she's also the most kind-hearted, loyal, fun-loving person I've ever met.'

'Thanks Dyl. That's definitely enough chat about me now.'

'But I haven't told Zach about our first house party. Remember? You drained all the alcopops, puked in your dad's wellies and . . .'

'NOT TODAY, SATAN.'

'Okay, okay,' Dylan holds his hands up. 'Actually, I might leave you lovebirds to it. The woman from earlier has messaged.'

I get up to give him a hug and watch as he and Zach give each other a frosty hand shake. We say our goodbyes and I ask Zach if he fancies one for the road.

'I actually have to be up early for work tomorrow. I've just taken on a new portrait commission and the client is coming for their first sitting in the morning . . .'

'Oh . . . no worries,' I say.

Zach finishes his drink and fixes his eyes on me. 'But perhaps I could walk you home first?'

As we walk through the empty streets, Zach hesitantly brushes my hand and I entwine my fingers in his. Normally I'd have batted the offer of being walked home away because been I'm strong, independent and perfectly capable of getting to places on my own. But I got the impression that Zach wasn't doing it out of any misplaced chivalry, or a means to an end, he just wanted to spend more time with just me, and I liked that.

'We're here,' I say, reaching into my bag to find my keys.

'Unmistakably Alice's house,' Zach says, looking up at my rented terrace.

'Why do you say that?'

'It's picture perfect . . . like you.' He looks at the cherry blossom growing in the little patch of earth out front, the hanging baskets either side of my front door, and the little picket fence around the tiny front garden.

'I know it's kind of twee but I love it. I painted the fence in rainbow colours because . . .' I trail off. We're so close now that I've completely lost the thread of what I was saying. Zach's started circling his index finger around my palm. As I move closer still I can smell fabric softener mixed with citrus fruits on his skin. I can feel the tips of his fingers retrace their steps from earlier, swirling around the patch of skin at the base of my back. Now they're walking up my spine and I hear his breath quickening. There are no interruptions now. No buses pulling up. No best friends with impeccably bad timing.

Just me and Zach.

I have never been the type to think you should wait for a guy to kiss you first. If I want something, I'll go for it.

And right now I *want* Zach.

I press myself against his body and tip my head up to his, my eyes trained on his full lips. Pushing up onto tiptoes, my whole body tingles as finally, finally, my lips find his. We kiss softly at first as if we're learning a new language together, before the kiss becomes more urgent, more passionate.

I pause, breathless.

Zach leans back, a smile curling at his lips.

'That was so good,' Zach says gruffly. He runs a hand through my hair, his fingers finding my earrings. 'I think we need to do it again. Just . . . um, to make sure it wasn't a first time fluke.'

'Excellent idea,' I murmur, folding myself back into him.

In this moment, I forget about sparks being potential fire hazards, letting them ignite through my body as I feel myself being drawn into his orbit. As far as first kisses go, I already know that this will never be bettered.

Dog Walk

Zach

Well *that* was worth the wait. There's been a definite spring in my step ever since Alice and I kissed and I suspect people are starting to notice. This morning the barista at my regular coffee haunt even commented on how "chipper" I seemed as she handed over my flat white and I found myself muttering something about the good weather before making a sharp exit.

I *am* chipper, though. I'd liked to have been the one to get in there first, so to speak, but there was something incredibly sexy about Alice initiating that kiss. I was busy panicking that I still wasn't sure how she felt when she decided to take matters into her own hands.

'What's up with you?' Raff says, pulling me in off the street.

'That's no way to great your one and only brother,' I laugh.

'You look like you're in a dream world.'

I'm about to tell him that that's exactly how I feel when we both hear the thud of not-so-little footsteps thundering down the stairs followed by an exuberant call of 'Uncle Zach!' Next thing I know, my nieces have leapt into my arms for their customary koala hug and I'm staggering back against the front door with the weight of twin 5-year-olds throwing themselves at me.

'Did you guys grow since I last saw you?' I puff as they finally jump back down.

'Can we borrow your phone to take selfies?' Fran asks, ignoring what I said.

'No phones! Not until you're older,' Raff butts in, doing his best stern dad impression. 'Honestly Zach, you wouldn't believe the stuff they can access on there now. Francesca, Sienna, go up and finish packing please. No more arguments.'

As they clatter off, I lean my arm around Raff in an embrace. 'Hello bro. You look . . .'

'Shattered? Like a shell of my former self?' Raff offers.

'I was going for "well".'

'I do not,' he laughs. 'I look like a man in his mid-thirties who is completely at the mercy of three fiery Italian women. You, on the other hand, look like you've just stepped off a Dolce and Gabbana shoot. You carefree bastard. I cannot wait to take the piss out of your beer belly and grey hair when you're in my position.'

'I think the term is "salt and pepper",' I smile, ruffling Raff's tangled hair. It's a wild and admittedly more grey version of my own.

'Thanks for doing this,' he says as we walk into the kitchen. 'The holiday cottage won't accept pets and I couldn't leave Tiny with anyone else.'

"Tiny" is anything but. Sienna and Fran came up with the name when their St Bernard puppy arrived and he outgrew it about three days later. He's now the size of a small pony and barking at birds in the garden. When he sees me through the French windows Tiny bounds in and I'm almost knocked over for the second time this morning.

Raff hands me a coffee and looks affectionately at his dog. 'It's bad that I'd prefer to be going on this holiday with just the hound, isn't it?'

'Yes it is. You've got a wonderful wife and two brilliant daughters you lucky git. You don't deserve them.'

35

'Things would be a lot more chilled though,' Raff says wistfully as I shake my head at him. Pulling up a seat at the table, I settle into the familiar feeling of being home. Raff moved out to a peaceful village in the Peak District not long after the girls were born and the life he's made here is awesome. I'm quite jealous, actually. It's a warm, chaotic home that has become the family focal point Raff and I never really had when we were growing up. I crave something similar for myself.

'You should be bloody grateful,' I tut.

'I know,' he yawns. 'And I usually am. You try to feel grateful when you're woken up by having two plastic dinosaurs poked into your eye before six in the morning. Anyway, there's food and beer in the fridge, dog food in the utility. Tiny eats a lot so you'll need to . . .'

'This is not my first time house-sitting, remember? Me and Tiny will be just fine.'

'Of course you will,' Raff's wife Ellie says as she walks into the kitchen. We greet each other with cheek-kisses. 'I've put some prosecco in the fridge in case you have guests,' she winks at me.

'Guests, plural? Jesus,' Raff looks baffled.

'All right, Grandad,' I laugh. 'There may be one guest, actually. I was thinking about inviting Alice out here.'

Ellie pulls up a chair and looks at me expectantly.

'Alice?' She repeats.

'Alice.'

Ellie's eyes widen with the promise of some news. 'Even saying her name has got you grinning like you just won the lottery. Care to share?'

'I take it she's new?' Raff prods.

'We met at my art exhibition and ended up hanging out afterwards, which sort of turned into a non-date kind of date. We've been on two more proper dates since then,' I say, blowing on my hot drink.

Ellie drums her fingers on the kitchen table. 'Come on, Zach!

Can't we have a bit more information than that? Your brother and I have been married for, like, six years now and all we talk about these days is who's turn it is to do the school drop off or which box set we're going to watch next. We need some excitement in our lives!'

'Hey! We both really enjoyed that chat about our pension plans last night.'

'I'm not sure "really enjoyed" is a fair summation, Raff. I almost fell asleep at the dinner table. So come on!' continues my best friend, looking encouragingly at me. 'Let us live vicariously through this new romance of yours please.'

I clear my throat. 'Right. Well, she's lovely. Intelligent. Funny. Beautiful.' And off I go, telling them about the alphabet dating idea. 'There's just one problem.'

'Oh?' Frowns Ellie as she pulls some hot croissants out of the oven.

'Yeah. She's a self-confessed cynic when it comes to love.'

Raff hoots. 'You really do know how to pick them to make life hard on yourself. Remember the last one?'

I roll my eyes. Of course I remember "the last one" as Raff charmingly puts it, but it strikes me that I haven't thought about *her* since Alice arrived.

'Stop teasing him,' Ellie says, poking my brother in the ribs.

Raff holds his hands up. 'All right, all right! I'm just pointing out the obvious. We all know that you're a die-hard romantic Zach, and now you're saying you've found yourself a cynic? Doesn't exactly sound like a recipe for success to me.'

I scratch my head. Raff's right. What makes me qualified to win Alice over when she already seems to have made her mind up that there's no such thing as the one? Back in the comfort of my family home, I decide I may as well lay all my concerns bare.

'It gets worse. On our last date she took me to a comedy gig, it turns out she's best friends with Dylan Smith . . .'

'Shut the front door,' shouts Ellie, croissant crumbs spraying from her mouth. 'I love him.'

Raff bristles on both of our behalf.

'Our Zach is even better looking,' he says, and I can't help but laugh. 'Is that the problem, then? You're worried that Alice used to be involved with her dashingly handsome and quite famous best friend?'

'Actually no, that wasn't the problem until you just suggested it.' Ellie punches Raff on the arm.

'Dick,' she says. 'Now you've made him paranoid!'

'Sorry bro. I'm sure they weren't . . . um. You know. I bet they never . . .'

And *now* I can't stop thinking about what Raff bets they never did.

'Ignore him,' commands Ellie. 'Everyone has a past and it's still early days for you guys, so you should just focus on enjoying that, right?'

'But what was the problem?' Raff presses.

'Well, we went out for a drink after Dylan's gig and when I came back from the loo I overheard Dylan saying something to Alice about a three date rule. As if she had this rule? I didn't pick up much more because they changed the subject as soon as they saw me, but he seemed to be joking about a three date limit or something. So now I'm wondering if she doesn't ever go on more than three dates with one guy and if that's it for us.'

'Oh man, there's a lot going on in that head of yours bro,' Raff taps my temple and I swat him away. 'You need to chill out a bit, like me,' he adds, getting up to check Tiny's food supplies for the third time this morning.

Genetically speaking, I have no hope.

'There's only one way to find out about that, Zach,' says Ellie. 'Ask her out here! Won't this be your third slash fourth date?'

I nod. 'I was thinking we could do a dog walk with Tiny for our D date.'

'There you go then. If she comes, you've got nothing to worry about.'

Later, as my bro straps Fran and Sienna into their car seats in the back of his tatty old Defender, Ellie pulls me to one side.

'Don't pay any attention to what Raff said, will you?'

'You mean about my ex?'

Ellie nods. 'You're my best friend as well as my brother-in-law and I know what you're like. You'll be overthinking what he said the minute we drive off. There's absolutely nothing to say that history will repeat itself, okay? We all make mistakes and we all fall for the wrong person at some point. Don't let that stop you from finding happiness again. So what if you and Alice are different? The best relationships I know are based on finding the joy in being together, not sharing the exact same outlook on life.'

She pats me on the arm as she strides over to the car and they all wave as Raff starts up the engine. Tiny bounds around at my feet, ready to play, and I take a picture of the loveable hound on my phone. Then I forward it on to Alice with a message.

Hi, I'm the biggest Tiny you'll ever meet. Fancy joining me and Zach for a dog walk this weekend? x

'I feel like I'm in that scene from *Titanic*,' Alice calls out, her arms splayed wide as she stands at the top of Mam Tor. I'd wrap my arms around her waist, Jack and Rose style, if it weren't for Tiny having decided to do a poo at this very moment. I shoot him daggers for scuppering my romantic moment with Alice.

She turns and heads back towards us, cheeks pink with the bracing wind. Alice even manages to make walking gear look good. Her hiking boots are topped with pastel socks, her bare legs stretching up to denim shorts. A soft green jumper makes the colour of her eyes dance. Her hair's pulled back today into a pony tail and I realise that my heart has set on fire every single time I've seen her.

'It is glorious up here,' she beams.

Tiny barks in agreement and gets a chin tickle for his efforts. Lucky pooch.

'So a walk was a good suggestion? You didn't mind the early start?'

'A great suggestion,' she says. 'Plus I'm used to getting up early with work, although you did rob me of my only lie-in of the week.'

'My apologies,' I grin. 'It can get really busy up here in the summer but there's nothing more beautiful than watching the sunrise over the Peaks.'

'You old charmer.'

I laugh at that. 'Am I?'

'Look at this place! It's stunning and super atmospheric. Anyone would think you were trying to woo me, Zach.'

'I am,' I reply, too fast.

Stop sounding so keen or she'll be out of here!

Alice had turned her face to the rising sun, eyes closed in the sunlight, but now she opens one eye and gives me a look, like she's amused by me. 'So you come here a lot, then?' she asks, deftly stepping past my awkwardness.

'I do, yeah. My brother Raff moved out here a while back with his family.'

'Are your parents nearby, too?'

'No, Mum and Dad split up when Raff and I were kids. They're both Italian and Dad moved back to Italy while Mum stayed here. They shipped us off to boarding school and then Mum moved over to Manchester for work.'

'I imagine boarding school isn't the kind of Harry Potter dream everyone thinks it might be.'

I laugh at that. 'I definitely didn't get an invisibility cloak or a half-giant for a best mate.'

She's paused, watching me with a gentleness in her eyes that makes me feel like she empathises. But somehow, I sense that now is not the time to ask her too much about her story, growing up. Besides, Ellie was right when she said I should focus on just having fun with Alice today.

* * *

40

'How about that one?' I ask, pointing up at a cloud puttering slowly through the sky.

'Easy,' Alice says, lying on her back next to me, our fingers touching as we watch the clouds float by. 'That's a rabbit.'

'No way!'

'All right Picasso, what do *you* think it is?'

'A frog, obviously.'

'It's definitely a rabbit and I'm speaking from a position of great knowledge. Don't tell me you need me to remind you about my A at art A Level again, do you?'

I pull myself up on one elbow and Alice shields her eyes with her hand, her face lit up with amusement.

'Well then, once again I find myself bowing down to your superior knowledge,' I grin, leaning down to kiss her. The warm summer sun's on my back, the light breeze whipping strands of her hair onto my face. There's a smell of . . .

OH FOR FUCK'S SAKE, TINY.

'Wow, twice in one afternoon. What have you been feeding him?' Alice has shot up from our spot on the grass, stepping away from the scent of Tiny's butt and wrinkling her nose. Can't blame her.

'Bloody Raff,' I huff. 'He did this last time I dog-sat. Gave Tiny loads of food before he left so now he's all, um . . . you know. Raff has a hard time accepting that I'm thirty-two years old and fully capable of looking after his beloved dog. It doesn't matter that I have gainful employment and a house of my own, I will always be a little kid to him.'

'Aw, that's kind of sad.'

'Nah, that's just him being a big brother. He's been looking after me all his life and it's kind of hard-wired now. Speaking of which, we should probably head back and get this mutt in the tub before long.'

'He is filthy,' Alice laughs as Tiny finds another patch of mud to roll in.

* * *

41

'This is quite an intense work-out,' Alice puffs, folding over and resting her hands on her knees. 'I'm pretty sure we've got our steps in for the day already. Not that I check my steps any more. I read once that 10,000 steps a day is what you should aim for, which is a lot, and for a while I ended up doing laps of my house before bed to make sure I hit the target.'

'That's commitment.'

'I know! So now I try not to look because no one wants to be running up and down their stairs ten times before bed. It was a very sweaty time for me.'

I laugh. 'So you're competitive, huh?'

'Very,' she nods. 'Race you to that tree?'

And she's off.

Tiny is thrilled. He bounds along in pursuit.

'You win, you win,' I hold my hands up as I pull up next to her.

Alice beams. 'How about you? Competitive too?'

'With myself, yes. I always want to do the best I can at work, and I try and smash my own PBs when I'm running or climbing.'

'You're full of surprises, Zach. I had you down as the kind of guy who survived on black coffee and eggs, and maybe spent his spare time reading intense literature or listening to some old records on your vintage record player.'

'Why's that? Because I'm an artist?'

'Well, yeah,' she admits, looking sheepish.

'It sounds like you have seriously stereotyped me,' I reply with a stern look. To be honest, I'm just happy she's been thinking about me full stop.

'And yet here we are getting sunshine and fresh air!' She teases.

'You make it sound like you thought I was a vampire or something,' I laugh.

'Not quite a vampire but definitely a fan of intense films and maybe, like, jazz?'

'You're killing me here! First you take down my art and now

42

you're making sweeping assumptions about my character. I mean, I know I wear a lot of black but . . .'

'I'm sorry,' Alice grins, reaching her fingers around my bicep. 'I'm sort of teasing. You do strike me as a bit of an enigma, though. Brooding and a bit intense but also into sunshine and Point Romances.'

'I was hoping you'd forget about my teenage literary choices.'

'Never,' she laughs. 'It's all part of your charm.'

She thinks I'm charming? My heart starts beating faster and I can already feel myself getting carried away.

'So you're pleased you came, then?' I ask.

'Very,' she smiles.

My next sentence tumbles out before I have a chance to check myself.

'Because technically, this is our third date. Or maybe even our fourth if you include the night we met,' I say.

'Excellent maths,' she says with a smile, though her expression's changed slightly.

'Thank you. I, um, heard you and Dylan talking about a three-date rule when we were out last week.'

'Ah,' Alice pauses. We're making our way back to the village now and I stop to put Tiny's lead back on, which he isn't thrilled about. Alice carries on talking but I notice that for the first time there's more hesitancy in the way she speaks. 'So . . . yeah. I don't usually go on any more than three dates with one guy.'

'Why's that?'

'Oof, where to start?' She says, kicking some cut grass off her boots. She's lost in thought for a bit and I find myself wrestling with a tonne of emotions. Does the fact that we've made it here mean she's into me more than anyone else she's dated? Or is she not counting the night we first met as a date? Will this be our last?

After a pause, Alice catches my eye with a wry smile. 'Listen, Zach, I'm not great at opening up about stuff or . . . talking about my feelings much?' She looks apologetic and I realise I'm holding

43

my breath. 'But basically yes, I generally don't date anyone for very long. It's kind of an unwritten rule of mine.'

Fuck.

Tell her you like her!

'May I make a case for myself?' I say.

She looks at me with that half-smile again, like she's trying to make up her own mind about how she's feeling.

'I completely respect the fact that you don't want to open up about stuff and I would never pressure you to do that, but I'd just like to put this out there. I really like you, Alice. I feel like we have a connection that is so worth exploring and I'd hate for that to be cut short. Being around you is amazing. I'd love for us to spend more time together, go on adventures, dance under the stars.'

What? MATE.

'Hang on, that sounded really cheesy,' I check myself, trying to find some words to make myself sound like less of a cheese ball when Tiny decides to take matters into his own hands. Tugging on the lead, he races towards Raff's house and I'm left with no option other than to race after him, leaving my ridiculous words hanging in the air.

I kick off my boots in the hallway and usher Alice inside, but she lingers at the door.

'There's some prosecco in the fridge,' I say. 'I thought we could celebrate your win.'

'Oh?'

'The race to the tree?'

She laughs, but I notice that she still hasn't taken her boots off.

'Actually, Zach, I think I'm going to head back into Sheffield.'

'No!' I clear my throat. 'I mean, I'd love you to stay. I was going to cook us some dinner later, if you fancy it?'

'That's really sweet of you but I'd better get back.'

'Okay,' I reply, failing to hide the disappointment in my voice. 'I can drive you back?'

44

'Nah it's fine, I got an open return . . .'

'Let me at least drive you to the train station, then?'

'It's not far away,' she smiles. 'I think I can manage a few more minutes on foot before I need a sit down.'

Crestfallen, I realise there's nothing I can do so I move to kiss her goodbye, but Alice has turned her attention to Tiny. Then she plants a kiss on my cheek and as I watch her leave, the doubt creeps in. That kiss felt perfunctory, the kind of thing you might give an elderly relative.

Shit. I came on too strong, didn't I? I've freaked her out and now she's left and I can't take it back, or make it better. Once she's out of sight I step past my boots and shut the front door, knowing very well that I'm going to be sweating over my mistakes and that kiss for the foreseeable.

Later, I make enough pasta for the two of us anyway, only now I've realised that I've lost my appetite. I stack the dishwasher despondently. I'd hoped to spend the evening here with Alice, just the two of us getting to know each other better. Instead it's just me and Tiny, who has clearly picked up on my mood. He pads over to Raff's booze cabinet and lies down next to it, his wet nose by the handle.

'Whiskey it is, Tiny. You're absolutely right.'

I knock one back.

'Do you think I'll hear from her again?'

Tiny barks.

'Me neither,' I sigh. '*Fuck.*'

The next morning I wake up with a distinct headache and a slobbery dog lying by my side. Stretched out on the bed, Tiny is almost as long as me. It's not quite the wake-up I'd been hoping for, I'll be honest. I'd allowed myself to dream of waking up next to Alice, our clothes dotted around the bedroom. Her face would be lit by the morning sunshine, her warm body curled into mine.

My heart feels heavy when I remember her leaving and that

goodbye kiss. The more whiskey I drank last night, the easier it was to persuade myself that I knew exactly what the kiss meant.

It's been nice getting to know you, but goodbye.

The thought of not seeing her again feels like a physical pain and I'm unwilling to put myself through any more misery, so I leave my phone on the bedside table and head downstairs. If I can't have Alice, I can at least get some work done. I take my sketchpad out into the garden and mainline coffee while I try out some new ideas.

I spend most of the day avoiding my phone, worried that I won't have heard from Alice or worse, that she'll have put into words what that kiss meant. But when my stomach finally gets the better of me and I head inside to raid the fridge, I find myself being pulled towards it like I'm seeking out the bad news.

I pick it up.

She *has* messaged.

A glimmer of hope mixes with the gloom of potential bad news in my head. I'm pleased that she's got in touch but . . .

Jesus just read it, Zach!

I open the message.

I'm sorry I hurried off. I'm a bit confused to be honest. I really like hanging out with you and I do definitely want to see you again, I just get a bit panicked when things get intense. Are you happy to just have fun together on our next date? No pressure? x

Eighties Disco

Alice

'Ooh, a shell suit!' Natalie coos, rifling through the piles of treble denim, leg warmers, oversized blazers and other eighties fashion staples currently strewn across my bedroom floor. I watch her over the top of my compact mirror, which I'm using to apply electric blue eyeshadow all over my lids.

'I love seeing that smile back on your face.'

'How can you not smile when you look this good?' She preens, fluffing the perm wig she's wearing.

'You are serving pure Kylie Minogue circa *Neighbours* tonight.'

'Charlene!' she gasps. 'I think that may be the greatest compliment I have ever received. You look absolutely banging, by the way.'

It's my turn to gasp as I step in front of the mirror and catch the first sight of myself in my outfit for the night. I'm wearing very few clothes. Black fish-nets and a gold lamé leotard with massive ruffled shoulder pads. That's literally it. Natalie loves a theme night even more than I do but I'm slightly regretting giving her free rein to choose my outfit now.

'You can see my ass. Is it a bit much?'

'Yes! In the very best way. You look like Joan Collins and Madonna had a love child. Zach's going to lose his mind when he sees you.'

Butterflies coarse through me at the mention of his name. I'm super excited to see him and also still in a bit of a tizz. 'This will be our fifth date, Nat.'

'Bloody hell. Going out on more than three dates with one guy is so off brand for you. You must really . . .'

'Don't say it!' I interject.

Nat drops down onto my bed and pats the space next to her. I sit down, feeling a bit like Raff's dog Tiny. Only slightly more obedient. The memory of him ruining Zach's romantic moments on our last date makes me smile so hard my cheeks hurt.

'What's going on?' she asks.

I flip open a shimmering bronzer, wondering if the answer to her question will find me in there.

'I don't know,' I say eventually. 'I had a miniature freak-out on our last date and I've felt all . . . tumultuous ever since. We were having loads of fun on a dog walk when Zach asked me about my three date rule.'

'You *told* him about that?'

'No! He overheard me and Dylan talking about it when we all went out for drinks. So then he started making a case for himself and talking about the connection we have and I panicked.'

'He made a case for himself? Alice, that's adorable!'

'It was too much!'

'Sometimes I forget that you're not a normal human being,' Nat laughs.

'Hey!' I protest.

'Kidding. Look, it just sounds like he's into you and that you're both coming at this from different angles, that's all.'

'I think you're right. I do really like hanging out with him, but that's the problem. I'm drawn to him like a moth to a flame and we all know that combination never ends well.'

'I think you need to stop seeing yourself as a moth, hun. They're the basic bitch of the insect world, don't you think? My Alice is a butterfly, make no mistake.'

48

'Butterflies *are* more colourful,' I concede.

'Listen, you've shut yourself away in your little fortress for so long now and we both know why you did that. Self-preservation. I won't dwell on all that but look at you now. You are strong, happy, successful. You have perfect taste in best friends,' she winks. 'You've made a gorgeous life for yourself and now, for the first time in forever, you've found a man who you wouldn't mind letting down the drawbridge for. You've not invited him all the way in yet, obviously, but you're happy for him to have a little look around.'

I bite my lip. 'How long's this fortress analogy going to go on for, Nat?'

She giggles. 'You get it though, right? This is all new for you and you're bound to feel a bit nervous about it. But there is no need to panic about flames and moths, okay? You are the first to point out that life is for living, so what I'm saying is, do that. Have fun and enjoy this!'

I nod, still laughing. 'Excellent advice, thank you. I actually chose a group thing for tonight's date so we could do exactly that. Just have fun, no pressure.'

Natalie beams at me as she turns her attention to gluing on some false lashes.

'You know that I'm bloody proud of you?' I add. The crime thriller Zach picked out for me on our bookshop date had been giving me some ideas for Jake's demise, but seeing my friend cope so well with their split means her ex is safe for now.

'Well, I'm definitely not crying on the sofa all the time now and that's thanks to you. Remember when I accidentally liked that old photo of Jake's and nearly emigrated? You told me I should start living in the present and you were right, Alice. Tonight, we disco.'

Natalie's crinkly shell suit is frankly exceptional. I took a snap of it before we left, sharing the green and pink diagonal stripes to my flower shop's Instagram stories and asking followers if they'd like to see an eighties-inspired window dressing next week. It was an overwhelming yes and my brain is already buzzing with ideas but I make a conscious effort to switch off from work, now. Because the dancefloor has well and truly claimed us. We're warbling eighties ballads to one another as the room fills with more incredible outfits. Blazers with huge shoulder pads, neon jumpsuits and so many shiny materials. Eve, her girlfriend Nicky and a couple of other friends have joined us and we're all singing 'I Wanna Dance With Somebody' to one another at high volume.

'This is all we need!' I shout, locking Natalie into a love-in and feeling so lucky to have this gorgeous woman in my life.

She makes an I-didn't-hear-you face.

'Friendship!' I shout. 'FUN! It's all we need.'

'You sure about that?' She asks, looking over my shoulder and spinning me around.

Zach's here.

He's walking across the packed dancefloor towards us and OH HOLY PHWOAR he looks good.

I'm thrilled to see that he's embraced the theme, ditching his usual muted palette for a bright green Adidas tracksuit, unzipped, with a white vest underneath and box fresh white trainers. He looks so eighties and also like he just stepped off a catwalk. I don't think I can handle it.

Zach doesn't take his eyes off me. Time slows right down as he approaches our hot, sweaty group. Finally he's here and I'm about to say something like, I don't know, hi. But his eyes are locked on mine and I realise I've stopped dancing.

'You look incredible,' he says, voice low.

The fireworks are back with a vengeance. I wrap my hands around his waist and kiss him hello. Our mouths are millimetres apart and I'm about to kiss him again when Marvin Gaye's 'Sexual Healing' comes on and we get the giggles.

'Hi,' I finally say.

'Hello.'

My ears feel hot. Never have I fancied a man in a shimmering tracksuit more. I motion to our group to see if he fancies dancing but Zach mimes getting a drink and once we've picked up drinks he leads me to a booth in the corner. A booth for just the two of us. ARGH! I need people around me or I may not be trusted with this man.

'So here we are at an eighties disco,' he says as he fidgets with his outfit like a fish out of water.

'Well deduced,' I grin. 'I had no idea you'd be able to pull off an acid green trackie so well. I'm kind of into it.'

You flirt, I think to myself. I need to calm down.

'Hah. Thanks. Fancy dress is definitely not my thing but I wanted to make an effort for you.'

Zach, I realise, makes me feel good about myself in a very cute way.

'Shall we dance?' I ask, eyes flicking to the dancefloor.

Shyness flashes across Zach's face. 'I'm not big into dancing in public,' he admits.

'Ah, okay. Was this a bad date choice?'

'Not at all! I'm enjoying the music a lot and your mates have some . . . interesting moves.' He laughs as we watch Natalie and Eve attempt the running man together. 'But confidence isn't my forte. Besides, I wouldn't mind spending the night wrapped up in your company.'

Butterflies! Or moths? No stop it.

'Well, Zach Moretti, the good news is that I have plenty of possibly misplaced confidence and I am more than happy for us to spin around the dancefloor like a couple of dorks for the night.'

'A couple of dorks, you say?'

I nod.

'Come on, then.' He takes my hand and our bodies tangle together as we move to 'Papa Don't Preach'. The glitter ball above sends shafts of light over us and I look up at Zach's face, lit up like a diamond. He looks hot and I like him. There's no need to

51

panic about that, right? Repeat after me: We're just having fun together. It's chilled. No pressure. We're just having fun together. It's chilled. No pressure.

Later I'm striking a pose around my face in what I hope is a mini Madonna masterclass for Zach. 'This is Vogueing. I can't believe you've never heard of it!'

'I know, what was I doing with my youth?' He grins, quite adorably poking himself in the eye as he attempts to copy me.

'I bet you were in a band.' I'm suddenly struck with an image of him as a guitar-strumming teenager. 'I can totally picture you writing love songs to your first girlfriend, heart bleeding all over the lyrics.'

Zach stops trying to mirror my dance moves and takes hold of my hands, inching me away from the middle of the dancefloor towards the less busy edges with a smile on his face.

'Incorrect. There wasn't much call for a piano-playing introvert in any of the bands at my school.'

'You play the piano?'

'Not for a long while, but yeah, when I was younger. Didn't write any love songs though. I guess you could say I was a late bloomer in that department.'

Another song comes on and Natalie bounds past us on her way back from the loos. 'What are you doing on the outskirts? Come on!' She calls, waving us back into the middle. I'm itching to join them but I don't want to be rude to Zach.

'Come on then,' he smiles. 'I can see I'm going to have to work hard to keep up with you, Alice.'

Thrilled, I lead him back into the throng where Natalie's unleashing the entire dance routine to 'Thriller'.

'I've been wondering about a career change,' she says, hands still clawed in the air. 'Serious question: Should I join a dance troupe?'

I snort. 'It's good to have goals.'

'It's this shell suit,' she grins. 'It's making me feel like a queen.

See that hot guy in the blazer over there? Just gave him my number. Why not, hey? Jake doesn't get to piss on my parade any longer.'

'That's the spirit!' I cheer, turning back to smile at Zach and spotting him trying to slink back to the booth again. I grab him by the hand. 'Oh no you don't!'

He smiles, kissing me firmly on the lips. 'I actually thought I'd leave you to it.'

'What?' I ask, crestfallen. I thought we were having fun and don't want him to go.

'Come on, you don't need me cramping your style any more.'

'No, you're not! I'm enjoying spending time with you. Why don't we head off together?'

'Alice, that's really sweet but I can tell you're having loads of fun with your girlfriends and you should make the most of that. Stay and enjoy your night, blow off some steam. Besides, it's been a long day and I am knackered. Can I see you again soon?' He asks, pulling me in for a kiss. My hand wanders inside his shell suit and I run a finger along the waistline of his trousers.

'Yes please,' I whisper.

'It's a date,' he says, looking pleased. 'Now go, have fun.'

I wave him goodbye then spin on my heels and head back to my girls.

'Everything okay with Zach?' Nat asks later. We've been dancing for hours and are taking a well-earned water break.

'I'm not sure he could keep up with us,' I say, kicking off my heels and rubbing my feet.

'I guess we can be a *bit* full on,' Nat says, nodding in the direction of Eve, who seems to be recreating some kind of Magic Mike moves in the middle of the club. I watch her for a while, letting my thoughts settle.

'Zach's actually earned some serious brownie points with me tonight,' I say. 'He knew that I was having fun here with you guys and he didn't crowd me out, or stay and be grumpy because it wasn't his thing. I offered to leave when he decided to call it a night and he insisted I stayed. I like that he was happy to give me space to do my thing.'

'Yeah, that is thoughtful,' Nat nods. 'Jake always insisted we did everything together. I'm only realising now how claustrophobic that felt.'

'Right? Couples often seem to merge into one person. I've lost count of how many of our friends now refer to themselves as "we" when I ask them how they are or what they're doing.'

'That's so true and I know I was guilty of that when Jake and I were together.'

'It's nothing to feel guilty about, Nat. I can see that it's cute, too. Feeling like a team, doing stuff together, being part of a little unit.' I pause, not wanting to bang on about couples right when Nat seems to have got herself into a good place after her split.

'Speaking of units, Jake was a total c-unit,' she grins.

I hoot.

'Zach, on the other hand, sounds like a winner.'

'You think?' I ask, unable to keep the smile from my mouth.

'I do. And I think you do too.'

'Well, I'm definitely feeling less freaked out about things now. I panicked on our last date but tonight he gave dancing a go even though it's not his thing. He didn't balk at a group hang out or insist on ending the night together. He totally put me first. I really appreciate that about him.'

'Face it, babes, you like him.'

'All right! Let's not get ahead of ourselves,' I laugh, pulling my heels back on and taking Nat's hand for one last dance.

Film Festival

Zach

The sun is high but there's still a freshness in the air when I pull up outside Alice's house. She's leaning against her front door wearing shorts and a jumper with a thunderbolt across it, her arms wrapped around her for warmth.

'Like your jumper.'

'Thank you. As you can see, I never did get the memo that you should stop dressing like a child when you hit adulthood. Plus this thunderbolt is made of sequins which change colour when you rub them.'

'Is that an invitation?'

'Steady,' she winks. 'Besides, that depends on whether you plan to leave this date early or not.'

'Argh, no, don't hold it against me. You guys were having so much fun at the eighties disco and . . . To be honest, dancing in public just takes me back to the primary school years where I was very, very far from being cool. I'd be the kid at the school disco sat on the side, eating all the cheesy wotsits while the popular ones were trying out their first slow dances in the middle.'

'Oh Zach, that's just melted my icy heart a little bit.'

'Don't worry, I'm over it now,' I grin, trying to extract myself from sounding like an utter loser. 'But you were the life and soul of the party that night and I didn't want to be the one to take you away from that.'

'It's okay, I'm just teasing you. I *was* disappointed when you headed off early but it was good to stay and blow off some steam with the girls. I really needed a fun night out. You were being very thoughtful and considerate.'

I doff an imaginary cap. 'Pleasure. Though I'm afraid I plan to be entirely selfish with you today. I've got a few tricks up my sleeve, actually.'

'Have you now?'

I gesture towards the bashed up old Golf GTI I've parked outside her house. If all goes to plan, today will be romantic *and* the chance for me to impress her. If I can stop talking about my geek days, that is. 'Alice, meet Gerty.'

'You've named your car Gerty?' She grins.

'Sure have. And she's in charge of getting you to Leeds and back today.'

Casually flicking the stereo on like I didn't spend hours painstakingly compiling the playlist for today's road trip, I realise that I'm hyper aware of having Alice in the passenger seat. She's fiddling with that ring on her middle finger again and I've noticed that she always wears it. I wonder if there's a story behind it. We're on date six and there's so much more about Alice I'm desperate to know.

'I love this song,' Alice says, reaching to turn the volume up.

Relief. The connection between us is undeniable even though we're different in so many ways and I'm pleased to see that my taste in music has hit the right note. She's started singing along and I'm so distracted by the sound of her lilting voice that I almost go through a red light.

'Easy,' she laughs. 'I didn't have you down as a rule-breaker.'

'I don't often have such a beautiful distraction in my passenger seat.'

56

Alice shoots me stern look. 'Am I a distraction to you?'

'Ah, no. That did not come out well. I meant . . .'

'Zach, I'm teasing.'

'I'm not sure if that's wise,' I raise an eyebrow. 'You know I'm not just your designated driver for the day, right? I'm also in charge of all the snacks. More wise-cracks, less snacks for Alice.'

She laughs again. 'What are we doing, anyway?'

'After you shared your love of cheesy eighties pop with me, I thought I'd share my own guilty pleasure. We're off to a film festival.'

'Is it going to be all arty films that win awards but never make any sense? Should I have packed my glasses and a black polo neck?'

'And there go the Hula Hoops.'

'Wait, no! Sorry, I can't help myself sometimes. I love Hula Hoops. And I can totally get on board with arty films. The more subtitles the better, I say.'

'That's better,' I grin. 'What's the best flavour, ready salted or salt and vinegar?'

'It's beef, surely?'

'Agreed. I bought all three, just in case.'

'Three packets of Hula Hoops and I'm yours.'

I don't tell her I think I'm already hers.

'*Notting Hill?* Are you kidding me? This was my favourite film growing up. When you said we were coming to a film festival I thought . . .'

'I know exactly what you thought,' I smile. 'I wanted to show Alice that I'm not just the intense artist she seems to see me as and, more than that, I just wanted us to have some fun in the here and now. I'm really happy and massively relieved that she seems genuinely excited about this date.

After parking up I pop the boot and pull out the cool bag I

borrowed, silently cursing Ellie. When she'd promised I could borrow it, I hadn't realised it would be covered in bright pink flamingos and putting a serious dent in my masculinity.

'Like your bag,' Alice grins, stretching her legs after the drive.

'It's what's inside that counts,' I reply. 'And we've already established that you've got three packets of Hula Hoops to get through. Shall we?'

I lug the cool bag over my shoulder and we head towards the entrance. The festival's being held in the grounds of an old stately home, a different film showing every day for the next few weeks, and a huge screen is erected at the bottom of a gently sloping hill. People are setting up camp all around it. The sky is dotted with clouds like cotton wool and the canopied areas are already filling up, so I lead us to a spot by an old oak tree and set down the bag, pulling a picnic blanket and a couple of cushions out of my rucksack.

'This is so cute,' Alice says, settling down under the dappled shade of the tree. We're lying on our bellies, legs kicked out behind us, when I realise that I feel more relaxed now than I have in a long time. Alice's soft skin brushes against mine as she sits up, pushing her sunglasses onto her head, and announces that she's off to get us a drink. When she returns with a prosecco and a soda water, she folds her legs underneath herself as she sits back down and we clink our biodegradable cups together.

'I'm kind of sad you aren't wearing your eighties tracksuit today. When Nat saw you that night she told me I should "get some".'

'Well now I just feel objectified.'

'Hah,' she giggles. 'I've started to realise that all of my friends are incredibly cringe. Still haven't forgiven Dylan for showing you those pictures of me at primary school.'

'The one where you looked a bit like Darth Vader?'

'Hey!' She protests, flicking a crisp at me.

I hold my hands up in self-defence. 'We all have one of those photos in our past. I've already sworn Raff to secrecy.'

Alice leans in. 'Does that mean I might meet your brother and sister-in-law one day?'

I'm not sure what to say, I'm just so surprised that this beautiful commitment-phobe has asked such a question that my words tumble into one. Style it out with a drink, Zach.

'Would you like to?' I say, finally recovering myself.

Instead of answering she decorates her fingers with Hula Hoops before biting them off, one by one. 'You do always pick dates where it's just the two of us. You aren't secretly ashamed of me, are you, Zach Moretti?'

'That could not be further from the truth. Anyway, you always pick dates where we're surrounded by your friends!'

'I guess I'm just more used to doing stuff in groups,' she shrugs. 'I don't really date much, so group activities and relaxed hangouts are more my thing.'

'Perhaps I'm being selfish, wanting you all to myself.'

She laughs at that. 'As an only child my mum refused to let me be selfish.'

'She sounds like a wise owl, your mum.'

Alice's eyes flicker, just for a moment. 'The wisest. Talking of my mates, what do you think of Dylan? I was worried you didn't like him.'

Caught off guard, again.

'Oh, um, he seems like a fun enough guy . . .'

'Hang on while I call his agent,' she deadpans. 'Dylan will definitely want to use your glowing "fun enough" review for his next promotional stuff.'

I find myself laughing again. Now that I think about it, we haven't had a date yet where Alice hasn't made me laugh, which is brilliant. I really like how funny she is.

'I'm just glad he didn't scare you away with all his embarrassing stories about me. He tends to hog the limelight, too.'

'He's definitely suited to being on the stage,' I say carefully. 'We're quite different I think. It can be a little intimidating when the girl you like has such a charismatic best friend.'

She's paused, watching me, and I worry that I've said too much but after a while her face breaks into that beautiful smile and she gives me a playful nudge.

An announcement tells us the movie will start in ten minutes and Alice heads off to find the portaloos, giving me the chance to set up the surprise picnic dinner I packed. Ellie came over last night to help me prepare it all. Savoury muffins in baking paper wraps, stuffed peppers, a goats' cheese salad. It looks pretty good all laid out now, even if being in the kitchen with Ellie was a terrifying experience. I'm still scarred by her shouting '*Don't scorch the peppers.*' '*Chop it FINELY.*' Not sure my nerves have recovered from the stress yet.

'Oh wow this looks so good! Did you make all of this?' Alice asks.

'I had a little help from Ellie.'

'It's lovely that you're so close with your brother's wife.'

'They actually met through me,' I say. 'Ellie and I studied together at uni. She's my best friend as well as my sister-in-law.'

Alice takes a plate and eagerly fills it with food, handing it over to me before making one for herself and licking her fingers. 'Please tell her I said thank you. I love goats' cheese.' Her enthusiasm warms me like the sun, which has just started to set and is casting a golden glow over Alice. She looks luminous. As she pulls her jumper off, I catch the briefest glimpse of her belly button and I want nothing more than to graze my fingers along it.

'Are you covering all possible weather bases with your outfit today? Thunderbolt jumper, rainbow T-shirt . . .'

'Sunshine necklace,' she adds, reaching for the delicate gold chain hanging under her T-shirt.

'That couldn't be more apt given that you are a ray of sunshine,' I say.

'Oh stop it,' she grins, sighing contentedly. 'I think this is the most perfect picnic I've ever had. Delicious food, one of my favourite movies about to start and the company isn't too bad either.'

'Steady there,' I laugh. 'My ego might not take any more. Okay, are you ready for a pop quiz?'

Alice claps. 'Love a quiz. Can I eat at the same time?'

'Of course. I'm going to throw some *Notting Hill* quotes at you and you can tell me who said them.'

Alice looks thrilled.

'Who said . . . "whoopsidaisies"?'

'Easy. William Thacker, played by Hugh Grant, as he struggled to get into the private park. Do I get extra points for detail?'

'Sure,' I say, pretending to mark down her score on an imaginary piece of paper. 'Who said . . . "demi capu".'

'I love that guy! Martin from the bookshop, I think his name is James Dreyfus in real life?'

'I'm impressed. "Surreal but nice"?'

'William again.'

'Very good,' I nod.

I look over at her, leaning in intently. That competitive streak again. And I think, it's now or never.

'"I'm just a boy, standing in front of a girl, asking her to love him."'

Alice pauses for a moment, looking puzzled. Then she shakes her head and says, 'You got that the wrong way round. It's Anna Scott, played by Julia Roberts, who says that. Remember? In the bookshop. She asks William to love her and he turns her down and it's just the most painful bit of the whole film. So the quote is: "I'm just a girl," etcetera.'

Deep breath.

'What if I didn't get it wrong? What if it's *me* talking, now?' I ask. 'What if I'm saying to you, Alice, that I'm here in front of you asking you if you want to spend more time with me. I like you Alice. I completely respect that you don't want to get in too deep, too soon but I'm trying to ask, very ineloquently, if you'd

61

be up for seeing each other exclusively? Christ, where is Richard Curtis when you need him?'

Alice smiles at this.

Please say yes!

Never have I wanted to hear a person speak more.

This silence is spreading out like the Ice Age.

'Zach, I . . .' she pauses and I realise I'm holding my breath. 'I don't want to get hurt.'

'I would never hurt you.'

'You don't know that,' she frowns.

'Alice, all my life I've doubted myself and I'm pretty bad at overthinking things, usually to the point where I decide I've said or done something stupid or embarrassing. When I'm with you all of that seems . . . quieter? Like my head's turned the volume down on all of the worry that can get the better of me. I think what I'm saying is that with you everything seems so much easier. You help to bring me out of my shell . . .' I pause, scratching my head and inevitably overthinking what I've just said. 'You're right, I can't promise that I won't hurt you but I can promise that I'll put my all into you and me. I think there could be something real here, if you wanted to give us a go?'

Alice breaks eye contact and stares off at the screen.

'The film's about to start,' she says absent-mindedly.

I take that as a no, feeling like a balloon that's just popped and is instantly deflated.

Turning my head towards the setting sun, a crashing sense of disappointment floods through me. That's when Alice scooches over, sitting down between my legs so that we're both still facing the screen. I wrap my arms around her and she turns to whisper in my ear.

'Go on, then.'

'Huh? Are you saying you're in?' I lean back to look at her, not wanting to miss this moment.

'I'm in. Just . . . go easy on me, okay? Let's take things slowly.'

'It's a deal,' I reply, not even bothering to hide the huge grin spreading across my face.

Two hours later as the film credits roll, she leans into my body and I breathe in the apple scent of her hair, realising that I've been smiling non-stop for the entire movie.

'Zach?'

'Mmm?'

'I love that you were Julia Roberts in that scenario,' she snorts.

'And you made a very beautiful William Thacker. I can't say I've ever wanted to kiss Hugh Grant before.'

'Hugh would readily accept that kiss,' she says, curling her body around until she's facing me. My mouth finds hers and we kiss under the oak tree. I'd happily stay here all night but Alice's phone beeps and she pulls it out of her pocket.

'Sorry, I should check this,' she says. 'I've got a couple of important orders tomorrow and need to make sure everything is ok. And look at the time! We should probably head back?'

I'm about to persuade her that we could stay for one more drink but she's already started rolling up the picnic blanket. So we walk hand in hand back to the car, pile our stuff into Gerty's boot and set off.

Alice is quiet on the drive back and I don't want to distract her when she's sorting out a few work things so I concentrate on the drive, replaying the best bits of tonight in my mind and feeling seriously chuffed that she's agreed to make our relationship official. I know it's a huge deal for her and I still can't quite believe that she's chosen me. I'd love the date to have lasted longer but with Alice, I'm learning to grateful for what's happening right now rather than rushing headfirst into the next thing.

Suddenly I'm aware of Alice's hand moving over to rest on my knee.

I allow myself a quick glance at her and she's leaning her head back against the head rest, a smile on her lips. The music's off, there's nothing but the sound of our breathing filling the space and the atmosphere in the car has intensified. The hairs on my arm stand to attention. I know she can sense it too, because we've spent all day in easy conversation and yet now, neither of us is speaking. We don't need to. The anticipation is enough.

I listen to the air whipping in through the open window. She's started oh so gently circling her thumb around my thigh.

Finally we pull up at Alice's house and I'm not sure what to expect, her request to take things slowly still echoing through my head. I follow her to her front door and she turns, grabbing both my hands.

'I've had the best day,' she says.

I kiss her then under the cover of twilight.

She pulls her keys out of her bag, opening the door before turning back to me.

'Do you want to come in?' she asks, eyes bright.

'Are you sure?' I ask, not wanting her to feel like she's under any pressure.

'I would very much like you to stay the night, Zach,' she says, hooking her fingers through the belt loops of my jeans. She pulls me in through the front door and every single one of my senses is now fully tuned to Alice. I reach out to circle my fingers around her wrists, running my hands up her arms and feeling the goosebumps on her skin as I pull her close. She backs up against the hallway wall and our bodies are pressed together, her head tipping up to meet mine. We kiss again and it's like a lightning bolt through my body. My heart's on fire as I reach up to stroke the soft skin at the nape of her neck. She's inching her fingers up and under my T-shirt. Suddenly she stops kissing me, looks straight into my eyes, and leads me up to her bedroom.

64

Garden

Alice

BREAKING NEWS. *Are you both free for a group chat?*

Natalie replies immediately. **Dyl's scrolling through his contacts to find "hot single celebrities" for me to date** 🙄. **Famous people bring me out in a sweat so YES I'm free and can we do it now please?**

I press call on our group WhatsApp and watch my friends' faces appear on screen. Natalie looks flustered.

'You okay?' I ask.

'She's fine,' butts in Dylan. 'The whole point of this weekend is to get her back out there.'

'I thought it was a chance for two old friends to catch up?' Nat says, biting her thumbnail.

'London is full of rich pickings. We might as well launch you back onto the dating scene again while you're here.'

'I'm not a boat!' She grumbles.

'Yes and not everyone is permanently randy, Dylan,' I say, standing up for Natalie.

'Says the girl who can't stop chatting about the new dude she's dating,' he grins.

'I wouldn't say I can't stop, thanks very much,' I pout, though in fairness I did expressly call them to talk about Zach. 'So, what have you guys been up to?'

'We went for a walk along the canals this morning, stopped for a brunch of hellishly overpriced waffles with bacon and tonight Dyl's insisting on going to some celebrity haunt,' Nat groans.

'We're going out out,' Dylan winks, which means a champagne-fuelled all-nighter is on the cards for my best friends and I feel a massive pang of FOMO.

'Stay safe kids! And don't miss me or anything.'

'Obviously we will miss you. Anyway, what's the breaking news?' Natalie asks.

'Oh gawd. Are you sitting down?' I watch Natalie and Dylan obediently drop down onto his sofa. 'Right, good. So, I'm officially seeing Zach now.'

Dylan and Natalie exchange looks.

I drum my fingers on the kitchen table, waiting not very patiently for them to say something. *Anything*.

'Oh shit,' Dylan finally says.

'Oh shit?' I frown. 'That's all you have to say?'

'Wow, Alice!' Natalie exclaims.

'I know! So . . .?'

'So . . .' Natalie nudges Dylan.

'You're obviously going to pretend that you don't, but you clearly like him a lot,' Dylan muses.

I squirm.

'Given that No Big Deal is the . . .'

'You've got to stop calling him that, Dylan!' I interrupt. 'I only said it back when we were coming to your Sheffield gig because I know how you can overreact.'

'Fine, *Zach*,' he says pointedly. 'Anyway, I'm pretty sure that Zach is the first guy you've properly dated in . . .'

'Forever?' Natalie suggests.

'Mmm hmm,' I nod.

'Huge,' Natalie exclaims, holding her hands out wide to empha-sise the point.

'Is that the size of his penis?' Dylan quips and the two of them

66

have a good old guffaw while I watch on, exasperated. Honestly, why they insist on acting like 13-year-olds when they're both 30 is beyond me.

Natalie's the first to straighten her face out. 'Sorry Alice. What I obviously meant was, this is huge *news*. I'm really happy for you.'

'The Bolter's got a boyfriend.' Dylan looks incredulous.

'Woah there. Calm down,' I say, breaking out into a sweat. 'I do not have a boyfriend. We just had the chat about seeing each exclusively, that's all. HANG ON. What did you call me?'

'You knew The Bolter is your nickname, right?' Dylan says.

'No I did not know that,' I smart. 'That's a bit . . .'

'Accurate?' Dylan offers.

'It is kind of true,' Natalie adds gently. 'Even a whiff of commitment and you usually bolt. Half-way through a wedding was your personal best, I think. Remember?'

I roll my eyes. Of course I remember. I'd only been on two dates with Matt when he asked if I'd be his plus one to his mate's wedding but I happily accepted because I love weddings! They're not right for me, obviously, but the chance to spend all day in a cute outfit, chatting to new people and toasting the happy couple is always a winner. Only, I didn't quite get to the toasts at this particular wedding.

'Didn't you bolt midway through the ceremony?' Dylan says.

'Not midway through, no! Just . . . immediately after,' I cough. 'In fairness, I'd thought Matt and I were very casual. I did not expect him to well up when the bride walked down the aisle, nor to clutch my hand as they said their "I do's". And I certainly didn't expect him to tell me that "we'd be next". It was literally our third date!'

'So you dumped him during the confetti throwing and left him to face a whole day celebrating someone else's wedding while he'd just been given the heave ho.' Dylan is shaking his head laughing at me. He loves this story. 'Wasn't that the start of your three date limit?'

'Yes it was,' I nod. I'd put a cap on the number of dates with one man after that, just so I didn't get startled again. 'I know I was brutal but I did speak to Matt after to explain myself.'

'And yet here you are, not only having broken your three-date limit but now you're exclusively seeing Zach. That's a big step for you, babes.' Nat's beaming.

I nod, pushing my hair out of my eyes and trying not to feel so clammy. Zach's shall-we-be-exclusive speech had been so sweet and I'm happy about where we are, if a teeny tiny bit scared. Surely I could have picked someone less intense for my first foray into proper dating. Like, I dunno, someone who isn't an incorrigible romantic? I suppose that's the point though. No-one has made me want to until now.

'Does he know that you're a butterfly who cannot be caged, Pickle?' Dyl asks.

'Um, I have told him that I'm not convinced about The One, or, um, love.'

'Ooh, lucky Zach. And he hasn't run for the hills yet?'

'Still keen, apparently.'

'Well, I think this is wonderful,' says Nat. 'You're being really brave Al, dipping a toe in something you vowed you never would. I've not had much of a chance to chat to Zach yet but he seems like a good guy. And he's hella hot.'

'Let's not forget his apparently "huge"—'

'*Thank you*, Dylan.' I butt in. He and Nat are roaring again.

'Okay, great chatting to you . . .'

'No, wait, don't hang up! You know we love you very much and we're only teasing. And who knows, this may just be the start of something brilliant,' Nat says.

Dylan does a thumbs up.

'Thanks guys. I do actually have to go though. Have fun.' I blow kisses at my two best mates and try to stamp down the thought that just popped into my head. That the very reason Natalie's in London is to get over her heartache. That the very reason Dylan is the perfect help with that is because he never bothers to linger too long for heartache to be a problem.

I roll my shoulders back and tell myself not to freak out, because I've got a date to get ready for and I cannot choose an outfit mid-panic. Let's just hope Zach likes the surprise I have in store for today's date.

Tomatoes bloom plump and red, green beans twist up bamboo sticks and bumblebees on a pollen hunt buzz through the air. I take a restorative breath, revelling in the scent of freshly dug earth mixed with bonfires. My little allotment is my inner sanctum. Dad has been the only VIP on the guestlist so far, but now Zach's on his way. Most people seem surprised when they hear that a woman in her late twenties keeps an allotment and I wonder what Zach will make of the fact that I'm just as happy digging up soil with octogenarians as I am twirling round the dancefloor. I'll probably lose major street cred points after this. Maybe he might even change his mind about me altogether – he seems to like the carefree and outgoing Alice, not the old soul version of me who is more sensitive than she likes to let on.

I weigh up how that makes me feel and part of me decides it would be a relief. It would be out of my hands then, before whatever we have together has the chance to venture into more dangerous territory. But if I was being honest with myself, I'd also be a bit gutted that I wouldn't get to find out where this could go, especially when the early signs are looking good.

A gust of wind catches the silk scarf in my hair. After this morning's chat with Dylan and Nat I'd stuck some music on and rifled through my wardrobe, jazzing up my usual gardening uniform of dungarees and a T-shirt by winding a bright orange scarf through my hair and slicking on some peachy lipstick to match my tee.

'Don't you look lovely!' ViVi, my allotment neighbour, pops over the hedgerow dividing our plots.

'Thanks!'

'Expecting someone special?'

'Maybe,' I say, pulling a face.

ViVi peers over her varifocals at me in delight. 'In that case, you'll be needing some of these.' She hands me a wicker basket filled with juicy strawberries.

'Oh ViVi, that's so kind of you. Are you sure?'

'There's not enough space in my kitchen cupboards for any more jam,' she chuckles.

'You've got a little . . .' Zach reaches out to brush my cheek and my skin tingles at his touch. 'Soil,' he grins.

'I *always* end up in a mess here.'

'When you suggested a Sunday spent gardening for our G date I was a little surprised. I figured after your previous form we might be gambling at a casino, or go-karting, or maybe going on a ghost tour. This is definitely unexpected.' Zach's eyes dart round my allotment. He's back in his uniform of dark T-shirt and turned-up jeans today.

'After you pointed out that all my previous choices were group activities, I thought we could do something a bit more low key, just the two of us. Though we can stick some eighties tunes on in the background if you'd like?'

'Honestly, I think I prefer listening to the birds tweeting and the bees buzzing.'

'Birds and bees it is,' I say with a wink. Zach's jawline tightens and he pulls me in for a kiss.

'I could get used to having you in my allotment,' I grin. 'Want to help me sow some seeds? I've had the best idea for a Halloween display at the shop and thought I'd try and grow some of my own pumpkins for it.'

'You know it's only June, right?'

'Yes I know it's only June! Things take a while to grow, Zach,' I roll my eyes playfully at him. 'Now how about you stop being sarcastic and get to work.'

'Oh I see, you just invited me along to be the muscles of the operation,' Zach's eyes are glinting.

'All I'm saying is, there will be absolutely no judgement if you want to take your top off while you're digging.'

Zach turns to me square on and folds his arms. 'And what will you be doing while I get my hands dirty?'

I gesture towards my potting shed, which I've turned into a cosy little den stringed with fairy lights. It has a mini bar and everything. 'Don't you worry about me. I'll be in charge of the drinks, the snacks and making sure my new gardener doesn't give me too much backchat.'

Zach doffs his imaginary cap and sets to work.

I feel like I'm in a Jackie Collins novel only on a slightly lower budget. I'm sat in a deckchair with a lemonade watching my new groundsman Zach get his hands dirty. There may be no pool and I'm not wearing any pearls or a wide-brimmed hat, but still, I like it.

Zach's not the most proficient gardener. He keeps getting the names of all the tools mixed up and I'm pretty sure he just decapitated a succulent I've been growing in my potting shed. But he is happy to muck in and I'm finding his willingness to try something new really endearing. A playlist of all my favourite feel-good tunes floats out from the speakers in my shed and we've been happily chatting about this and that. I'm humming along to a song that takes me right back to school days when I realise that Zach is humming too. I smile, realising how relaxed I am here with him. It's a relief to feel like this part of me is okay, too. I can be my true self with Zach, not just the woman who likes noisy nights out but also the woman who's happy spending a chilled weekend down at my allotment.

'What got you into gardening?' Zach asks when the song comes to an end. I take a deep breath and decide that I'm ready to open up to him more, and talk about my past for the first time in a long while.

'My mum died when I was fifteen,' I say. Instantly he reaches out to hold my hand, his finger stroking my thumb as I talk. 'She was diagnosed with an aggressive form of cancer and within weeks I was sat by the hospital bed we'd had moved into our house, saying goodbye to her as she lay there, dosed up on morphine. One minute she was there, the next she was gone.' Zach squeezes my hand and as I lean forward in my seat he reaches across to place a tender kiss on my forehead.

'I remember so clearly feeling like a stranger in my own body at the time. How could this be happening? It didn't feel real. We were dragged along on a wave of funeral plans and sorry-for-your-loss cards and it was only later, when the flowers stopped coming, when the cards stopped landing on the doormat, that it truly sank in. She'd gone. Just a few weeks which would change my life irrevocably.'

My eyes sting with tears and I blink them back. I don't think there will ever be a time I can tell this story without being that 15-year-old girl who lost her mum at the age when you need her the most, and it still feeling like it happened yesterday.

'Alice, that's awful,' Zach says. He's kneeling right next to me now, and pulls me towards him where he holds me tight. I nestle into him, feeling soothed by the sound of his heart beating right by my ear. There's something calming about his presence and I feel reassured by the fact that he's happy just to listen.

'Dad and I soldiered on as best we could but we both struggled. I went through a stage of being incredibly angry with everyone and everything. Dad would sit there quietly while I raged, letting me vent, soothing me when I had nothing left to give. He was as solid as a rock and worked so hard to look after me, always putting me first. But I knew that his heart was broken beyond repair. I'd find him quietly crying to himself, long after he thought I'd gone to bed.'

'As a kid, there's nothing more difficult than knowing that a parent is upset but feeling like there's nothing you can do to help,' Zach says, sitting down on a patch of grass and encouraging me to do the same. 'I'd overhear my mum and dad having bitter arguments after Raff and I had gone to bed. They seemed to save it up until we were out of the way but we could still hear them. They'd rage at each other and I remember lying in my bedroom, feeling so helpless. I think both Raff and I blamed ourselves for what happened to them for a long while.'

'Oh Zach, that's so sad. Their divorce wasn't your fault. You were just a child!'

'I know that now,' he says softly. 'Things are confusing when you're little though. And for you to lose your mum at fifteen . . . Ah. Alice. I can't imagine how tough that must have been for you.'

'It was tough,' I admit. 'One day, when Dad and I decided we felt brave enough, we'd started going through some of Mum's things. Touching the clothes she'd once cherished felt like breaking a spell. We'd made piles to keep and piles to take to a charity shop and after that I decided that we deserved some fish and chips from the van that used to drive through our village. When I got back, Dad was still up in their bedroom, holding onto one of her favourite dresses. I remember clearly that his knuckles were white, like he couldn't ever let go of it. I knew then that Dad would never be the same again. He'd lost the love of his life.' My voice catches in my throat.

'And you'd lost your mum,' Zach whispers.

'From that point, I became fiercely protective of my dad. Still am! I didn't want anything to ever hurt him like that again. So I focused a lot of my energies on that, giving him the space when he needed it.'

'It must have been so hard to be at home without her, especially at first,' Zach says sympathetically.

I nod. 'That's why I ended up round at Dylan's house, eating all his mum's food a couple of times a week. Things got easier for us, in a way that almost made it worst. In many ways you don't want something like that to get easier. But even with time, everything at home reminded us of Mum. The dip on her side of the sofa where she'd sit in the evenings. Her favourite coffee cup. The photos of us dotted all around. When I went to uni, Dad decided to sell our house. He bought a place not too far away, but far enough to feel like a fresh start. We talk all the time and he likes to send me poorly taken photos of his dinner, or a wonky selfie of him and his mates at the pub,' I grin.

Zach and I stand up together now, his arms still circled around my waist. 'No doubt your dad is incredibly proud of you.'

'He definitely tells me that a lot,' I smile. 'Remember when I told you that Dad always used to bring flowers home for Mum every week? It was such a simple, honest gesture of love and that's where my own love of flowers came from. I mean, I was nearly sick of the sight of them after the funeral. The house was stuffed with white lilies for weeks afterwards. But when the dust settled, gardening became my way of reconnecting with Mum, in a way. She had huge success with a rosemary plant in the garden one year and after that there was always a little pot of something she'd be tending to, so after Mum died gardening became my way of . . . I don't know, kind of carrying that love on? Keeping a little piece of her with me, I guess.'

'The fact that you're doing all of this to be close to your mum is really beautiful, Alice. She would be so proud of you.'

'Thanks. I hope so. When I was at uni I read about how much gardening can help you to cope with stress, or sadness, so I joined a community garden project. The minute I started raking through the soil, I got it. We transformed vacant sites into flower gardens and veg plots and there was something so positive about seeing things grow like that. I came back to Sheffield after uni and once the flower shop was up and running, I realised how much I missed it, so I decided to get an allotment of my own. This probably sounds really snowflakey of me but coming here is one of my self-care rituals. It means I can be the life and soul of the party *and* have some space for downtime too.'

'Not snowflakey at all,' Zach smiles. 'I'm a big fan of taking time for yourself when you need it. For me it's getting out into the Peaks for a big climb or heading out for a run. You can't beat that freedom and the sense of escaping from your everyday stuff. Clears the head, you know?'

'Absolutely,' I nod, relieved he's not been scared off by my sudden outpouring of emotions. 'God, sorry Zach. I've just realised how much I've talked. I bet you never expected a simple question about what got me into gardening would end up in a massive explanation about all the emotional baggage behind it!'

He squeezes my shoulder in response. 'Please don't apologise. I'm genuinely touched that you've felt comfortable enough to open up to me about this. I can't begin to understand how it must feel to lose a parent, but I can relate to your need to give yourself some headspace. You know, Raff and I spent a lot of weekends being shipped from one parent to the other and it was hard. I felt like I never quite had a place where I properly belonged. Other kids at school would talk about their family Sundays, where one parent would take them to football and the other would cook a Sunday lunch. We never really knew where we'd be from one weekend to the next so I just didn't have that sense of . . . grounding, I guess? I'd cry every time I had to say goodbye to Dad after a weekend, and the same with Mum.'

He grabs another deckchair and unfolds it so that we can sit down together. 'But you know, divorce happens a lot,' he shrugs. 'And we're all safe and well, so I really have nothing to complain about.'

'It's bound to have had an impact on you, Zach.'

'I think so. I shouldered a lot of the blame for it when I was younger and I'm really quick to judge myself on stuff now, still. I can sometimes get stuck in my own head and that's when the trainers come out and I head out for a run. A good dose of fresh air makes everything feel better.'

'Well, I can relate to all but the running bit of what you

just said,' I laugh, only now realising that I've been twisting Mum's wedding ring so much that the skin's gone red around my middle finger.

Zach notices and asks if it was Mum's and I nod.

'It's nice you can wear something that always reminds you of her. And that now you have this place too where you can feel close to her.'

'Don't tell Mum, but my rosemary plant is actually doing even better than hers now.'

Zach mimes zipping his lips and I laugh. This feels so good.

'Honestly, I never tell anyone all of this stuff,' I say after a pause, feeling suddenly shy and a little exposed. 'You know you're the first person apart from Dad who I've ever invited here?'

'Well I'm honoured to be only your second guest here. And I'm really glad you felt comfortable enough to share this with me,' Zach says, leaning in to kiss me.

Our moment is interrupted by ViVi popping her head over to say hello. I knew she wouldn't be able to resist the prospect of catching a glimpse of my new guest. Zach tells her that the strawberries were the best he'd ever tasted, his usual understated charm at play, and I watch her whole face light up with the compliment. He seems to have that effect on people.

We all chat for a bit, pottering around our respective allotments, before ViVi announces that she's heading home for the day and beckons me over to her, handing me a crop of runner beans wrapped in newspaper. Zach's turned his attention back to watering the newly planted pumpkin seeds and she mouths *'Phwoar!'* to me.

'I know, right?' I giggle. What Zach lacks in gardening skills he more than makes up for in appearance. He's rolled up the sleeves of his T-shirt which now sit tightly over his strong arms and frankly, I am very much here for it.

* * *

'I think we deserve a break,' I say later. Zach straightens up, wiping his forehead with his left arm.

'We?' He scoffs. 'Pretty sure you've spent the afternoon sunbathing!'

'I prefer to use the term "art directing",' I grin. 'Lemonade?'

'Because today couldn't get any more British?'

'Hmm, it is all quite quintessential isn't it?' Gardening, strawberries, lemonade. I'm still clutching a bunch of runner beans. 'I might as well stick on some cottagecore while we run through the Peaks, Jane Austen-style.'

'Cottagecore?' Zach's eyebrows shoot up in confusion.

'It's a fashion thing. Long, blowy dresses with cute paisley prints. Perhaps I should have included something Italian to make you feel less like you've stepped into *Last of the Summer Wine*.'

'I don't ever like to be too far away from an espresso or a gelato,' he teases.

'I can hear the Italian coming through,' I say, melting like a gelato at his delicious pronunciation.

'That's my Nonna for you. Once Dad moved back to Italy Raff and I would spend our summer holidays over there with him and our grandma . . . I remember counting down the days until summer term ended. We're still really close with her now and she loves a video call. Last time I spoke to her she'd found my childhood teddy in a cupboard she was going through – hang on, that's embarrassing. I definitely didn't have a teddy growing up.'

I laugh at that. 'Finally! I've been hoping for some balance ever since that picture of me as a kid emerged.'

'Darth?'

'Shut up.'

We're back on the deckchairs sipping lemonade and I snuggle into Zach, his familiar scent mixed with strawberries. A day in the garden has cleared my mind of all its usual hang-ups and I feel so peaceful, listening to his heart beat.

The sun's dipping behind one of Sheffield's many hills and the fairy lights I strung up along my potting shed start to glow.

'All the colours of the rainbow,' Zach smiles. 'It sounds like you got your love of colour from your mum.'

I'd told him earlier how Mum was a magpie for anything bright. She'd worked as an interior designer and was never happier than when she was pottering though vintage shops, hunting for treasures. As a result, our house was a riot of colour and an absolute mish-mash of styles. A squishy pink sofa from the sixties sat next to a blue velvet armchair in the living room, we ate our meals off bird of paradise plates, my muddy wellies stood next to a clementine-coloured coat stand in the hallway. 'The walls must stay white!' she'd insisted. 'Let the furniture do the talking.' I think that's one of the reasons we'd been able to sell the house, after she died. It would be years before we'd dig her furniture out again, but that's where her joyfulness lived.

'I finally unwrapped the bird of paradise plates,' I say to Zach now. 'Not that long ago, actually. They're in my house and I think of her every time I eat. I imagine her approval if I'm tucking into something nutritious, or the maternal tut if I'm eating instant noodles for dinner. Meanwhile Dad now spends most of his evenings stretched out on the pink sofa.'

'It sounds like you're in a good place, Alice.'

I pause at that, realising that I am. Zach's legs are stretched out beyond his deckchair and I've twisted to rest mine on his. Paper cups filled with lukewarm lemonade gently fizz at our sides. His arm is still around the back of my neck. Instinctively we rest our heads together, our hands linking as we sit side by side. I let my eyes close and enjoy the feeling of real happiness washing over me as we kiss.

Happy Hour

Zach

Alice is leaning against the kitchen counter in her tropical palm print pyjamas. The coffee machine is whirring into life and the smell of cinnamon buns wafts from the oven. I pause in the doorway, not wanting to disturb her while I take in every moment of this scene. It's easy, happy, relaxed . . . so many of the things I've yearned for over the years. I was really chuffed that Alice opened up to me yesterday at the allotment. It can't have been easy to talk about her mum the way she did. Knowing her background and understanding how much she'd had to overcome at such a young age has helped me to fit together some of the missing pieces from her jigsaw puzzle. Now I understand why she's kept love at arm's length. Because she's afraid. She's seen how easily love can tear you apart and she's protecting herself. Those barriers of hers are there for a good reason.

I remain a firm believer in love, though. And finding out that Alice has such a big heart makes me even more hopeful that there will be room for me in it.

She spots me standing in the doorway and pads over, a sleepy smile spreading across her face.

'Good morning.'

'Good morning. Your bed felt very empty without you in it so I came down to investigate.'

'I am pleased about that,' she says. 'It's not often I have a man wearing nothing but his boxers in my kitchen.'

'And I am pleased about that,' I laugh.

'Zach, prepare yourself. This morning I am going to make you the best coffee of your life. It's a big statement, I know, given that you are Italian and used to work in a coffee shop. But I've been watching YouTube tutorials for the past twenty minutes so I think that means I'm now a trained barista in my own right?'

Amused, she leads me over to her kitchen table, motioning for me to sit down while she weighs out the ground beans.

'I'm already impressed,' I say as she tamps them down.

'Nat brought all this coffee kit with her when she moved in,' she explains. 'Pretty sure she nicked it from an event she'd organised. Wait, no. Natalie is very professional and never steals things from clients,' she spins round, pulling a face.

I pretend to look shocked. 'Should I check around your house for any of my artwork?'

Alice grins. 'Nah, I'm into bold colours and more than one, preferably. Lots of them, splashed onto a canvas.'

'Pollock?'

'There's no need to be rude.'

'No, I meant Jackson Pollock. The artist. I thought you did art for A level?'

'I did! Renaissance art was my thing, though. And photography. Do I need to hunt out my polo neck again while you give me a modern art lesson?'

'Always teasing,' I sigh. 'How about you pipe down and bring that coffee over, woman.'

'And that, m'lord, was the last thing renowned artist Zach Moretti said before he disappeared and was never seen again.' She's waving the coffee tamper at me and I hold my hands up in surrender.

'Okay, okay, I take it back,' I laugh as Alice hands me the coffee.

80

'Please don't ever pipe down. I mean it. I love to hear you talk. It's like plugging into my own personal uplifting podcast.'

I take a sip. 'Well?' She asks.

Hmm. 'It's good,' I offer.

'The best coffee of your life?' She prompts, hand playfully on her hip.

'Um . . . Yes?'

She laughs. 'You are very bad at lying, which I suppose is a good quality. Listen, I'd love to laze around with you but I've got a meeting with a potential new client this afternoon. Mondays are normally pretty quiet in the shop, and Eve's opening up this morning, but I'd still like to get in and do some prep work before the meeting. It's for a wedding and I always like to be prepared. You're welcome to stay, if you'd like?'

What I'd really like is to be spending the morning in bed with Alice, but her drive and passion for her career is one of the many reasons I'm drawn to her.

'You go and smash it,' I say. 'I could do with some time in the studio, too. And, since I'm in charge of our next date, are you free tonight?'

'Nat's not back until later and I have no plans . . .'

'An old friend of mine has opened a new bar and it's their launch party.'

'What's this? You're inviting me to a bar? You know there's a chance we might see . . . other human beings there?'

'I'll have less of your cheek, thank you very much.'

She beams. 'A bar sounds great, especially as our last date was very wholesome. Two dates in two days, Zach! But there's one big problem . . .'

'There is?' I ask, worried now.

'Very big,' she says.

I'm flummoxed.

'Our alphabet dates?' She says, eyes wide. 'Don't tell me you've forgotten! And I thought you were the romantic one in this situation.'

'Right,' I laugh, relieved. 'If you'll let me finish. H for Happy Hour. Sound good?'

'Early drinks? Now you're talking!' She runs her fingers through my hair and kisses my earlobe before heading off for a shower.

With Alice on my mind, I wonder if it might be hard to focus when I arrive at the studio. She'd very sweetly packed me off with the last cinnamon bun 'in case you need a mid-morning boost' and I'd been so touched by her thoughtfulness. Spotify playlist on, I settle onto the stool by my easel, fully prepared to end up with sketches of Alice on the paper in front of me, rather than the commission I'm meant to be working on. The freckle on the inside of her left thigh. The scar just above her belly button. The way her chestnut brown hair crashes like waves over her body when we're in bed.

Obviously all of the above has been running through my mind on repeat, but it seems to be helping rather than hindering my creativity. Now charcoal sketches are strewn across the floor at my feet, paintbrushes dipped in colours I don't usually use by the sink. When I finally check the time I realise I'm only an hour off our date and I definitely want to change out of my paint-splattered clothes before I see her again, so I dash home for a shower.

It's a mess in here. I've been meaning to start properly renovating the house ever since I bought it earlier in the year but finding the time isn't easy with so much to do in the studio. I pull on some fresh clothes and am about to leave the house when I feel my phone vibrating in the back pocket of my jeans. I wonder if it's Alice after directions to the bar.

But the screen is lit up with a different name.

Clara.

I frown. It's been a while since she's called now. I figured I got the message when I'd ignored her the few times she rang in the days after we split, leaving her WhatsApp messages unread and deleting her voicemails.

What does she want now?

I shake my head. It doesn't matter. Automatically my thumb goes to decline the call and I put my phone on silent, not wanting any disruptions.

Theo's standing at the door of the bar when I arrive, greeting people with a huge smile across his face.

'Zach, it's good to see you! It's been a while.'

Theo and I used to work together at a coffee shop in Sharrow before he set up his own café and my art started taking off, meaning I didn't need to work the extra job.

'Congratulations, man,' I clap him on the back. 'A successful café and now a bar, too. The empire grows!'

'Hah. Not quite an empire, yet. Give me time though. Come on in and take a look around.' He leads me inside and I take in the exposed timber floors and Scandi-style tables, teamed with plush furniture and deep blue walls.

'It looks really good,' I say.

Theo smiles. 'I've reserved a table for you. Drinks are on the house for old friends. I'll come and catch up again later!'

I pick up the cocktail list and entertain myself by wondering which one Alice will like the best. In the end I go for something called a Hugo, made using elderflower, prosecco, club soda and mint leaves, because it sounds botanical and I now know how much she loves growing things in her allotment.

Back from the bar, I settle into my seat and smile as Theo masterfully does his meet and greet thing with the rest of the guests. I know for a fact that Theo isn't the kind of guy who'd feel awkward if he was sat waiting for a date in a busy bar, like I am right now. He's got the same easy confidence as Alice. It's been a while now, the prosecco in the cocktails I ordered no longer fizzing. Where is she? I hope she's okay.

Remembering I left my phone on silent as I dashed out of the house earlier, I pull it out to check if she's messaged.

And that's when I spot them.

Four missed calls and a voicemail from my ex.

Clara was never in touch this often even when we were together so it's out of character for her to call so much, which makes me worry it could be an emergency. I reluctantly press play on the voicemail.

'*Zach, hi, it's me . . .*' I bristle at the sound of her voice, once so familiar to me. It acts like a time machine, taking me away from my life now and back to the days when it was Clara and me. I listen. '*I know this is all out of the blue and I'm sorry to contact you like this. You've made it clear that you don't want to hear from me and I understand that. I just had to get in touch because there's something you need to know. I'm sorry to tell you this over voice message but if you won't pick up the phone there's no other way. So here it is I guess. Zach, I'm engaged. I know it's soon—*'

I drop my phone onto the table, not wanting to hear any more. My mind feels like it's going at a thousand miles an hour, thoughts coming in and out so fast that I can't grab onto them for long enough to process anything.

She's engaged?

I should clear my head, get some fresh air. I should not give this any more thought. Taking a sip of my cocktail, I try to get myself back into the here and now but it's not easy. Like a dick, I pick up my phone and scroll through Instagram until I find Clara's profile, which I'd long-since unfollowed.

There it is.

A typically stylish black and white photo, but this one's of her. She never normally shares photos of herself on social media. Or, shared, I correct myself. I don't know her any more. It's an image of Clara leaning into him, the ring on her finger sparkling more than the lights in the background.

I seek out the caption even though I know I shouldn't.

Starting the week with a spring in my step! This weekend I said yes.

It was posted earlier today, the likes already pouring in as her friends wish them all the best in a conveyor belt of congratulations.

And what stings the most is I know who her fiancé is. He's the man who Clara had been secretly seeing the entire time we were together. A sharp intake of breath and another sip of my drink. An elephant has just walked straight into this bar. Alice is on her way and I *still* haven't told her about my messy last relationship.

Alice brings a waft of fresh air with her as she sits down next to me, her face breaking into a huge smile as she spots the two empty glasses on the table. 'Easy tiger! Did I take so long that you had to drink all the cocktails?'

'Ah, sorry,' I say, attempting to laugh back. 'I was thirsty. Let me get some more.' I head over to the bar and order the same again, my head feeling slightly woozy from necking two drinks in quick succession. 'They're called Hugos. I thought you might like them because they contain lots of things you can grow,' I explain when I get back.

'Zach, that's sweet,' she says, taking a sip. 'Mmm, it's good.'

She looks even prettier this evening. Her hair falls around her shoulders and she's wearing a navy silk shirt with yellow polka dots tucked into loose-fitting jeans, a pair of butterscotch block heels on her feet.

I crack my knuckles, willing the tension I can feel throughout my body to dissipate.

'Are you okay?' She asks tenderly. 'You seem a little on edge.'

Pull yourself together, Zach.

'I'm fine thanks,' I nod, trying to soak up Alice's positivity. Why am I letting Clara get to me like this. She's in the past.

'*Okay*. Everything all right in the studio?'

'Um, yeah, it went well actually. Thanks. How was your day?' I ask, trying to shift the conversation away from me. There's no point dwelling on this, I tell myself.

Alice claps her hands together, excitement lighting up her face.

'Remember that bride I mentioned to you this morning? We had the best meeting. She brought her fiancé too and they were just the cutest couple. And they're keen, too. They only got engaged on Friday but she's already so on it, she's got a clear vision of what she wants and the best bit is that she's a fashion director, so this could have a massive impact for my business.'

A fashion director who got engaged only a few days ago? You've got to be kidding me.

Alice is asking me if I've heard of the magazine where she works, which of course I have. I shift uncomfortably in my seat, willing this conversation to move in a different direction.

'So anyway,' Alice charges on, 'she found my work through an interior blogger they featured in the mag, who I've collaborated with before. How cool is that? So she's already been into the shop and knows that I get booked up quickly, especially during wedding season, which is why she got in touch so fast. This could be huge exposure for the shop, Zach. She's super influential and I already know that their wedding is going to be stunning.'

She pauses to take a sip of her drink and I find myself unable to think of anything to say.

'They're such a sweet pair. They decided to make it Instagram official this afternoon, just before our meeting, and she kept checking her phone and getting all excited when she saw the comments coming in.'

My ex is getting married and the woman I'm now seriously into is doing the wedding flowers. I can't believe this is happening – just as I was over it and finally moving on too.

Alice is so full of enthusiasm and I shake my head, hoping to shift the thundercloud that's gathered there, but it's not working. I've just found myself slap bang in a very awkward situation.

'That sounds good,' I say trying to muster some enthusiasm to support Alice on her important new client.

Alice takes a long sip of her drink.

'Zach, I feel like I'm missing something. You seem . . . off.

Is there something on your mind or are you annoyed with me because I'm late?'

'No, it's not that.'

'Because it was only twenty minutes!'

'Like I said, it's not that.'

'Well, what is it then?' She bristles. 'Am I boring you with my work chat? You've barely said a word to me since I got here.'

'I'm not the same as you, Alice,' I find myself snapping. 'I'm not always full of the joys of spring, okay?'

Alice flinches.

Stop being such an idiot.

'I didn't mean that to sound like a character assassination. Sorry. I'm just . . . You're always so positive. So perky. I can't match that today.'

'I never asked you to match that,' she counters, ruffled. 'Everything was fine this morning. Has something happened?'

'Uh . . . no.'

'No? That's it? I just get grunts of one-word answers now?' She's folded her arms now, looking hurt and confused. I know I should be back-peddling but Clara's news is painful and I'm lashing out at the person who least deserves it. Worse, the picture has reminded me that I need to be completely upfront with Alice and when I do that, she'll run a mile.

I take a deep breath.

'I'm really sorry Alice. You're right, something has happened but I don't really want to talk about it right now. Let's just enjoy our evening.'

Alice nods sympathetically and I feel like an absolute dick. So much for "happy" hour.

'Whatever has happened, I'm here to help when you feel ready. It sounds like you need some time to process things and honestly, Zach, I wouldn't have minded if you'd cancelled tonight. I'm pretty easy-going, you know?' She gives a little laugh and I smile back at her, frustrated with myself for messing this up. 'Listen, why don't we call it a night? We can catch up properly when you've had some time.'

She's right. Better to call it quits before I act like even more of a fool and completely put Alice off me.

'Okay,' I say, frustrated with myself. 'Sorry again.'

'You don't need to apologise. I'll see you soon, if you want to.' Softly, she kisses me on the cheek and leaves.

You still in your office? I'm in a bar just round the corner and I've royally fucked up.

I finish at 6 tonight so can be with you in ten mins x

Nine minutes later and Ellie bursts through the doors.

'Please tell me you didn't you drink all of those yourself?' She demands, eyeing up the empties.

'I got here at five for happy hour and in fairness, Alice had one,' I say.

'Is she here?' Ellie looks around excitedly.

'She left, that's my problem.'

'It's not over is it?' she asks, grabbing my hand.

'No, she's just giving me some space.' I explain about Clara's news and the fact that my mood just ruined a date with Alice.

'Oh Zach,' Ellie says, pushing a glass of water towards me. 'Don't be too hard on yourself. That is a lot to take on board.'

'I feel like such an idiot. You know I had no idea that Clara was in a relationship when I met her. And then I found out there was this "ex" on the scene and she swore she'd broken it off with him. So how come just months after we break up, she's getting engaged to him?' I shake my head.

'She straight up lied to you, Zach. You don't deserve to be treated like that.'

'I'm really annoyed with myself, Ellie.'

'It wasn't your fault!'

'But I let it affect my time with Alice. Turns out she's now doing their wedding flowers and she's all excited because Clara's such a high-profile client. For a second I thought about telling Alice that I knew Clara but it just felt weird. And then I couldn't even muster any enthusiasm and probably seemed so rude and standoffish when she was telling me about work, which is so important to her. It's all a big fucking mess and now she's gone.'

'That is awkward,' Ellie says sympathetically. 'But it's not beyond repair, right? It's possible you're being a tiny bit over-dramatic, just like your brother. Maybe it is time you told her about Clara? I think it would help to give you peace of mind. And you can always make up for tonight by cooking Nonna's zucchini pasta for her another time.'

In spite of myself, the reference fills me with comfort. Raff and I insisted on zucchini pasta as often as possible during those brilliant summers at Nonna's. It's a family recipe that has been passed down through the generations and is still a firm favourite. Raff and Ellie handed out hot plates of it for their wedding breakfast, explaining to all the British guests that zucchini is Italian for courgette.

'I'd murder for a bowl of that right now,' I say with a half-smile.

'There we go! You're feeling better already. Zach?'

'Yeah?'

'When you saw the photo of Clara's engagement, did a part of you wish it was you? Asking her to marry you, I mean?'

My answer is immediate and honest.

'Absolutely not.'

I'm surprised by how much I know this to be true even though when we were together I had allowed myself to wonder if we might get married one day. I clear my throat and look at Ellie. She's studying me closely. 'It's funny how your feelings for someone can change so quickly. I'm not saying I'm not shocked that she's getting married now, of course I am, but you know what? Seeing that picture made me realise that I am completely over her. I've known it the whole time but ... I dunno. I guess seeing that photo has cemented it. But, fuck, Ellie, I feel like such a dick for how things are playing out now. It's obvious how much I like Alice but that scares me.'

'Why?' She asks, concern etched across her face.

'Because I don't want to feel like a fool again.'

'You aren't a fool, Zach. Being vulnerable isn't foolish. It's just a part of loving someone and unfortunately, the last person you fell for took advantage of that. That doesn't mean that history will repeat itself and it certainly doesn't mean you should stop trying. It sounds to me like you're simply upset to have found out about Clara, which is understandable. So you know what you have to do now, right?'

I shake my head.

'Go get your woman.'

Ikea

Alice

If I thought perusing the bread section of my corner shop would take my mind off things, I was wrong. There's only one loaf left for a start. (Wholemeal, as if I need that in my life right now.) Even small talk with the guy behind the till can't stop me from thinking about the abrupt ending of our Happy Hour date earlier this evening. Zach and I would probably be out for dinner by now, if only he hadn't been so preoccupied with whatever it was. I think giving him some space was the right thing to do, I just hope he's okay. As I unlock my front door and I'm immediately hit by the smell of a thousand scented candles.

'Home so soon?' Natalie asks.

'Zach was a bit off so I'm going to make cheese on toast for dinner. I'd offer you some but I've a hunch you might be going out?' I say, taking in the fact my best friend is currently striding around in her bra and pants while my living room has been turned into a mood-lit walk-in wardrobe.

'Sorry to hear that, hot stuff. Want to talk about it?'

I shake my head. 'What I'd really like to do is help you get ready. This looks fun.'

'Good because I cannot decide what to wear. Dylan was right, it's time to launch myself back out there and I now intend to date all the eligible men of Sheffield. I'm quite excited about this guy,' she says, wriggling out of the jeans and top combo she'd just rejected while I rifle through her impressive selection of hairbands. 'He's very cute *and* we're going for ramen.'

'How about this then?' I ask, handing her a band T-shirt and leather skirt. 'Sort of cool and cute all rolled into one?'

As Natalie pulls the outfit on I run upstairs to grab my make-up bag. 'I follow this amazing make-up artist on Instagram who does incredible things with eyeliner. Shall we watch one of her videos while I try it on you?'

'Obviously yes,' Nat says, sitting down obediently as I walk back into the room.

I grab my phone to set up our tutorial.

Oh.

'You okay?' She asks.

'Just got a message from Zach. I'll read it later.'

'Nice try, but you should read it now,' she commands.

I open the message and read it. 'He's apologising for being off with me. Says he wants to explain things in person and is asking if he can come round.'

'Well I'm heading off soon. Sounds like he has something important to tell you.'

'It does, doesn't it?' I say, full of curiosity and concern.

When Nat's fully made up and looking divine, she gives me a squeeze and says: 'I'll keep my phone on so if you need me, call me, okay?'

'Thanks,' I say, suddenly feeling nervous.

Zach is leaning against the fridge, his hair mussed up and his brows knitted together. He looks so anxious that I just want to kiss him better but I sense that he needs to talk first.

'I'm sorry again, for earlier,' he says, holding his hands out as I make us both a cup of tea.

'Are you okay?' I ask.

'I, er . . .' he rubs his fingers along his forehead. 'I've got something I need to tell you.'

'Grab a seat. Cheese on toast?'

'Yes please.'

'Those cocktails were strong, huh?' I say with a little laugh. I don't know what he's got to tell me but seeing how nervous he seems to be is making me worried. I place the plates of cheese on toast down and pull up a seat opposite, biting at a crust and realising that I'm not that hungry after all.

Zach clears his throat.

'Alice, I'm sorry I was off earlier at the bar. It wasn't that you were boring me by talking about work at all.' He pauses to take a deep breath. 'It turns out that the wedding client you had a meeting with today is my ex-girlfriend.'

'Clara? Oh God. That's awkward, sorry Zach, I had no idea.'

He takes a sip of his tea. 'Really, you don't need to apologise. This is on me. I didn't know she was engaged so it all came as a bit of a shock.'

'Yeah, I can understand that. Had you two been serious, then?'

Zach nods, catching my eyes ever so briefly. 'We'd been together for about eighteen months.'

'Was she your first love?' I ask, wondering if that explains why they'd fallen out of touch. I mean, I know not many people remain close after they split up but I'm surprised that he didn't know she was in a serious relationship now.

'It's more recent than that. We only broke up a few months ago.'

Ouch. Clara must have moved on quickly. No wonder he's upset. Though now that I think of it, I swear she and James said they'd been together for a couple of years. Something doesn't quite add up here and I frown, trying to make sense of it. Zach's watching me, a mixture of embarrassment and unease written across his face and just like that, it dawns on me.

'But Clara told me that she and James had been together for

years. So does that mean you were seeing Clara while . . .' I say it as a statement, the reality of it sinking in.

Zach takes another deep breath, looking over at me through those dark lashes of his.

'That's right,' he admits.

I lean back, pushing my plate away from me. Zach's last relationship was an affair. I can feel my defences inching back up around me, locking in place to try and keep me safe.

'Will you let me explain?' He asks.

I nod, folding my arms in front of me.

'Okay,' he clears his throat. 'A couple of years ago Clara's magazine commissioned me to do some pen and ink drawings to run alongside a fashion shoot and that's when we first met. She invited me out for drinks when the issue published and one thing led to another. We started dating, things were going well, we started to get serious, you know how it goes. Only, about a year into the relationship I found out that she'd had this ex.'

'James?' I ask, joining the dots.

'Yeah. Clara insisted that they were no longer together when she and I met, and that he was only still on the scene because they worked together. There were a lot of red flags, like how she wanted to keep our relationship low key, how she never invited me to her work events . . .' Zach lets out a low, deep sigh then. 'But I liked her, I even thought I loved her so I wanted to believe her. It was only earlier today when I finally figured it out. She left me a voice message telling me that she was engaged and then I saw the photo of her and James together on Instagram . . . she never did split up with him. I was just, I don't know, an extra.'

I bite my thumbnail, my heart breaking for how sad he looks and for how sad I feel, too.

'Today was just . . . confirmation, I guess, that she hadn't been straight up with me,' he adds.

'I had no idea, Zach. So when did you two split up?'

94

Zach's elbows are on the table now, his thumb rubbing his jawline as he looks down at the cheese on toast he's left untouched.

'She broke up with me on the day of my exhibition,' he says, wincing.

'The day we met?'

'The day we met,' he confirms.

I stand up, then, the legs of my chair screeching across the wooden floor. I don't want to hear any more.

'I know you're upset but Alice, please—' he's up too, moving around the table towards me but I hold my hands up and step away from him.

'I just need some space to think about this. It's a lot to take on board. I think you should go.'

'Of course. I'm sorry, again. I . . . I really like you, Alice.'

I smile tightly as I usher him to the front door, my head spinning and feeling more confused than ever.

The next morning I hear a knock on my bedroom door, followed by a stage cough.

'Don't mind me!' Natalie calls through. 'I don't want to interrupt any shagging. Just to say I'm off to grab some breakfast from Forge Bakehouse, text me if you guys want me to bring you some back!'

'You can come in, I'm alone,' I shout, chucking on some joggers and opening the door wide.

'No Zach?' She asks, peeking into my bedroom. 'I thought he was staying. But from the look on your face, last night didn't go great?'

'No it did not,' I say. 'Give me five minutes to brush my teeth and I'll come with?'

Baggy joggers, flip flops and a gardening T-shirt isn't my best look ever, but today already feels like a CBA kind of day and I'm just grateful to get outside with Nat. I've filled her in on everything Zach told me on our way to the bakery and now we're feasting

95

our eyes on breakfast potentials. I order a cardamom snurr and a cappuccino to go, throwing in a custard tart at the last minute for good measure.

We're waiting in line for our hot drinks when my phone buzzes with a message from Zach. The preview on my lock screen reads:

Alice, I just wanted to say that I know my last relationship was messy and I regret so many things about . . .

Nat's reading over my shoulder. 'Aren't you going to open it up and read the rest?'

'But then he'll see that I've read it.'

'So?'

'I'm pissed off, Nat! I don't even do relationships and right when I decide to give them a go, right when I find myself liking a guy, he ends up having a whole lot of history and bringing a load of drama to my life.'

'So you're just going to ignore him?'

'Urgh,' I say, in lieu of some actual words. I already know that I'm not going to ignore him even though I feel frustrated for finding myself in this situation. I open up WhatsApp and together we read the whole message.

Alice, I just wanted to say that I know my last relationship was messy and I regret so many things about it, but my main regret is that I feel like I've messed things up with you. I feel awful for letting it impact our Happy Hour date. The truth is, I've never felt this way about anyone before. I really, really hope I haven't messed this up x

'How do you feel?' Nat asks.

'Annoyed. I don't love the fact that his last relationship ended *hours* before we met. I'd say that's a bit soon for him to be moving on, right?'

'Sounds to me like Zach knew his last relationship wasn't right and it had probably been over long before it ended. I think he's painfully aware of how his past looks but it's also made him want to tell you how strongly he feels for you.'

'But I don't want to be in a relationship with drama! I didn't even want a relationship in the first place, remember? And then along came Zach with his intensely cool ways and talk of love and . . . And now I *like* him and it turns out he liked someone else until right before we met? If he can move on that quickly, he could end up hurting me, right? I'm risk averse, Nat and this is suddenly very risky.'

Natalie hands me a coffee and steers me back onto the street.

'Take a deep breath,' she says. 'It's a lot to take on and now it's your turn to have some time. But if you want my opinion, I'm impressed that he's trying to be honest with you. That's a good thing, no?'

I huff.

'It's taken guts for Zach to tell you this. I think he's been really brave.'

'Maybe. It's a great big red flag though, isn't it? He was dating someone who was already in a relationship! Regardless of what she told him, it's not great. And what's weird is I really liked Clara when I met her. She and James seemed like such a sweet couple.'

'Just goes to show that none of us have any clue what's going on behind the scenes, hun. Relationships are complex and hard, sometimes. And yes, it's a red flag for Zach but you'd been getting so many green flags from him, too. The way he's been honest with you about the whole thing is a big green flag, right? So maybe this is just a bump in the road.'

I pause to take a bite out of my cardamom snurr as we walk.

'This is so annoying. Why am I even worried? I should have got myself out of this situation ages ago because that's what I do, right? But you're right, there have been lots of green flags from him. He has been honest about his ex. He's been incredibly sensitive about my mum. He makes me feel like I can be my whole self around him. He's kind, he's thoughtful, he makes me laugh. The butterflies in my stomach when we're together . . .' I pause, realising I could go on and on.

Natalie is grinning at me.

'Shut up.'

'Didn't say anything,' she says, her smile getting wider.

I roll my eyes. 'So, yeah, there are lots and lots of positives. But because of all the good things I've started developing . . . bloody . . . *feelings* for him and look where I am now! Panicking! What's happening to me?'

'What's happening is that you like him and that's new for you. I know you built up this wall after your mum died, but it's about time that wall came down, and this is what happens when you meet someone. Everyone has their own baggage, you know.'

I sniff, cradling the takeaway cup in one hand and my pastry in the other. Sugar and coffee will be my saviours.

Nat insists on a morning pamper session to take my mind off things and I definitely feel much calmer now I've smoothed a leave-in conditioner through my hair, while my best friend applies a clay face mask.

'I haven't asked how last night's date was?' I say, feeling guilty.

'Let's just say that the ramen and my outfit where the highlights.'

'That bad, huh?'

'He was just boring, that's all,' she says. 'It's nice to be back out there, though.'

'You're kicking heartbreak right in the nuts, Nat. I'm proud of you.'

She shrugs.

'Seriously. From now on I'm going to call you Bounce because of how well you're bouncing back from this. I don't want to spend all morning talking about men because obviously we've got more pressing items on the agenda, like our plans to conquer the world . . .'

'Or where we're going on our next holiday . . .' Nat adds.

'Or whether we should move to New Zealand because they seem to have it sorted over there . . .' I suggest.

'Or if we should eat lasagne or pappardelle for dinner . . .'

I snort. 'See! So much to discuss. But if I may just briefly go back to men again, I did want to ask how you are finding dating post-Jake?'

Natalie's mask is crusting over like a salt-baked cod so she tries to talk without moving her lips. 'It is a bit weird, but only because it's all so new still. Sometimes I find myself thinking how much I'd like to go back to what Jake and I had but honestly Al, I think that's because our relationship had turned into a habit. What I really miss is the comfort of knowing what was going to happen, if that makes sense? Having everything planned out felt safe. But I feel like I've adjusted to my new normal pretty quickly. You can't pick and choose when life-changing things happen to you.'

I'd fallen quiet as I listened to my best friend and notice now that she's trying to wiggle her eyebrows but it's not very easy with a mud crust all over her face so she ends up nodding her head up and down instead. 'In case you can't tell, this is my this-story-is-relevant-to-you-too face,' she says.

'You can't pick and choose when life-changing things happen to you?' I repeat.

'Exactly. I know you're worried that you and Zach hooked up too quickly after his last relationship but you don't get to decide the perfect time to meet someone new. Especially when that person is a glorious ray of sunshine called Alice. It took guts for him to tell you all that and I bet he's worried you'll . . .'

'Do not say bolt.'

She presses her lips closed.

'So . . . will you?'

I pull my hair into a messy bun as I think about it.

'No,' I say eventually. 'You're right, it did take guts.'

'No one is baggage-free, Alice. We all have stories to tell.'

She's right. And now that I've calmed down a bit I'm ready to reply to his message.

I appreciate your honesty Zach. I just want to make it clear that if I'm in this, then I need to know that you are too. I don't want what happened in your last relationship to happen again with us.

Alice, I am so in this. He types back instantly.

Meet me at 9 a.m. next Saturday, then?

It's a date. You won't regret this x

'Gerty! I've been very much looking forward to seeing you again,' I grin, patting the car bonnet affectionately when she's parked outside my house a week later as instructed. 'Glad you brought your chauffeur, too,' I nod towards Zach.

'Objection, your honour. I'm also a gift-bearer,' Zach says, nervously handing me a large paper bag.

'Shall I open it?'

'That's sort of the point,' he teases.

I reach inside, pulling out a framed piece of art. Bright splashes of colour cluster together like an abstract bunch of flowers. I trace it with my finger. It's signed by Zach.

'You painted this?'

'I was in the studio thinking about you and playing around with colour. I thought you might like it?' He looks so hopeful.

'I love it. I'm really touched you made this for me.'

'It's my way of saying thanks, I guess. For giving me a chance. I want you to know that I am so into what we have.'

I look over at him, struck with how much he seems to care, and feel instantly like I've made the right decision.

'Plus you said you were redecorating so I thought you might like to have something new to hang on your walls when you're done?' He's leaning against Gerty and watching me nervously.

'That's really sweet, Zach. So, shall we?'

'Let's. You might want to tell me where we're going first, though.'

'Clue: cheap meatballs.'

'IKEA?'

I high five my date. 'Hells yes. Have you seen *500 Days of Summer*?'

Zach nods. Of course he has.

'Well, I was writing a list of stuff I need to decorate when it struck me that there's no bigger test than going to IKEA with the guy you're seeing. And you're convinced I'm a commitment-phobe so . . .'

'Are you going to prove to me that you're not?'

'I'm definitely going to pretend I'm Zooey Deschanel and also eat a lot of meatballs.'

Laughing, Zach opens up the passenger door and I hop in.

'Tiny pencil?' I ask.

'Check.'

'Store map?'

'Check.'

'Trolley?'

'Do we really need a trolley? I thought you said you only needed a couple of bits . . .'

'Let me stop you right there,' I interject. 'It is a truth universally known that you cannot go to IKEA and only buy "a couple of bits". Even the most focus-minded people get side-tracked by all the stuff. You just wait.'

'All right, but you're pushing,' he grins.

'Ooh, what a gentleman,' I joke.

Now I'm making it my mission to plonk my bum down in every single room set-up we walk past, pretending that I live in each perfectly styled Scandinavian haven. Zach's joined in and we're making up role play scenarios in every one. Currently I'm Devil Boss, perched on the swivel chair in a home office set-up. I swing round to face Zach and bark: 'What makes you think you're qualified for this job?'

His eyebrows raise in amusement as he plays along. 'Could you remind me of the job specifications, please?'

'Dating me,' I say, pulling my most stern face. 'It's a full-time commitment. I'm very high maintenance. I expect calls at least

101

once every ten minutes during the day, a good morning message the minute you've woken up and to be lavished with adoration at every opportunity.'

Zach mimes making notes as I march on with my pretend checklist.

'Absolutely,' he squares his shoulders. 'I'm fully on board. I will always agree with everything you say and will never argue, even if you do decide to become high maintenance.'

He holds up the store map. On the back he's scribbled: 'You're cute and I like you.'

I laugh. 'That is very inappropriate for a job interview.'

He scribbles a new note and holds it up. 'You deserve to be happy.'

'So soppy,' I scoff, rolling my eyes even though my heart is pounding. My date is charming and it's a joy to feel like we've fallen back into the swing of things together. Spinning back to my imaginary computer, I start pretend typing and say, 'I'd ask you to send me your CV but we all know what *that* looks like.'

'What's wrong with being a successful artist?'

'I meant your love CV.'

'Low blow. How about you stop ribbing me and buy me something pretty instead?'

'Uh uh, no way,' I say, swerving the trolley out of Zach's reach.

'What do you mean?' He asks, mock-crestfallen eyes looking at me. Those eyes.

'There is no way you're putting anything in my trolley.'

'Oh it's *your* trolley now, is it?'

'It's always been my trolley. Ever since you scoffed at the idea of needing one, remember? Or have you conveniently forgotten now you too have discovered a load of stuff you don't need and yet have to buy?'

He looks down at the ceramic soap dish in his hand.

'It's possible that I was wrong,' he grins.

'Mmm hmm. So what are you going to do now?'

102

'Use yours! It isn't even yours, Alice. It's IKEA's.'

'I foresaw the need for it, like a bargain basement fortune teller.'

'Then you'll have foreseen this, too.' Zach's up against my body before I know it, his chin resting lightly on my forehead. Instinctively I circle my hands around his waist and he moves his lips close to my ear. 'I've missed this,' he whispers and my heart continues its gradual defrost. Suddenly Zach's stepping back, untwining my hands and looking triumphant. I cast around to figure out what he's up to. He's put the soap dish in my trolley!

'Hey! You tricked me,' I grumble. I'm not usually befuddled by sexiness like this. Whatever's going on, I quite like it.

'Players gonna play,' he says, face crumpled in amusement.

I fold my arms, stifling a giggle.

'In that case, I'll race you to the restaurant. Last one there buys the meatballs,' I call, blocking him in with the trolley as I run off.

With Zach and the clunky trolley in hot pursuit, I finally screech to a halt at the canteen, plonking myself down at the nearest table and throwing my hands into the air with a double victory sign. I'm about to shout something triumphant when I realise that I've got a stitch. Ouch. Zach pulls up next to me, his thick dark hair looking extra messy from the run.

Finally catching my breath, I say: 'I win!'

'You cheated,' he objects, leaning against the table.

'I merely saw an opportunity.'

'You hemmed me in *and* left me with a trolley that won't turn on its wheels.'

'Excuses, excuses. How does it feel to be a loser?'

'I will be getting my own back on our next date, you just wait.'

'Oh really?'

'Really. Well if you'd still be up for another date that is?' He grins, eyes twinkling and I nod. 'Why are you sticking your fingers into your side like that?'

'I got a stitch from the run,' I admit.

'So you thought you'd treat a sharp, stabbing pain under your ribs by poking it?'

'What can I say, the medical profession was my second career option if floristry didn't work out.'

Zach laughs, easing my hand away from my side and instructing me to take slow, deep breaths. He kneels down next to me, matching his breathing with mine until the pain starts to ease. It's the sweetest moment.

'Better?' He asks after a while.

'Better. That actually worked. Thanks!'

'Glad to be of assistance, ma'am. Now, I believe I'm buying. What do you fancy?'

I rub my hands together. 'I can't decide between a hotdog or a plate of meatballs so I might go for both?'

Zach stands up straighter. 'Both?'

Seems reasonable?

He checks his watch. 'It's not even eleven a.m. so what you're saying is, you'd like a hotdog *and* meatballs for brunch.'

'Yes,' I cheer.

I can't tell if Zach is impressed or incredulous as he walks towards the canteen.

Predictably, Zach opted for a more stylish elevenses of coffee and cake which he wolfed down within minutes.

'Who's laughing now? You're all done while I've still got a lot of balls to get through,' I say before pulling up short. Smirk.

'Looks like you're doing a pretty good job to me,' he grins, eyebrows raised. 'I was wondering if you'd let me have a bite of that sausage. You've got a lot on your plate, after all.'

'It's what the Swedish people would want.'

'So can I? Try your hot dog?'

'Fine,' I smile, holding it out to him. He takes a bite and a little bit of American mustard smudges on his lip so I reach across to brush it off.

'And the winner of today's All You Can Eat competition is . . .' Zach drumrolls his fingers on the table. 'Alice O'Neill. Congratulations, Alice, how do you feel?'

He holds an imaginary microphone to my mouth and I giggle. 'Mouth . . . still . . . full!'

'I'm sorry, ladies and gentlemen, but it appears our winner is still eating. What an impressive appetite she has! No doubt we'll be seeing much more from Ms O'Neill through our packed summer schedule of All You Can Eat competitions.'

Finally finishing my mouthful, I take a bow. 'Thank you so much.'

'And the crowd went wild!'

We're laughing, eyes trained on each other as we play out my apparent victory.

'As Chief Judge, I wouldn't mind taking you home now,' he grins.

'Wouldn't that blur the boundaries between competitor and judge? I'm sure there are rules about that,' I tease.

'Funnily enough I wrote the rules.' Zach pushes his glasses up his nose and pretends to read from an imaginary rule book. 'Here it is. Under Category B, Subsection C, I can see that it is definitely ok,' he beams, holding out his hand. I take it, both of us still giggling as we make our way to the car park.

Jogging

Zach

Something's not quite right with my brother, I think, studying his face on my phone screen over a spoonful of cereal and trying to work out why he looks different today. 'Are you wearing lipstick?' I ask eventually.

Raff looks distracted. 'Hmm? Oh, yes I am. Fran and Sienna have been giving me a makeover this morning. They said something about Daddy needing a glow up? I don't know what that is.'

'Suits you.'

Raff laughs. 'It's been a while. Is this really my long-lost brother calling?'

'Very funny. Listen, man, I'm sorry I've been quiet. Work's gone crazy but I finally finished a commission this week so I'm treating myself to the weekend off.'

'Want to come and visit?'

'Ah, I'd love that but I'm seeing Alice later.'

'Things back on track then?'

'I think so. She brings out the best in me, she makes me laugh and I swear I'm working better now as well. I definitely feel at my happiest when I'm around her but we haven't seen much of each other recently because Alice has been really busy with wedding season too; this is a hectic time of year for her.'

'Are the alphabet dates still going strong?'

'We went to IKEA for the last one,' I reply, smiling thinking of how we'd acted like a couple of dorks, pretending to live in the show spaces.

Raff grimaces. 'I haven't been there since the twins were three. It was so busy and the girls decided to entertain themselves by having a farting competition. I don't think we'd be welcomed back. I take it yours was better?'

'You could say that.' I say with a big grin, thinking back to how eating £1 meatballs was not half the story, with us spending the rest of the day in bed once we got back to Alice's house.

'The smile says it all,' Raff tuts. 'Lucky bastard. So you haven't seen her since?'

'Yup. It's been two weeks now and I can't wait to see her later. I've missed her but I've also felt strangely cool about it. I like that we've both got our own things going on and that we're not living in each other's pockets. With Clara I constantly wanted reassurance from her that she was going to find time for me but I think that's because I knew we were on rocky ground.'

Ellie's head pops onto the screen as she sits down next to Raff. 'That's because Clara was a crazy demonic . . .'

'Person,' Raff sensors.

'Not quite what I was going for, but yeah,' Ellie grins.

I take another mouthful of cereal as my brother and sister-in-law settle in next to each other.

'With Alice I feel like I can get on with my own stuff without worrying.'

Ellie slaps her hand down on the kitchen table, making us all jump. 'Well, well, well. Alice may be the first person who has chilled you out!' She exclaims before pulling a face. 'Listen, I've been worried about this, Zach.'

'Here we go,' Raff sighs.

'Be quiet,' she instructs.

'Worried about what?' I frown.

'That you've moved on from unattainable Clara to a fixer-upper.'

'A fixer-upper? Ellie, you've been the one championing Alice and I from the start. What's changed?'

'Don't you think it's weird that she's never had a serious relationship before?' she says. 'Like, don't get me wrong, I am all for people prioritising themselves and their careers but . . .' I can hear her drumming her nails on the table. 'But she's also told you that she's a cynic when it comes to romance and doesn't believe in "the one". For me that rings alarm bells. I don't want you to get hurt again.'

'Have you been reading some amateur psych memes on Instagram again, my love?' Raff teases. He gets barged off his seat.

'Look, I appreciate your concern Ellie. Alice really opened up to me at her allotment a while back and I think I understand why she's swerved relationships. And she definitely doesn't need fixing, okay? She's perfect as she is. I'm just trying to live in the moment for a while, to be more like Alice, because being around her makes me happy.'

Ellie looks like she approves of that. 'That's the main thing. I'd very much like to meet her at some point.' An image of Alice under a spotlight while Ellie fires probing questions at her fills my mind. 'So . . . watcha waiting for?'

'A time when my best friend doesn't give the girl I'm seeing a massive grilling and scare her off?'

Ellie rolls her eyes. 'Please. I'll be divine. Let's get it in the diary!'

'All right, I'll mention it to her and see what she says. Now, Raff, go and enjoy your glow up. Tell Fran and Sienna that Uncle Zach thinks some sparkly eyeshadow would look really good on their dad.'

'I will say no such thing,' Raff tuts.

'But I might,' grins Ellie, blowing kisses down the phone.

By Saturday afternoon Alice is walking towards me in a pair of lilac leggings with a matching crop top, her hair bouncing in its high ponytail as she walks. I lean against a tree, trying to match her effortless cool while similarly feeling like the luckiest man in the country, which isn't easy.

'I cannot believe I was so keen to see you that I've agreed to a jog, Zach,' she says, wide-eyed.

'Oh really?' I reply with a raised eyebrow. 'You were keen to see me?'

Alice tightens her ponytail.

'I didn't say that,' she mumbles, trying to shrug it off.

'You definitely did. Who'd have thought Ms Play It Cool was, and I quote, "keen to see me".'

She playfully rolls her eyes.

'Did you miss me?' I grin.

'Please.'

'Because I missed you.'

'I might have missed you but only the tiniest bit so don't let that head get too big.' It's hard to believe that this awesome woman actually likes my company and I use retying my shoelaces as an excuse to let her sentence sit for a while.

'You ready? It's the perfect day for a nice long run,' I eventually say.

'When you say nice and long you mean . . . '

'Maybe a 10k?'

Alice's eyes widen in horror. She motions towards her lilac lycra and bright white trainers, her ankles edged with pink running socks. 'Let me break this down for you,' she says as I swallow hard, trying not to get distracted by how good she looks. 'I am not a runner. This is the only sportswear I own and I put it on to do yoga on YouTube with Natalie. And when I say do, I mean *watch*. We'll roll out our yoga mats and sometimes we'll try a bit of the breathing but mostly we just sit and eat snacks before chanting "ohm" at the end.'

I laugh. 'I didn't realise I was dating a fitness-phobe.'

'I prefer the term fitness-averse,' she giggles. 'I'll do a bit every now and then but to be honest, I'm on my feet all day at the shop as it is. You, on the other hand, are apparently the kind of man who talks about running in terms of distance which is alarming.'

'Not alarming,' I try to put her at ease. 'Running's a massive endorphin boost and a nice way to switch off from stuff, but don't panic because there could be cake at the end of it. I'm combining a jog with junk food for our J date.'

'Oh now you're talking,' grins Alice. 'You know me so well.'

Five minutes in and Alice is already asking if we've hit 10k so I suggest we reset our goals and go for five instead.

'No way. Nuh uh. I am no quitter. You said ten and I will give you ten,' she puffs. 'How long does one of those usually take when you're running by yourself?'

'Just under an hour,' I reply as we jog along the river in Millhouses Park.

'Ooh, is that a pedalo?' Alice asks, distracted by a swan-shaped pedal boat floating across the boating lake. 'We could do that instead? Look, those guys have got an ice cream on theirs.'

'I'm afraid neither pedalo nor ice cream begin with a J.'

'Hang on, rewind. Did you just say a 10k takes you an hour? OF RUNNING? Are you kidding me Zach?'

I shake my head.

'Fine, I can totally run for an hour. No probs.'

As we run along I realise that Alice is not only competitive but also incredibly stubborn. I set a slow pace at first, not wanting her to get too tired too soon and thinking that we might jack it in after half an hour or so, anyway. Alice has other plans. She's taking great pride in racing past me as we jog through Ecclesall Woods and while running behind Alice in her lilac leggings has its obvious perks, I don't particularly enjoy being elbowed out of the way when we come to a narrow bit so she can go first.

'You're kind of a rude runner.'

'I like to win,' she pants. 'Surely we're nearly there now?'

'About half way through,' I say, listening to her groan. 'Just think of the end game. I'm ordering burgers on Deliveroo.'

She shoots me a look, her cheeks pink with the effort. 'Talk dirty to me,' she says between exhales.

'Beef patty covered in melted cheese.'

'More.'

'Grilled bacon on top.'

'Keep it coming.'

'Brioche bun. Crinkle cut fries. A cool beer on the side.'

'Yes. YES. YEEEEEEEES,' she calls out and I feel like I'm watching Meg Ryan at the diner in *When Harry Met Sally*.

A dog walker overhears and looks flustered as they walk by and I laugh to myself, even more spurred on to catch up now.

'I can do this, Zach!' And off she goes again, jogging past brambles, jumping over fallen trees and at one point actually turning back to me and clapping, as if she was the seasoned runner and I was the newbie. The more time I spend with Alice, the more I realise that she never fails to surprise me.

We're knackered by the time we get back to Alice's and she emerges from the bathroom in a cloud of steam, a little white towel wrapped around her hair and her skin still glowing from the run. I jump in after her, borrowing her apple shampoo, which I can smell on me now as I pull a fresh T-shirt and jeans out of the bag I'd packed earlier. I didn't want to assume I'd be invited to stay tonight but going for a run seemed like a cheeky cover to bring some overnight stuff, just in case.

'STITCH,' Alice calls out as I head downstairs to find her lying on the sofa. 'I'm taking deep breaths like you taught me but it still hurts.'

'Jesus, what *have* you two been up to?' smirks Natalie, joining us from the kitchen.

'Zach just made me run ten entire kilometres and now I'm never moving again.'

111

'Bit melodramatic,' Nat laughs.

'Agreed,' I say, smiling at Alice. 'Also funny because the way I remember it, you insisted that we carried on even after I'd suggested stopping.'

'Oh yeah, she gets like that,' says Nat as she potters between us in the living room and their kitchen. 'One minute you're suggesting something and the next Alice has to be the champion at it. It's quite annoying, actually. Remember our school leavers' ball?' A snort of laughter comes from the direction of the sofa.

'Quiffs were a big thing back then,' Nat explains to me. 'The bigger the better. Alice and I spent the entire day of the ball backcombing our hair and right when I thought we were done and started getting dressed, Alice began shoving in more hair pins and misting more hair spray. The next thing I knew I was going to the ball with Marie Antoinette. Hair so high she had to slide down the back seat of her dad's car so it didn't hit the roof.'

'Har har har, very amusing, thank you for sharing,' Alice says.

'I bet your date loved that,' I say.

'Dylan thought it was hilarious,' Nat adds.

Oh, so Alice and Dylan *did* date when they were at school. It figures, I guess. I feel my shoulders tense up and try to relax because whatever happened back then, Alice and Dylan are just friends now. I'm trying to style out the pang of jealousy but Natalie must have noticed my reaction because she's already backtracking.

'Not like that. Not *date* date. We all went together. Kind of a three-way. Hang on, I'm making it worse,' Natalie shakes her head. 'None of us could get real dates because we were quite an insular little gang of three so we did a lame friend date thing instead. We actually had the best time, apart from the bit where Alice out-quiffed me.'

'That explains Alice's race to the canteen at IKEA.' I tease, although I'm quietly relieved to hear that Dylan wasn't Alice's first love. 'Has she always been happy to win at any costs, even if it involves cheating?'

'Oi!' Alice protests as Nat heads back into the kitchen. 'It wasn't cheating just . . . making the most of an opportunity with the trolley.'

'Sure, you tell yourself that,' I grin, checking the time. 'Well you did make it through the run so I guess I owe you junk food as promised.'

'Nat, do you want to order a burger?' Alice shouts after her friend. 'Wait, sorry Zach, I should have checked first. Is that okay with you? I just don't want her to feel left out.'

'Of course it's okay, I'm the third-wheel here,' I whisper to Alice, giving her hand a squeeze before calling back to Natalie. 'You're welcome to eat with us!'

She pops her head back around the living room door. 'I'm actually heading out so I'll get out of your hair soon but thanks for the offer. Just going to finish this tea.'

'Ooh good idea, you're meant to rehydrate after a run, right?' Alice asks, hopping off the sofa. 'Fancy a juice?' She asks me. While Alice is out of the room I ask Nat how work is going, not wanting us to sit in silence until she comes back. Nat seems really nice and it feels important that we get on well together.

'It's okay, thanks. Bit quiet. A lot of our clients are on summer holidays so there aren't many events to plan. The run up to Christmas is always the busiest season for us. So I'm twiddling my thumbs a bit, which I hate.'

'Doesn't help that your boss is a douche,' Alice comes back in and places the drinks on the coffee table before rearranging some cushions and falling onto the sofa. Nat and I budge up to make space. I realise Alice's place gives me the same kind of feel I get when I'm at my brother's house. It's so cosy and welcoming. I notice with pleasure that she's hung my painting above the fireplace. It's definitely motivation for me to sort out my house, finish the half-arsed renovation attempts and get all the boxes unpacked so Alice likes coming around to mine too.

Natalie pulls an exasperated face. 'Douche is probably a bit unfair but Sid's very comfortable in his position, he's on a great salary and has a decent amount of responsibility without it being too much.'

'And he takes all the glory for all of your work . . .' Alice points out.

'There is that. But basically, I want his job and I'm pretty sure he isn't going anywhere any time soon.'

'That's difficult,' I say, not wanting to butt in but also hoping to show Alice's best friend that I'm listening and trying to be supportive. 'Who's his boss? Can you talk to them?'

'That would be Bruno, the company is his start-up. Client liaison is his thing so he's hardly ever in the office, which means Sid picks up the day to day running of it all.'

'Yeah, Sid swans around with his Breitling watches while Natalie puts in the leg work. All of the event ideas come straight from Nat. She's so tuned in to what their clients want and then Sid turns up to the parties with his posh accent and a glass of champagne in his hand and takes all the praise.'

'Alice seems to be more annoyed about my work situation than I am,' Nat grins at me.

'It's because you're selling yourself short,' she calls over.

'We can't all knock out 10k runs with no prior experience or set up a successful business *yaknow*,' Nat sighs.

'I know, I know, I'm great at everything,' Alice laughs.

'Including cheating,' I tease. She throws a cushion at me and it hits me square in the face. I readjust my glasses, wondering whether the thought that's just crossed my mind would be over-stepping the mark. My gut tells me to just say it. 'Have you two ever considered working together? It sounds like you'd make a great team. Alice's flowers and social media knowledge, Natalie's event planning. You could make a killing.'

Alice sits up at that, cushions tumbling around her. 'That's actually quite a good idea.'

'I'm going to think on this,' Nat agrees. 'And that can be my cue to leave you lovebirds to it.'

'I'm pretty sure this is how you're meant to refuel after a big run,' Alice says confidently. 'In fact, I think I read about it in one of those fitness magazines.'

'Burger and chips?'

'And beers. Something to do with replacing all the lost . . . calories?'

'Definitely,' I nod. 'You should consider a job as a dietician.'

'I intend to,' Alice laughs, dipping a chip in mayo. We're sat on brightly coloured outdoor cushions in her back yard and I'm learning that Alice has the ability to make anything look like it should be in a magazine shoot. She's thrown an old tablecloth over an upturned palette which we're using as a makeshift table. Jam jars filled with leftover flowers from her shop are dotted on top of it, just like she used to do with her mum and dad as a kid. I felt a pang of sorrow as I watched her place them on the "table", knowing what memories such a simple act must bring back for her.

'Do you ever wonder what you'd have done if the floristry hadn't work out?' I ask.

'Like a back-up plan? When I was little I thought I might follow in Mum's footsteps as an interior designer. I used to love arranging the furniture in my Sylvanian Families house.' She smiles and I find myself smiling along with her. 'But really, I think my dream alternative job would be something that meant I could travel loads. Maybe I'd be fluent in another language and work as a private tutor to some super rich family, living in their mansion in Monaco and teaching their kids an hour's English a week.'

'So basically, minimal output for maximum job satisfaction.'

'Exactly!' She laughs. 'In reality, I'd probably go crazy with boredom, but it sounds good doesn't it? How about you?'

'It would have to be something arty, I think. I can't see myself in an office environment at all.'

Alice chuckles. 'Zach in a suit, working through spreadsheets? Or in a bank shouting about profit and loss and throwing back champagne at lunch?'

'Not really an option, right?'

'You would look good in a suit,' Alice concedes. 'Now, speaking as a future dietician, I wondered if it would be too much of an artery risk to have pancakes for breakfast tomorrow. That is, if you want to stay over?'

'In a heartbeat,' I say, feeling like I lucked out. Music floats out from the opened kitchen window. The bees are going nuts for some honeysuckle climbing up Alice's garden wall. I could quite happily picture myself spending more weekends with Alice, just like this.

Karaoke

Alice

The past month has been a steady stream of two weddings a week *plus* running the shop full time and I am ready to let off some serious steam. I'm fidgety for it. Tonight's the night, baby! As the last customers leave the shop, arms stuffed with bouquets, I decide to delay tidying up for a while and turn up the volume on our Sonos, prancing around the floor instead.

'I should probably film this,' Eve laughs when she sees me. 'We could call it "Dancing with Dahlias".'

'Or "Flexing with Fuschias"?' I suggest.

'"Tango with Tulips".'

'"Rumba with Ranunculas"! Sounds sexy.'

'I can see it going viral now,' Eve's leaning against the counter. 'Seriously, where do you get your energy from? We've been working like dogs all week and I am so ready for a bath tonight.'

'What? You're going home for a bath on a Friday night?! You Gen Z-ers are beyond me.'

'Self-care is very important.'

'I totally agree with you there,' I nod, already hoping to get out to the allotment this weekend. 'But also, it's Friday night! You should know that Zach and I are going to karaoke later . . .'

'Ooh,' her eyes light up. 'Now I feel torn. Do I love karaoke as much as I love my new bath oil? What a dilemma.'

'Mmm, totally. Singing cheesy hits with your mates or stewing in the tub . . . it *is* a tough call.'

Eve rolls her eyes. 'You are such an enabler. All right, count me in.'

'YES! Bring Nicky if you like, the more the merrier.'

'Not sure if it's her thing but I'll ask.'

'Yeah Zach's the same. I'm sure they'll warm up to it.'

I'd actually hesitated about asking Zach to this in the first place, because I know that he can feel awkward in big group settings. I've loved the past few dates we've had, spending time just the two of us has been the best chance to get to know each other better. But work has been non-stop recently and I'm desperate for a night out. Besides now that we are well and truly dating I need to feel like I can be completely me around him. I like to let go and be silly sometimes. So I'm hoping that karaoke night for our K date might give us both a chance to have some fun.

As soon as Zach arrives at the karaoke bar I can tell that this genius plan might backfire massively. His expression is pure fear. 'Tell me I'm in the middle of a nightmare and about to wake up,' Zach says as I shimmy around under the neon sign at the entrance to the bar.

'I'm afraid I cannot do that.'

'Singing in public? Alice, have we met before?'

'I thought you'd react like this but there's good news. I booked a booth so there's only going to be a handful of us in there.'

'When you say us . . .'

'Me, you, Eve and her girlfriend, and Nat's coming with another date,' I reply.

'Great, humiliation in front of your friends. That's much better than humiliation in front of people I've never met before.'

'Oh Zach! Don't panic, okay. I just thought that we've both

been working so hard and a night out would be the perfect chance to let off some steam. You never know, let yourself go and you might actually have some fun,' I wink.

Zach stands with his hands on his hips, looking up to the sky before seeming to resign himself to a night of karaoke. He readjusts his glasses and gives me a super cute look, as if to say: 'I'll do this, but only because it's you.'

'All right, then,' he gives me a lopsided grin. 'But you will owe me.'

'I'm still recovering from those ten kilometres you made me run. Consider this payback.'

Zach runs his hands through his hair. 'The things I do because I want to spend time with you,' he sighs and I feel a warm glow inside. I link my hand through his and lead him into the venue.

It felt so nice to get properly dressed up for tonight. My dress is made of bronze sequins and cut low at my back.

'You look beautiful,' Zach says as I slide my coat off, his fingers grazing my skin.

'This old thing?' I beam, trying to play down the butter-flies as Natalie bounds in. She's come dressed like Beyoncé circa 'Telephone' in a stars and stripes bustier and skirt, the date she's brought with her looking evidently thrilled to be in her company.

'Fit,' I whistle, ordering our drinks while Natalie chucks me a microphone and cues up the first song. It's inevitable, really, given what she's wearing. The first bars of Beyoncé and Gaga's 'Telephone' fill the room, a song which Nat and I may or may not have spent a drunken night replaying while learning all the moves to. We're cool like that. We start singing and out of the corner of my eye I see Zach watching us with a smile on his face. He's enjoying it! He sips at his bottle of beer, looking incredibly hot in a green T-shirt. Zach wears colour now, apparently. He really is becoming more chilled out. The green sets off his lightly tanned skin and green eyes so well I'm borderline distracted from my moment.

When our duet ends I motion to him to come on up.

Zach shakes his head.

I turn my microphone back on.

'Ladies and gentleman, may I present to you Zach Moretti!'

He's holding his hands up in the universal sign for *stop*.

Eve starts a chant. 'Zach! Zach! Zach!'

Her girlfriend's joined in. Natalie and her date are chanting too. Reluctantly, Zach sets his beer on the table and comes up to join me.

'You are very much in my bad books,' he whispers in my ear. I try to look remonstrated but to be fair, I'm just thrilled he's actually here.

'Would you like to choose a song?' I ask.

'Er, no.'

I press on. 'It needs to be a duet because obviously I'm joining you. How about Robbie and Kylie's 'Kids'? Do you know it?'

Zach gives me the side eye. 'Remember my Point Romance days? I was also quite into Take That,' he whispers.

I could squeal with glee. I love this about him!

'Take That forever!' cheers Nat.

Zach looks up, horrified.

'Ah, yeah, I forgot to say that our mics are still on,' I point out, biting my lip.

Zach gives me a jokey death stare and I give his hand a squeeze, starting the music. I fully expect Zach to just close his eyes and mumble through it as quickly as possible, but oh how wrong I am. Zach is the gift that keeps on giving. It turns out he already knows all the words to 'Kids' so he doesn't need the lyric prompts on screen. He's even prompting me when it's Kylie's turn.

He can sing! His eyes are on me and I channel Kylie Minogue for a minute, visualising those gold hot pants and wondering if Zach ever went through a guyliner phase. My guess is yes.

It's been a while since I listened to this song in full and I had completely forgotten about Robbie's rap. But it turns out Zach hasn't. He's rapping away with a Stoke on Trent accent just like his favourite Take Thatter and I am *deceased*. Literally folded over in hysterics as Zach throws himself into it. I manage to pull myself together for the final chorus.

'SO COME ON, ju-u-ump on board,' booms Zach, so into it now that his hands are in the air and our entire booth has jumped to their feet, singing and dancing along.

This is amazing! And pretty sexy, actually. I wrap my hands around his waist as we sing.

'GET A ROOM!' shouts Nat as we get to the end.

Still hot from singing, Zach and I collapse down next to each other while Natalie whips the rest of our mini-crowd into a frenzy with her rendition of Lizzo's 'Juice'.

'How do you feel about Nelly and Kelly's 'Dilemma'?' I ask.

'Huh?'

'For our next duet?' I pant. 'That was so much fun!'

Zach scratches his forehead. 'It was fun but I'm not sure I can face another one.'

'Why not? Everyone loved it!' I say, taking a sip of my drink. Zach frowns.

'Okay fine, you pick the next one,' I concede.

'I was hoping that might have been enough,' he says and instantly I realise that I'm pushing him too far.

'I've made you uncomfortable.'

'No, well, not really,' he replies, grabbing my hand. 'I think there's only so much public singing this introvert can take, though.'

'I get it. You're a really good singer though, Zach. Maybe you could put on a little private show for me later.'

He runs his fingers along his jaw-line as he takes a slug of beer.

'Maybe,' he smiles wryly. 'I hope you don't think I'm a killjoy. Sometimes I worry that I'm not good enough for you in situations like this.'

I take a sip of my own beer and realise I am quite tipsy.

'That's not true at all. I'm definitely more of an extrovert but did you see yourself up there a minute ago? You're a secret entertainer, Zach.'

He laughs at that, looking bashful.

'It was fun,' he admits. 'Just go easy on me, okay. I'm not a natural life-and-soul-of-the-party kind of person like you are.'

Not long ago I was asking Zach to go easy on me in the romance stakes. How funny that things can turn around so quickly.

'I actually think we complement each other pretty well,' I say.

'Agreed.' We clink beer bottles and it feels like we're enjoying a moment together when Natalie flops down next to Zach and readjusts her boobs. 'We've got one song left so we've got to make it count. Only the Spice Girls will do now. Zach, do you know the words to 'Wannabe'?'

Argh, Nat, don't interrupt!

But Zach does something that surprises the heck out of me. Eyebrows raised in amusement, he shoots me a part-resigned, part-playful look. 'Yes I do, Natalie.'

Nat leaps back up, taking his hands in hers. The fact that they get on so well makes me super happy.

'Are you sure?' I whisper to Zach now.

'Why not,' he says with a look of playful resignation. Thrilled, Nat marches us up to the front and Zach wraps his arm around my shoulder, handing me a microphone and quickly throwing himself into Mel B's A-Z wrap. Instantly I'm reminded of the business card he gave me when we first met. How he'd boldly announced that we should work our way through a whole alphabet worth of dates and how I'd found the idea hilarious. As if we'd get past C! And yet here we are, on date K. The intense, brooding artist I thought might interest me for a couple of dates is now the man I'm seeing exclusively and currently to be found belting out Spice Girl lyrics at the top of his voice. Either the sequins on my dress are reflecting some serious light, or there are actual fireworks dancing above my head.

* * *

122

'We're calling it a night,' Natalie winks at me as she and her date grab their stuff. 'I'm going back to his.'

'Text me his details so I know where you are, okay? And ring me when you get there. And stay safe. Have you got condoms?'

Natalie titters. 'All right, Mum! I will be just fine, he's a guy I know through work so don't panic. This means you'll have the house to yourself,' she adds with a nudge.

I cast a glance at Zach, currently deep in conversation with Eve and Nicky about which Spice Girl is the best, and feel anticipation ripple through me. Home alone with my date. The last time we went for a big night out he left early but tonight's he's the last man standing.

'You're so lucky to have lived through all of that the first time around,' Eve is saying, hanging off Zach's every word. 'I wasn't even born when they had their first hit.'

'Oh my god, I hate you a little bit,' I laugh.

Zach's grinning. 'Apparently the Spice Girls are having a huge renaissance,' he tells me. 'As is *Friends*.'

'Another classic,' I nod.

'Guys, I could stay and listen to you talk about old people stuff all night but Nicky and I need to get some beauty sleep and I haven't even made my overnight oats yet.'

'The kids of today! See you at work.' I laugh, waving as they head off and turning to Zach. 'Well, well, well. Fancy taking this ancient twenty-nine-year-old home for the night?'

'Yes I do.'

'I'm a tiny bit tipsy.'

'Me too. Don't take advantage now,' he smoulders.

'Never! Though I should probably warn you that I found your secret karaoke side very sexy.'

He laughs. 'I knew my Take That days would come in handy one day.'

'See! It's not all that bad, is it? Letting yourself go can be very fun.' I'm swirling my finger around on his chest now.

123

'Well, let's just say that I have no regrets. Can I take you home now?' He pulls me into a kiss which takes my breath away and as we head outside to grab a taxi, I'm filled with this warm, fuzzy feeling. It's been amazing to go out and let off some steam tonight, and now it feels just as good to be heading home with Zach. To know that I'll be waking up next to him tomorrow morning.

Lunch

Zach

Like all good Italian boys, family is a massive part of my life, probably all the more so because the importance of *famiglia* seemed to skip a generation for my parents. I remember overhearing a conversation Mum had on the phone with Nonna when I was a kid, telling her mother-in-law how she didn't want to spend the rest of her life putting her kids first like Nonna had with Dad. It still stings to think of it now. If only she'd known that Raff and I never wanted her to put us first, we just wanted her to show us that she cared.

When Raff met Ellie, I watched my older brother make sense of his life with her by his side and now that they have the girls, we make even more of an effort to see each other regularly. They've made this awesome home together, not to mention two great kids, and as much as Raff pretends to grumble about being a down-trodden dad I can tell how proud he is to have such a strong bond with his own children. It's exactly what we didn't have growing up. Raff, Ellie, Fran and Sienna. The people here today are my family.

Tiny barks at the bottom of the ladder I'm up.

'Are you telepathic, Tiny? Don't worry, you're part of my family too.' He sits down by the bottom step and sticks his tongue out.

'Now you ask, I'm a little overwhelmed to introduce Alice to the rest of this bunch.'

Tiny licks his lips.

'You're right, it is a big deal. It wasn't for Alice, you know? She welcomed me into her circle the minute I met her. Now I think about it, she's shown such a willingness to let me in. I think that sums her up perfectly. Happy to give things a go, to be open and kind. God, I must seem so reserved in comparison?' Tiny barks up at me and I'm convinced I can see a frown on his face. 'She was really keen when I suggested meeting you guys.'

More barking.

'No I hadn't expected that either. I thought she'd run for the hills.'

'Having a heart to heart with the hound again?' It's Raff, coming towards me with a huge bowl of apricots.

Tiny looks up at me conspiratorially. He knows so many of my secrets.

'I'm not sure we need bunting,' I say, choosing to ignore Raff's question. I've been stringing triangles of colourful fabric around the garden for the past twenty minutes and there's still reams of the stuff left.

'Ellie's going all out,' Raff shrugs. 'And you know what she's like.'

A force to be reckoned with, which is probably why I've put this off for so long . . . in case she scares Alice away.

'She's never got the bunting out for any of my ex-girlfriends,' I point out.

'I think we can all sense that Alice is different.'

'Why's that?'

'You're into her, that much is obvious, but you haven't got tunnel vision like you have had in the past. How do I put this? Alice seems to be bringing out the best in you.'

'Oh, right,' I scratch my head. 'Well that's good news, I think?'

Raff laughs. 'Don't look so worried! The sun's out and there's enough food to feed the entire village. Today's going to be a good day.'

*　*　*

126

'She's here!' Fran and Sienna run into the kitchen from their vantage point in the living room. They've been staking out a spot by the window for the past five minutes, desperate to catch the first glimpse of Alice.

Christ I'm tense.

'Right, um, excellent,' I say, mindlessly picking up a tea towel and putting it back down again.

'So sweet that you're nervous,' Ellie pinches my cheeks and I frown. She's my best friend and honorary big sister rolled into one but bloody hell, she can be annoying.

The doorbell rings.

'You should probably get that,' Ellie grins.

Why am I faffing about? I make for the front door but it's too late, Fran and Sienna have already opened it. I can hear them chatting away and quicken my pace.

'You're called Alice and you're Uncle Zach's girlfriend and he's nervous about you meeting us but there's no need, Mum says, because we're actually very sweet and not at all intimidating.'

Girlfriend? Oh *god*. I cannot believe they just blurted that out. To me, it feels like Alice is my girlfriend already but we've not had The Conversation yet and I'm already worried that she'll be scared off by my noisy family. Now we've got the G word to deal with as well?

Flustered, I rush to the front door and there she stands, framed in the hallway like a painting waiting to happen. Her summery dress is an explosion of yellows and oranges, her hair in plaits twirled around her head. She's carrying a bouquet in one hand and a shopping bag in the other, which she sets on the floor as she greets my nieces.

'Alice, hi.' She turns her gaze to me and I'm fixed to the spot with her wide smile. She doesn't *look* too freaked out so that's good. 'I see Sienna and Francesca have made their introductions already. Do you want to come through?'

127

'I'd love to,' she replies as I kiss her on the cheek. I pick up her bag and we head into the kitchen, Fran and Sienna chatting non-stop as we go.

'The famous Alice,' Ellie pulls off her apron and kisses Alice three times on the cheeks.

'That's the kind of introduction I can get on board with,' Alice laughs. 'Ellie? It's a pleasure to meet you.'

The two women take a few steps back from one another and I realise I'm holding my breath. Raff's standing next to me and I get the impression that he's doing the same.

'Thank you so much for inviting me today,' Alice says after a pause. 'I asked Zach if I could bring a dish but he said you've got that covered so I bought these instead.' She hands Ellie the bouquet of bright yellow sunflowers tied together with brown paper.

'These are beautiful,' Ellie says. 'Thank you. Now come in, come in! Make yourself at home. We're having a picnic lunch outside a little later.'

'L for lunch,' Fran pipes up. 'Uncle Zach told us about your alphabet dates.'

'Oh did he? Well, he told me that you guys are into colouring at the moment and guess what? So am I! I brought some felt tips and colouring books with me if you fancy . . .' Alice is being dragged outside by Fran and Sienna before she has time to finish her sentence.

'Well, she's definitely a hit with the girls,' laughs Raff as we watch Alice pulling the gifts out of her bag and placing them on the play table in the garden. The girls have dragged a sun lounger over so Alice can sit down next to them and now they're fighting over who's closest to her, so Alice seems to be diplomatically making sure both Sienna and Francesca feel like they're getting plenty of attention.

'She's a natural with kids,' Ellie says, following our gaze.

128

It's true. Raff, Ellie and I stand for just a minute, watching the sweet scene outside before the timer goes and Raff's put in charge of pulling the lunch together.

The table is heaving with food. Sliced focaccia sandwiches stuffed with salami and aubergines. A fresh tomato salad dressed with herbs and olive oil. Artichokes and roasted peppers. A taleggio frittata in the middle. Jugs of peach juice making crackling noises as Ellie tips in handfuls of ice.

'This is heaven,' Alice sighs as Raff hands her a plate laden with food. 'Did Zach warn you that I'd eat you out of house and home?'

'I bought some Hula Hoops just in case,' I tease and she chuckles.

'We're foodies here Alice, you will fit right in,' my brother smiles and I could convince myself that Alice looks pleased at that.

She runs her hand along the gold cutlery and colourful plates. 'This looks so effortlessly stylish.'

'Thank you,' Ellie says. 'When Raff and I got married, his Nonna sent us a huge box of mismatched crockery as a wedding gift. It's been in the family for years.'

'The lemon prints on these plates are too pretty,' Alice enthuses.

'Apparently there's a lot more back in Italy ready for Zach when he—'

Don't mention the M word! We've already got the G word to contend with.

'More frittata over here please!' Raff cuts across his wife and I'm eternally grateful for his timing. Thank goodness for brothers. I give Ellie what I hope is a shut-your-face look.

'Did you guys marry over there?' Alice asks.

'We had a legal ceremony here and then a big celebration in Amalfi. My family are Italian too so I think we'd all have been disowned if we didn't celebrate over there,' Ellie says.

'How did you meet, then?'

'Through this legend,' Ellie waves at me. 'Zach and I met at

129

uni, we were in the same halls in first year. Zach had found the only decent Italian restaurant in Newcastle, made friends with the owners and charmed his way into free food at the end of each service so most of our time at uni was spent eating bowls of pasta late at night.'

'That sounds perfect!' Alice flicks her eyes between us.

'It would have been if I didn't have to spend it with this chump,' Ellie jokes.

'Come on. There's no way we'd have handed in our dissertations on time if Angelo hadn't kept us stocked up on limoncello on the night before our deadline,' I point out.

'I met Ellie on their graduation day,' Raff pitches in. 'I'd heard so much about this best friend of his so I knew she'd be brilliant to hang out with, I just hadn't expected her to set my heart on fire as well.'

'Oh you two! That's so cute,' Alice says.

'Adults are gross,' announces Fran. I ruffle her hair.

'You just wait, kiddo. Besides, as best friend of the bride and brother of the groom I got to go on both the stag and the hen do,' I grin, reaching for another piece of focaccia.

'You weren't looking so pleased when my friends suggested you strip and serve us shots,' Ellie laughs.

She's right. *That* was embarrassing.

Suddenly Sienna's setting both her elbows on the table and looking very serious. 'What are your intentions with Uncle Zach?' She asks Alice.

The focaccia drops down onto my plate.

I look at Alice in panic, wondering how she'll take being interrogated by my 5-year-old niece over lunch. If anything, I thought Ellie would be the overprotective relative today. She's going to freak out, isn't she? Alice places her glass of juice back down and looks around the table. I follow her gaze. Raff and Ellie are silent-laughing, their shoulders heaving. Sienna looks thrilled with herself.

130

Alice bursts into laughter and the whole table erupts.

'Did Uncle Zach bribe you to ask that question?' She asks once everyone has quietened down. Sienna giggles gleefully, hanging on Alice's words.

Alice pauses, catching my eye. 'Can you keep a secret?' She stage-whispers to my nieces. They bob their heads up and down, thrilled. 'I do like him quite a lot,' Alice says.

Fran and Sienna cheer while I savour those words of hers. 'The feeling is very mutual,' I say.

'So,' Raff says, breaking the spell. 'No doubt that you're not just here for a bit of lunch, Alice. I expect you'll want all the dirt on Zach from when we were younger and Ellie and I are here and ready to share. Shall we start with the teddy bear years?'

Alice clasps her hands together with glee while a little bit of me dies inside. 'Yes please. My friend Dylan showed Zach some deeply embarrassing photos of me as a child and I've been waiting for this moment ever since. It's payback time'

Dylan again, I think. He peppers her conversation so often and I need to stop finding it annoying.

'Photos, you say? I can do one better,' Raff turns to me with a grin. What's he up to? 'I was going through a load of storage boxes in the garage the other day and found Zach's comics. You probably think I mean comics that you might buy in a shop but in fact I mean comics that he'd drawn and starred in himself.'

I am going to kill Raff. He's rushing back into the kitchen with a look of pure joy on his face. He's not fetching them, is he? I don't usually blush but I can feel my skin going a deep shade of crimson right now.

'Just a friendly reminder that I'm due to dogsit Tiny again soon, bro,' I call after him. 'You wouldn't want me to cancel at the last minute with a severe case of mortification, would you?'

Raff's hearty laugh echoes out from the kitchen. Ellie, Alice, Sienna and Fran are sat around the garden table on tenterhooks and I'm wondering if it's too early to crack open the vodka, especially when I see the smug look on my bro's face when he comes back out.

'Alice, may I introduce you to Captain Zach the Brainiac,' Raff says.

If the ground could swallow me up right now, that would be great. I haven't thought about Captain Zach the Brainiac in years and yet here's Raff, handing a copy over to Alice.

I clear my throat. 'I'm just going to go and check the . . . oven's off.'

'No!' Alice protests. She looks up at me from the comic in her hands, a brief frown casting a shadow over her face. She motions for me to sit down next to her and as I do she whispers: 'I don't want you to feel embarrassed. Shall I put this away?'

I'm so touched by the fact that she's checking in on me that I'm briefly out of words.

I sigh good-naturedly. 'Thanks, but it's only fair that you should read it. Just . . . promise you'll still like me once you've taken a look inside the mind of a teenage, angst-ridden boy? In my defence, I was listening to a lot of emo at the time.'

Alice laughs. 'I can picture you now, smudging charcoal liner around your eyes with My Chemical Romance playing in the background.'

'Were you spying on me?' I joke.

'The eyeliner phase! I'd forgotten about that,' Raff's roaring with laughter. 'Really Alice, we've so much to share with you.'

Lunch turned into dinner, peach juice turned into white wine and now Raff and Ellie are persuading Fran and Sienna that it's bedtime.

'But I don't want to,' Sienna groans for the fifteenth time.

'Can Alice come again?' Fran asks, eyes mournful.

'She is more than welcome any time,' Ellie grins as she finally shepherds the girls indoors.

It's just Alice and I sitting in the garden now, solar-panelled lights draped along walls. I have loved seeing how easily she's fallen into step with my noisy, nuts family but it's nice to have some one-to-one time too. I listen as she breathes a contented sigh.

'They've really taken to you,' I tell her.

'The feeling is mutual. Raff and Ellie are raising some strong girls there.'

I nod. 'I'm proud of them.'

'You should be. They obviously adore their Uncle Zach.'

'Ah well, being an uncle is great because I get all of the fun and none of the shit.' I'm interrupted by a bellow coming from an open bedroom window upstairs.

'THAT'S *MY* TELESCOPE SIENNAAAAARRRRRGGGHHH.'

'Right on cue,' laughs Alice.

'They can be a handful. Like earlier, when they dropped a certain G word as soon as you arrived?' I say tentatively, wondering if she picked up on it.

Alice catches my eye.

'You mean when they called me your girlfriend?'

I clear my throat. 'Yup. I was wondering, um, how it made you feel?'

She's doing that thing where she falls silent again, lost in thought.

'Because we've been seeing each other for a while now and I was hoping . . .' I pause, still haunted by her three-date rule and the constant fear that she might grow tired of me soon. But fear isn't going to get me anywhere, is it? And now that I've started, there's no way I can stop. 'I was hoping to ask if you'd like to have me as your boyfriend?'

It's out. There's no going back. I can't even look at her. She's going to panic that I've pushed her too far and run for the hills, right?

I feel her hand reach out to hold mine and I chance a look at her.

'Zach, I would very much like to be your girlfriend,' she says, a huge smile reaching across her face.

Lucky doesn't cover it. I wrap my arms around her, pulling her in close and feeling the warmth of her body next to mine as I let it sink in. Alice leans up to kiss me and I'm not sure today could get any better.

'There I was thinking my nieces might have thrown me under a bus and it turns out they did me a huge favour,' I laugh after a while.

'Ha, I bet it's not the first time they've done something like that.'

'They've been a handful since day one,' I say, still high on the fact that Alice is my girlfriend now. I can't believe it! 'Apparently twins run in the family. Ellie and Raff hadn't expected it and I know they've found it challenging, especially when Fran and Sienna were babies.'

'I bet. Kids must be the ultimate test of any relationship.'

Would Alice like kids one day? My brain is shouting the question so loud I'm surprised she can't hear it.

Mate. Chill out.

Just enjoy this moment and for fuck's sake do not ask that question.

Ellie bustles out through the French windows, saving me from diving in way too deep. 'I've left Raff in charge. The girls turn into monsters at bedtime. Sorry, did I interrupt?'

'We were just talking about how tough it must be when you have kids, but you and Raff seem to be doing an amazing job,' Alice says.

'That's down to a mixture of love, patience and a fully stocked wine cupboard,' Ellie grins.

Alice laughs. 'No doubt. You make it look very easy.'

'For me, becoming a mum was something I knew in my bones I'd love to do one day, if I was lucky enough to. I'm aware that not everyone feels the same way though. I've been listening to a fascinating podcast about women who've decided not to have kids for whatever reason.'

'You'll have to give me the name of it,' Alice says, leaning into the conversation. 'For so long motherhood has been seen as the ultimate achievement for a woman and it's just bollocks, isn't it? What about career success? Or opting out for ecological reasons? Or just simply not being maternal? It really annoys me when motherhood is seen as the defining feature of being a woman.'

'You should definitely listen to this podcast then,' Ellie says.

And I guess I have my answer. I know that we've made huge progress today. Alice is officially my girlfriend which is something I've wanted for a while now. Still, as lucky as I feel, I can't help but worry that I want a family one day and maybe she doesn't.

Mini-Break

Alice

'He is definitely no alpha,' I say as Nat throws an assortment of miniature shampoos into my travel bag. I've been thinking back to Zach's teenage comics at lunch last weekend and Captain Zach the Brainiac may be my favourite thing about him. Each black and white square of the adorable comics was filled with images of his anime alter ego being super cute. Not fighting dragons or rescuing princesses or any other misogynistic crap. His cartoon character had superpowers like standing up for the kid getting bullied in class, or whisking grannies in care homes off on fun adventures, or building massive dens for him to store his comic collection. *I mean.*

'A soft bro,' she nods knowingly.

'A what?'

'It's the opposite of an alpha. Let's take a look at the evidence. Is Zach charming?'

'Yes.'

'Sensitive?'

'Definitely yes.'

'Thoughtful and into talking about his feelings?'

'Yes and yes.'

'Classic soft bro, babes.'

136

'Is that a good thing?'

Nat rolls her eyes good-naturedly. 'What do you think? Remember Jake? Every time one of his mates had a break-up they'd go out "celebrating" with a night on the lash. They'd be necking shots and eyeing up women in bodycon like the emotionally stunted fuckboys they truly were. The kind of men who'd suggest a few "brewskis" after work.'

Brewskis. I cover my hands with my ears.

'Toxic, the lot of them,' she says.

'I'm sensing you still feel a bit raw, Nat.'

She considers this. 'It's more that I'm annoyed with myself. Why did I dedicate a chunk of my twenties to putting up with that behaviour? Jake was a boisterous dickhead and I went along with it. Worse than that, I actually wanted to spend my life with him. I should have listened when you voiced your concerns right from the start. But I dismissed them because you weren't looking for a partner so you didn't get it, or that's what I thought. Turns out that none of that mattered, anyway. It was his character that was the problem, not the circumstances.'

'Oh love, don't be hard on yourself. Jake was a fool but he did have a certain charm and it seemed like you were happy.'

'That's the worst bit. I was happy. I thought being with the man who'd buy drinks for the entire pub when he hit his work targets was the height of sophistication. The man who'd deliberately order the steak when we ate out with vegan friends just to be provocative. What was I thinking?'

'When you're in it, you can't always *see* it. You've been able to step away and get some major clarity this summer, Nat. The guys you've been seeing lately have been so different to Jake, I guess it's opened up a whole new world.'

'All right, Katie Price,' she laughs.

'Shut up. I'd obviously be Peter Andre.'

'Har har. You're right though, it's been nice to get some perspective.'

'So which lucky man are you seeing while I'm away this weekend?'

Nat pops a couple of mini conditioners into my bag. She was given a tote filled with samples after organising a beauty brand's launch event and I am forever grateful for the perks of her job.

'No one, actually.'

I stop shoving shorts into my rucksack. 'No one?'

My best friend shrugs. 'I'm going to take some time for myself.'

'Are you sure you're okay?'

'Just a bit of Tinder fatigue, I think. I fancy some me time. Don't look so worried! I'm going to catch up with mates, go to the cinema and take myself out for pie and mash. Meanwhile you're going on a minibreak with your boyfriend this weekend. We've basically swapped roles,' she giggles.

I laugh at that. She's right.

It's just Zach, Gerty and I cruising through the Lake District with another of Zach's impeccable playlists providing the soundtrack. I'm into his eclectic taste in music. Some stuff I recognise and some stuff that sounds like it might be played on one of those ultra-cool French radio stations that are impossible to find. The minute we hit Cumbria the landscape opens out into expansive views of windswept hills and exposed crags, a patchwork quilt of browns and greens. I wind my window down (*that's* how old Gerty is) and shout out into the wild, 'WOOOOOOOOOOOOOOOH!'

'It's like going for a drive with Tiny the dog,' Zach laughs.

'Rude. I'm just expressing my enthusiasm.'

Zach winds his own window down. 'WOOOOOOOOOOO-OOOH!' he calls, before quickly pulling his head back in as an articulated lorry trundles past on the other side of the road. His hair's all mussed up from the wind.

'Feels good, doesn't it?'

He grins and my insides somersault. A whole weekend with Zach. I'm really, really excited. It's been ages since I've had a

Saturday off but Eve kindly offered to take on the wedding we had booked in for this weekend and when the clients saw what she was capable of, they were more than happy to let her run the show. I'm the first to admit that I can be a bit micro-manage-y when it comes to my flower shop. The business is my baby and I'm definitely guilty of wanting to be involved in everything. But Eve is brilliant and has such a natural flare with her styling. So here I am, taking time off and going on a mini-break with an actual man I like.

New me who dis?

'Left or right?' Zach asks as we approach a fork in the road.

'I'm guessing left?'

'You're *guessing*?'

'That sign says Windermere so . . .'

'Alice, did you print off a map before we left?'

'No I did not, Grandad! I'd forgotten that Gerty doesn't have satnav,' I add sheepishly.

'What about a map on your phone?'

I check. 'No signal.'

'Perhaps now's the time to tell me where we're going? Two heads are better than one and all that.'

'You're going to love it,' I say confidently. The artist's residency I found online has Zach written all over it. Floor-to-ceiling windows with views of the lake. Minimalist interiors. Its own jetty! I cannot wait to see it.

I cannot see it. That's because it's pitch black by the time we arrive. The place is literally in the middle of nowhere and with no satnav or phone signal, Zach and I had to stop at every village we drove through to ask for help. Hardly anyone had heard of it. Eventually we found an old lady chasing after chickens in the garden of her remote cottage and Zach was so charming with her, offering to help round them up for the night, that once she'd given us directions she handed us homemade cheese, a dozen eggs and a packet of sausages as we left. Now that we're finally here, the owner of the residency is less pleased. We were meant to check in at 4 p.m., he keeps grumbling. We offer sincere apologies and let him harrumph for a bit longer before I shepherd him towards the front door. It's time to light some candles, open some wine and get our mini-break on.

'Just look at that view,' Zach says, relaxing in a chair as I sizzle our free sausages on the outdoor grill. I pad over and plonk myself on his lap, following his gaze. The sky is so dark now and without the glare of any big cities, we find ourselves under a canopy of stars.

'It's beautiful,' I whisper.

Zach wraps a blanket around both of us and I settle my head on his chest. I feel peaceful and still and quite frisky to be honest. But first, sausages.

I'd have happily spent our first morning in the Lakes scoffing breakfast and admiring the view but Adventure Pants has other ideas. Swimming *in the lake*. It looks absolutely freezing in the water and Zach is not doing a very good job of pretending otherwise.

'It's exhilarating,' he calls back at me, teeth chattering. I've a big fluffy towel wrapped around my body and I'm pretty cosy thank you very much. However Zach has a gentle persuasion technique . . . it's called his face. Droplets of water trickle from his forehead down to his jawline. There's a smile curling at his lips. Frankly I'd be a fool to resist, so I let my towel drop to the floor and dive in head first.

'ARGHHHHHHHHHHHH,' I splutter as I surface.

Zach swims over. 'I probably should have said that getting your head wet isn't the best idea.'

'I. Can't. Feel. My. Limbs,' I gasp.

Zach wraps his arms around me as he treads water.

'Is my bikini still on?'

'Sadly, yes,' he grins. 'Are you warming up?'

'I think so. Either that or hypothermia has set in.'

140

'Follow me,' he says, taking long, strong strides out into the lake. I splash along behind him, mesmerised by the grass-covered mountains all lit up with the morning's golden glow. The water's a dazzling blue as it reflects the cloudless sky above.

'This is actually very refreshing,' I announce after a while, flipping onto my back and staring at the birds of prey soaring overhead. He does the same and we hold hands like otters and my heart feels full.

'I think it's illegal to visit the Lakes without eating sticky toffee pudding,' I explain to Zach as we stumble upon a shop selling very little else. After drying off this morning, we warmed up with a long, hot shower together before hopping in the car, driving alongside the majestic lake until we reached Ambleside, where outdoorsy shops nestle next to chic delis.

'I wouldn't want to break the law,' he says, grabbing a basket and promptly *filling it* with puddings. I definitely like this guy. 'Perhaps we should get something else for dinner though?'

I blink.

'It's just a suggestion,' he says, the lines around his green eyes creasing in amusement. 'But a main course wouldn't go amiss. Or are we really just going to eat a sticky toffee pudding each tonight?'

Now he's said it out loud I realise it's perhaps not the sexiest plan I've ever had. So much stodge. 'Okay fine,' I concede. 'There's a deli over there to sate your savoury tastes.'

After paying for our puds, we walk hand-in-hand across the road and spend a lot of time admiring everything behind the deli counter. Sensing that we're in no rush, the shop assistant offers us a selection of cheeses to try and when we both like the blue one best, Zach seems genuinely thrilled. I find myself chuckling at his reaction. 'One of the things I love about you is how into food you are,' he says. Then he stops talking and stares immediately at the ground.

He definitely just used the word love.

Do not panic Alice.

'I will basically eat anything,' I say, trying to ease how awkward we both feel. But seriously, love? We're not there yet, I tell myself. I think back to the first time we met at Zach's exhibition, to how he told me that he's an 'I love love' kind of guy right before he asked me on twenty-six dates. I'd fully believed we wouldn't get past date three and yet here we are, on a mini-break for our M date. Just last week he asked me to be his girlfriend and now he's talking about love? I pretend to be fascinated by the cheese counter while suddenly feeling like our relationship has gone from zero to 100 in the space of seven days. I like hanging out with Zach but I can't help but feeling like I'm on the verge of a freak-out.

The rain comes down in fat droplets just as we finish dinner on the jetty. Zach piles the plates up on his toned arms while I grab the wine glasses and we dash inside, laughing. 'That one was like a missile,' I shout as a raindrop splashes on my nose. Inside he's wiping his glasses on his T-shirt, a glimpse of torso on show. He hands me a tea towel with a lopsided grin and we busy ourselves making things cosy inside the little living room. It's too hot to light the fire but we dot more candles around and keep the lights down low, snuggling up on the sofa and gazing out of the vast windows. Every time I look at the lake something has changed. It's magical.

I top up our wine glasses up. An Italian red because *obviously*.

'I don't think I've told you how much I enjoyed meeting Ellie, Raff and the girls at lunch,' I say as I curl back into his body.

Zach turns his head to listen.

'Really? They can be quite full on,' he says.

'In the best kind of way. I especially enjoyed it when Raff challenged Ellie to a washing up competition at the end of the night. They're like a pair of kids.'

'So competitive,' Zach grins. 'And I think they wanted to give us time to ourselves.'

'They wouldn't let me help! After I'd eaten all their food and lounged around in their garden all day. It was bliss.'

I can see Zach smile at this.

'It's lovely that you're so close,' I add.

'We always have been. After my parents divorced it was pretty much just the two of us. Mum and Dad have always been career driven and I admire that, you know? But Raff and I always felt like an obligation to them, rather than anything else.'

I run my hand across his chest in sympathy.

'It's fine,' he says. 'I'm very aware that I had a fortunate upbringing in so many ways. Mum and Dad's cold approach to parenting was more than made up for by Nonna. But she was in Italy and Raff and I kind of became each other's emotional support. I feel very lucky to have him and his family, now. I would love to have that for myself one day.'

With my head now on his chest, I can hear Zach's heart beating faster while mine feels like it has stopped still. This setting is so perfect for romantic declarations of love, for promises of future lives shared. The house. The kids. Suddenly I can hear Natalie's words when she was reeling from her split with Jake echoing around in my mind. How her main source of heartbreak was that she felt like their future of monogamy, marriage and multiple children had been stolen from her.

That feeling of being on the edge of freaking out rears its ugly head again, only this time I'm too close to the edge. My stomach lurches as I realise that I can't stop myself from falling.

And I panic.

My heart rate shoots up and I can feel it pumping against my ribcage. My palms are clammy and the walls are closing in around me. Zach shifts, sensing the mood change.

'Are you okay?'

'Just a bit hot,' I mutter. 'I'm going to grab some fresh air. You stay.' I pull on my shoes and rush outside.

* * *

143

I'm pacing up and down the jetty, oblivious to the rain blasting my face and soaking my top through to the skin. I'm too busy trying to get my breathing straight. In. Out. In. Out. With every steadying breath I can feel my heart-rate begin to settle but the questions in my mind won't follow suit.

What are you doing, Alice? You don't date. And now you're in a relationship with the ultimate romantic who split up with his ex hours before you met and who wants a family one day.

Am I messing with his emotions as much as my own? And if so, why? Suddenly I feel like I've got us both into such a mess. I tip my head up to face the rain and cry.

'Alice? It's getting late. Are you okay?' Zach looks full of concern as he steps outside.

'I'm fine,' I sniff. 'Just needed some space.'

'You're soaked,' he says tenderly.

'I don't mind,' I say with as much of a smile as I can muster. 'Honestly, you head back in. I'll be in soon.'

But I stay in the rain trying to gather myself together. Later, when I see that he's turned all but one of the lights off, I tiptoe back indoors, slipping into bed next to him.

'Hey,' he says sleepily, his arm reaching around me in a way that feels so familiar now.

'Night, Zach,' I whisper, knowing I'm shutting him down and feeling bad for doing it. I turn my back to him and pretend to fall asleep.

After a predictably sleepless night, I'm up at dawn, creeping out of bed and throwing my things into my travel bag. I wash my face as quietly as I can and slink back into the bedroom, pulling on some clothes when Zach starts to stir. The duvet's half kicked off his body and his hair's all messed up. I feel a visceral pull towards him but I push it back down. I need some space and I need it now.

'Morning,' he says, sitting up. 'Why are you dressed? I was

144

hoping we could spend the day in bed together.' He stretches out his arms for a hug but I move away.

'I can't, I need to leave.'

His smile fades and he's looking at me with concern and confusion.

'I'm so sorry but I'm going to have to go,' I say, feeling like an idiot as I zip my toothbrush into my cosmetics bag.

'Alice, please don't. I don't understand what's happened. Have I done something wrong?'

'Not at all,' I say, attempting a breezy smile. 'Eve texted me first thing. Bit of a work emergency to deal with.' I feel awful for lying, like, proper shit.

Zach's pulling on yesterday's jeans. 'Give me twenty minutes to pack and I'll drive us home,' he says.

'No need, I've booked a cab. I didn't want to ruin your last day here and we don't need to check out until this afternoon so . . .'

'Honestly, it's not a problem. I want to help.'

'No,' I'm firmer this time and I can see it catch him by surprise. 'I don't want this to ruin your weekend too. You should stay, get out for a walk, maybe do some sketches? I know how you love the fresh air.'

'I'd rather spend time with my girlfriend,' he says, and at the mention of *that* word, the air around me feels thinner, and the cage I've built for myself even smaller.

It's too much. The space is closing in around me and it feels harder to breathe.

I'm filled with relief when my phone buzzes to let me know the taxi's arrived. 'Here it is now. You stay and enjoy yourself.'

He's scratching his head, dejected, but I can't focus on that right now. I have to get out of here. I don't even kiss him goodbye as I pull on my trainers, sling my bag over my shoulder and leave.

There's a message pinned on the fridge from Natalie waiting for me when I get back.

'Cannot wait to hear the details of your bonk fest SOZ

145

mini-break! While you've been away with your boyf I've spent the weekend working and seeing mates so our role swap continues. See ya later!'

I sling my bag on the floor. No debrief with Natalie just yet then.

HELP PLEASE. I panicked halfway through my trip with Zach and now I'm back at home already. I message Dylan.

The Bolter's at it again!

This is serious. I feel awful.

Do you?

YES.

Uncharacteristic of you. Usually you just ditch them and move on.

I haven't ditched him. I have genuine questions about what I'm doing with my life and his and this is one huge mess.

Pickle, I'm sorry to hear that. I'm about to go on set but will be free later if you want to chat then?

Dylan's busy. Nat's away. Which means there's only one option left. Today, it's time to bring out the big guns.

'Daddy?' I say down the phone. I still call him that, okay? Let's move on.

'Hello, love! How are you?'

'I'm . . .' Great? Really good? I find none of my usual replies to this question will work. *What is the matter with me?* 'I'm a bit confused to be honest, Dad.'

'Oh dear, are the business accounts getting the better of you again? I told you to hire an accountant. It might be an extra expense but if it means . . .'

'No, not that,' I say, laughing in spite of myself. 'It's about the guy I've been seeing.' Dad knows Zach and I are dating because we talk all the time, but I don't often bring up the topic myself and I can practically hear the cogs turning in Dad's brain now. 'I know you're away for the weekend but have you got a minute?'

'Of course! My friends are still at the beach but it was getting too hot for me so I'm back at the hotel reading my book.'

I smile at this. Dad's in Cornwall with his pals and his delicate Celtic skin has never fared well in warm weather.

'Why are you confused, love?'

Pfft. Where to start? I take a deep breath. 'We've been on thirteen dates now, Dad. I only know that because we're doing this alphabet dating thing and I had no intention of it getting any further than, like, B.' Dad chuckles down the line. 'But I've just left our mini-break in the Lake District early. It was all going so well until I basically clammed up, made some rubbish excuse about a work emergency and left.'

'Don't you worry, my love. There's not always a right or wrong way to go about things. But it seemed like it was going well and you liked spending time with him. What made you panic?'

I explain to Dad about how Zach talked about his family and how much his parent's divorce has made him crave a family of his own. How his brother's picture perfect family are exactly what he wants for himself. 'I totally understand that, Dad. And the thing is, I really care about Zach but I don't know if I want those things myself. Until recently I didn't even want a boyfriend and now I feel like I have all these big bloody life decisions to make. Like, I want Zach to be happy but can we find a common ground for our fundamentally opposing views on what we want out of life?'

'Alice, these are some big questions,' Dad says eventually.

I scratch my head. 'Can you answer them for me please?'

'Now if there's one thing I know for certain about my clever daughter, it's that she likes to make decisions for herself. You are strong and independent, Alice. It sounds like you and Zach are more similar than you think. You've both had childhoods which have made you want to do things differently for your futures. For Zach, his parents splitting up has made him yearn for a family of his own. For you . . .' Dad pauses and I can hear the crack in his voice.

'For you, losing Mum has made you vow never to put yourself in a situation that could risk you feeling such heartache again.'

My eyes pool with tears and I look up, blinking them away.

'I wish we could have a cuddle,' I say.

'I'm back on Tuesday,' Dad rallies. 'Are we still on for pie and mash night?'

'Yes please. Will you bring some Cornish clotted cream back?' It's as if I haven't indulged enough over the weekend.

Dad laughs. 'Already earmarked the shop I'll stop at on the way home,' he says. 'Alice?'

'Yes?'

'Not everything is black and white. Sometimes, there is joy in the unknown and the unexpected. Sometimes we have to open up our hearts to things that feel scary because if we don't, we might miss out on the journey of a lifetime. You've spent your whole life being strong, I just hate to think that you might miss out on things because of what happened. Ask yourself how Zach makes you feel. What does he bring to your life? Is it brighter and bolder with him in it? Or do you feel happier and more content by yourself?'

I fall silent as I think about what Dad's said. Zach makes me feel like I can be all the parts of me. The woman with clinical FOMO who is always out and the woman who's happy pottering around her allotment like a 60-year-old. He makes me laugh so hard I end up doing that weird cry-laugh noise that I used to find embarrassing but he says is endearing. He's sensitive and thoughtful and, now that I've been put on the spot, I do like my life more now that Zach is in it.

I swipe at the tears that are now dribbling under my chin, feeling so caught in my conflicting emotions.

'I'm just scared, Dad. Of being hurt.'

I can hear the smile in his voice. 'There's nothing wrong with that, Alice. I am always here for you and so's your mum. She's in your heart and she will help you to make the decision that feels best for you.'

I say my goodbyes and rest my hand over the place I'm pretty sure my heart goes, even though I wasn't a biology buff at school. Closing my eyes, I listen to the voice in my head.

Don't let him be the one that gets away.

Netflix

Zach

It's been three days since we, sorry, I got back from our mini-break and perhaps the most unproductive three days of my career so far, but the fact is that I just can't focus on work. The canvas remains stubbornly blank. I've lost count of the number of times I've stepped away from it, hoping for inspiration to strike, only to find myself staring hopelessly at it once again. I'm too distracted thinking about Alice and whenever my mind lingers on her, I'll inevitably grab my phone and open up our message chat. The last message I sent her was the night I got back from the Lakes.

Alice, whatever you're going through, I'm here for you. It seems like you need some space right now but please know that I'm just a phone call away xx

The double tick turned blue tells me she's read it but she hasn't replied. And I know I can't send her another one, because I'm afraid that she'll think I'm being too intense. So instead I keep reading and re-reading the message, torturing myself with how and why it all went so wrong on our trip. Obviously I did or said something to upset her and even though I was desperate to try and fix it, she could barely get her shoes on fast enough that Sunday morning.

I thought Alice and I had something worth pursuing but

maybe I was wrong. It wouldn't be the first time I've made a major miscalculation like that.

I chuck my phone back down onto my work bench and take a slug of coffee, which it turns out is cold, so I head over to the kitchen unit in the corner of my studio and tip it down the sink. I'm filling up the kettle when I hear my phone ring and, assuming it's Ellie ringing to check up on me again, I leave it go for a minute while I put the kettle on.

Eventually I pick it up. Alice's name flashes on the screen.

A million thoughts race through my head as I answer it, not wanting to let her ring out and make things even worse for myself. Is she going to end this? Is this the call to make it officially over?

Stay strong.

'Hi, Alice,' I say, clearing my throat.

'I'm sorry it's been a while.' It's only been a few days but I've missed the sound of her voice.

'There's no need to apologise. I figured you needed some space.'

'Well, thanks Zach, I did and it was sensitive of you to understand that.' She sighs then and I imagine the words that are about to come next. *I'm sorry it's over. I've realised that this isn't for me. We're done.*

The kettle has started to hiss.

'Did it help?' I ask.

'I think so. I wanted to apologise for leaving our trip like that . . . with such a bad excuse, I mean.'

'I can't say I was totally sold on the "work emergency" thing.'

There's another painful pause, filled only by the low rumble of boiling water.

'Yeah, that wasn't great. I should probably explain myself. I feel torn, Zach, like I'm being pulled in two completely different directions. On the one hand, there's you and how much I like you. On the other, there's this fear. I think the weekend was just a bit too much and the scared voice in my head was getting louder, asking me what I'd got myself into with you and telling me that

151

it would only end badly. I don't want to mess you around but I don't want to miss out on this, either.'

'Why do you think it's going to end badly?' I ask quietly.

'Because I'm worried that we want different things.'

'Alice, you're not messing me around. I'm a big boy and I chose to be here. Christ, I'm happier here than anywhere.'

'I feel like that too.'

'Was it me talking about families that made you panic?'

A pause, then: 'Yeah . . .'

'Honestly, I could kick myself.'

'But you shouldn't have to and that's the point. That's what you want from life. The problem is that I don't think I do. Or, at least, I haven't made my mind up yet.'

'Alice, *you* are what I want from life right now. All that other stuff . . . those are big questions but we don't need to deal with them. All we really need to know is that we have fun together and that we like each other.'

There's silence down the line.

'That's what I think, too.'

'I know you want to take things slowly and I know why you want that, too,' I say, trying to reassure her. 'Just because we've put a label on our relationship now doesn't mean we're on a one way ticket to getting married and filling a house with kids. I'm not going to lie, those are things that I think I'd like for myself in the future but I'm not dead set on anything. Life throws you curveballs, right? And suddenly you find yourself looking at things differently, maybe realising that where you are right now is where you want to be.'

There's a pause while Alice processes what I've said. 'Are you calling me a curveball, Zach?' I can hear the hint of a smile in her tone and it feels like a massive confidence boost. All I can do is be honest because I owe that to myself. I don't want to be too full on for Alice, but I also need to be true to how I feel.

'I don't think either of us were expecting what happened on

152

that night at my art exhibition,' I say. 'I've had the best summer of my life getting to know you. I'd like for that to carry on because this thing we have is fun. We don't need to worry about what the future has in store just yet. So, what I'm saying is, can we just stick with what we have?'

'I'd really like that, Zach. And I have to admit that this summer with you has been pretty great.'

I punch the air in relief. 'Does that mean you fancy our N date?'

'Depends,' she laughs. 'What is it?'

'I figured that something with no pressure and no grand gestures could be good. Netflix this weekend? And as we always hang out at yours, you'd be very welcome to come to mine for a change.'

She giggles. 'I am so up for that.'

The only problem is that I still haven't got very far with the house. Every time I peel at some flaking wallpaper or pick at a loose carpet thread, I realise I should really be in the studio. My house looks like the grey-washed before pictures of one of those house makeover TV shows.

When the doorbell rings the following weekend I take a last quick look around. There's music playing in the background and I've gone big on low-lighting which makes the place looks less like it's desperate for a paint.

I open the door and Alice is standing there with a smile on her face. She's wearing stone-washed jeans and a white T-shirt with a pair of red lips on it, handing me wine and flowers as she steps inside. I haven't seen her since our fated mini-break and we both stand there for a moment, the weight of what happened when we last saw each other seeming to hang in the air.

Suddenly Alice is in my arms, reaching up to kiss my cheek, and everything feels right with the world.

'I've missed you this week. Sorry about the drama,' she says almost sheepishly, her body still against mine.

153

'Please, there's no need to apologise,' I say, steering her into the living room. 'I'm just glad it's all out in the open and that you're here. I've missed you too.'

'I've been looking forward to this. You might have guessed that work's been mental since I got back from our trip.'

After three days of silence and our conversation mid-week to clear things up, Alice has mostly sent me a string of head-exploding emojis ever since. 'I figured from your messages,' I grin.

'I haven't been the most communicative,' she says, clinking my glass with hers and catching my eye. 'Nat and I have been working on your idea.'

I must look confused because she carries on. 'You know, joining forces? You mentioned it in passing a while back when we were talking about Nat's awful boss. You were right, flowers and events do go hand in hand so we've been staying up late, brainstorming ways to combine our talents and turn them into a business opportunity.'

'Alice that's awesome.'

'I'm really psyched about it,' she nods happily. 'It would be a side hustle for both of us at first which would mean even longer working hours, but I really believe that we could make a go of it. And it feels like everything else is in place. Eve is brilliant at the shop already so I'd have no concerns about her potentially taking over one day. Meanwhile Nat is so ready to tell Sid and Bruno where to stick it.'

'I can picture her doing that,' I laugh and Alice joins in.

'Zach?'

'Mmm?'

'What's for dinner?'

'Never not thinking about your stomach,' I smile, hopeful that tonight might get us back on track. 'Fancy making pizzas together?'

* * *

154

The look of concentration on Alice's face is adorable. She pats her floury hands on the apron she's borrowed from my coffee shop days and suddenly stops in her tracks, shaking her head.

'No Zach. NO. This is not okay.'

Shit.

'What is it?' I pause, looking at her in concern.

'You're putting pineapple on your pizza, man. You're Italian! The whole of Italy is weeping right now.'

Relief floods through me as I laugh. 'Pizza is a safe space, Alice. Somewhere we can express our personalities *without judgement.*'

'There are so many ways to express yourself when it comes to pizza,' she nods thoughtfully. 'Pepperoni or salami, mozzarella or burrata, mushroom or pepper. But pineapple? That's just plain wrong. I can't believe I didn't know you were a dirty pineapple pizza lover. What's next . . . ham?' She wrinkles her nose.

I nod towards the packet of ham hiding behind an empty box of pizza dough.

'Oh my.' She holds her hands up in horror and I love how quickly we've got our rapport back. After the mini-break I thought that was it but I understand that Alice has never been big into dating before. I guess she's bound to have wobbles along the way and all I can do is be here to ride them out with her.

'Surely you're not going to dump me because of my pizza preferences? That would be very short-sighted of you. Besides, people in glass houses shouldn't throw stones.' I look pointedly towards her own pizza. She's making a smiley face using two slices of salami as eyes, halved olives as the pupils and a mouth made out of sliced peppers. She's currently adding hair and eyebrows with grated mozzarella.

Alice follows my gaze and bites her lip.

'I'm going to call her Penelope,' she announces.

'I think my five-year-old nieces could make something more professional.'

'Pipe down,' she retorts. 'Penelope could do with some contouring. Could you pass me the passata, please?'

We muck about contentedly, putting our pizzas in the oven and drinking our wine and just being. It feels good.

Later, we're settled on the sofa grabbing slices of pizza when Alice gives me a devilish look.

'You must never speak of this,' she declares as she takes a bite of mine.

Quick as a flash, I grab my phone and snap her mid-bite.

'Oh no you didn't?'

'Just a little evidence of the fact that you're currently eating my pineapple and ham taste sensation and enjoying it.'

'It's really good,' she whispers.

'I see. Perhaps I'm owed an apology then?'

Alice bites into the crust with a raised eyebrow.

'You did just tell me I was a disgrace to my Italian heritage,' I point out.

'Oh yes. Sorry about that. I bow down to your superior knowledge, Zach Moretti. Would you like a slice of Penelope?'

I look down at Alice's own creation. 'Do you think she'll mind if I eat one of her eyes?'

'Nah,' Alice laughs. 'She's cool like that.'

As we flick through film options on Netflix, Alice seems genuinely thrilled to discover that my recent watches are mostly romcoms, chuckling about me being 'too cool for school' on the outside but a 'giant softie' on the inside. It's the kind of thing that I might normally feel mortified about but to be honest, I'm just happy to know that I've made her smile. Her hair is loose again tonight and she keeps absent-mindedly pushing it behind her shoulders when we talk.

'I think we should go for a Nordic crime,' she says eventually. 'I loved that book you chose for me and look, this film's got murder and snow. Sounds cosy!'

'A cosy murder?'

'Exactly,' she laughs, grabbing the remote. 'Shall I put it on?'

'Alice?' I say, turning on the sofa so I'm facing her.

'You'd prefer a romcom, right?'

'No, a cosy murder with some snow sounds good. I just wanted to say that I'm proud of you. I hope you don't think that I'm out of line for saying it. I just . . . I don't know. You've been through a lot and yet you're this incredible ray of sunshine. You're smart and funny and kind of dark. I mean, who names their pizza Penelope and then demolishes it with glee?' Alice is laughing now and I pause to take a drink. 'And you're successful and determined, too. So I just wanted to say that I think you're great.'

I rub the back of my neck, suddenly embarrassed.

Alice has inched closer to my body and we're pressed up against each other now.

'Thank you,' she whispers, lips close to my ear. 'You know, I reckon you and I are more similar than we think. You're smart and funny and kind of . . . light, actually. Underneath this achingly cool exterior of yours lies a romcom loving snuggle fan.'

'I do enjoy snuggles,' I murmur, wrapping my arms around her and pulling her on top of me.

'Maybe we're pieces of a jigsaw puzzle,' she suggests, her hair falling down onto my shoulders as I lean up and kiss her.

That might just be the closest reference Alice has made to us fitting together, being together, working together. I will take that.

Oysters

Alice

Natalie's crouching down by the washing machine, muttering to herself when I walk into the kitchen.

'Oh here you are,' she says accusingly, holding up a pair of my pants with a right look on her face.

'Just coming to empty out my washing but it seems you beat me to it?'

She bats my comments aside, nodding furiously towards the pants in her hand.

'What are these?'

Oh no, she's lost it. Breaking up with Jake, going nuts on the dating scene, taking a man sabbatical and setting up a new business . . . all in the space of a few months. I guess it was only a matter of time but I'm mad with myself for not seeing it coming.

'These are pants,' I say, edging towards her. 'Shall we put them down and make a hot chocolate?'

'I'm fine!' she says indignantly. 'However these so-called pants are not. They're beige. What the eff are you doing with your life, babes?'

'Well that's rude! I'm quite busy running a business you know.'

Nat tuts, throwing the knickers into the laundry basket and sitting me down. 'These pants are not the one. How can you have the wardrobe of a stylish rainbow when all the while you're hiding this dirty magnolia-coloured secret underneath?'

'They're just pants,' I argue.

'"Just pants" indeed. Please. You need to get some lingerie and you need to do it now. The type that errs on the side of too expensive.'

'I think I'll stick to buying basics from M&S. The last thing I need is to be dealing with a wedgie when I'm at work.'

Nat's looking more violated by the minute. 'I know what you're thinking and you can stop right there. Wearing beautiful lingerie is empowering. It's not about who might see it, it's about how it makes you feel. If your tits are happy then the rest of you will follow, that's my motto.'

'Is it though?' I laugh. But as I retrieve my knickers from her withering gaze and head upstairs to hang out my laundry, I wonder if Nat has a point. A little sexy lingerie couldn't hurt, right? Especially as I have some Serious Plans for Zach on our next date.

So I take the tram out to Meadowhall. And yes, I do buy sexy underwear for a guy and yes I will have to repent at my next feminist meeting but honestly, it will be worth it. I arrive back at home with three new sets and a large dent in my bank balance. Later, I find myself wearing a peach plunge bra and briefs trimmed with tulle while I cook up a romantic storm in my kitchen.

Since my massive meltdown Zach and I have settled into a pace that suits both of us and I really feel like we're connecting. Not long ago the thought would have had me running for the hills but now I'm actively enjoying it. I'm into Zach and I haven't given the bolting option a second thought for ages. I like it. And tonight, I am planning the ultimate romantic dinner date to celebrate. Dylan's back for the whole week and Nat's staying at his parent's house, leaving my house empty for Zach and me.

Somebody pop a Barry White playlist on, quick!

* * *

'Oysters?' Zach says, his eyebrows raised in a sexy-as-hell way. He looks good tonight. He's wearing a T-shirt with an actual motif on it which feels ground breaking. The T-shirt is pale grey (sure) but across the front stretches a snow-capped mountain with a red sun setting behind it. Red! I love that he wears less muted colours now.

'Oysters,' I nod. 'Shucked them myself.'

'Lucky them,' he says in that low voice of his, running a hand through his hair then down to his stubbled jawline.

Quite frankly I'm tempted to sack off cooking altogether and skip straight to the bedroom.

'Champagne?' I offer, my peach lacy boobs and I (plus the pale pink shirt-dress I threw on over the top for decency purposes) making our way to the fridge. I take two of Mum's vintage champagne saucers from the kitchen cupboard and pop the cork while Zach leans against the counter, watching me.

'Cheers,' I say.

'Saluti,' he replies, and as we clink our glasses together I feel my whole body relax. How can someone give you goosebumps and make you feel content in equal measure? Is he a wizard?

We move easily around the kitchen together, him with a tea towel slung over his shoulder as he takes charge of cleaning up my mess, me with a bowl of homemade garlic butter in my hand and the temptation to just chuck a baguette into it and call it a night. But no, I will find some restraint. I've nestled the oysters into little salt houses on a baking tray and am dolloping a helping of garlic butter into each on. Grill on, I pop them under for a couple of minutes.

'Smells amazing,' Zach says appreciatively.

'Let's hope they taste as good,' I reply. Full disclosure, I searched 'how to eat oysters' on YouTube earlier so that I could look like I know what I'm doing when it came to the crunch.

Zach's chatting about his latest project as we sit down at the dining table. 'I'm only in the early stages but it's kind of inspired by you,' he says, looking at me nervously.

'Is it?'

'I've been pushing my own boundaries a bit. My latest work definitely makes use of a wider colour palette.'

I feel honoured. 'I'd love to see it,' I say.

'You would?'

'*Yes!* I know I was super critical of your work in the early days but I was just being a brash buffoon. Just because I don't necessarily understand something doesn't mean I should rule it out, right?' Zach raises his eyebrows as we both realise that sentence has relevance on a much wider scale. 'Anyway, I loved the painting you did for me. Besides, you've been so involved with my job and so enthusiastic about the project with Nat that now I just feel kind of rude for not showing enough interest in your artwork. Forgive me?'

Zach sits back in his chair, flashing those delicious green eyes at me.

'Seriously, there's nothing to forgive. I'd love to show you the new stuff but I'll need a bit more time before I'm happy with it.'

'I'll attempt to be patient, them,' I grin, placing the oysters in the middle of our table. YouTube taught me to take a sip first, chew then swallow, which is not at all like I'd thought, but I am so ready for the aphrodisiac!

Hmm. I'm not sure. It's kind of like chewing garlicky slime. Still, Zach looks genuinely impressed so I'm happy. Plus my go-to pasta dish takes minutes to make so I know the main course will be a winner. I literally bake a camembert and then chuck the molten cheese into some linguine. Not the healthiest, I'll admit, but still pretty tasty if I do say so myself.

After the oysters I serve up steaming bowls of pasta and top up Zach's glass. He's smouldering at me from across the table and I take a moment to marvel at how every element of tonight seems to be combining into a melting pot of romance. An empty house. A sexy AF dinner date. Oysters to start. Champagne. Lacy bra. I think I might be the unexpected queen of romance? Me! A commitment-phobe.

I feel a tingling sensation as I watch Zach expertly swirl pasta around his fork. His eyes meet mine as he takes his first mouthful.

'So good,' he says.

Is it the oysters or is it just Zach? I'm going to have to insist that he gets naked quite soon. For once the plate of food in front of me seems too big. Why did I pile so much pasta on? It's going to take ages to eat and I've a right frisk on.

I take a bite but I'm distracted. My stomach somersaults like it's taking part in some gymnastics. Bloody hell, one plate of oysters and one hot date and I've turned into a complete melt! I swear I can feel butterflies and everything.

Then I hear a growl and slowly but surely, I realise that these are no butterflies. This is the noise of a stomach which no longer wants to be acquaintances with the oysters I've just introduced it to.

Rumble.

OH HELL NO.

I race up to the bathroom as fast as my shaking legs can carry me. There, I frantically turn the tap on to disguise the sound of my dinner making an unwelcome reappearance.

I'm face down in the toilet, retching, when I hear a knock at the door and groan.

'Alice, are you okay?'

'Um . . .'

BARF.

'Can I come in?'

'No?'

'It sounds like you could do with some help.'

I cast a hopeless look around the bathroom which does not look good. My clammy forehead is resting on the toilet seat as I reach out my foot and nudge the door open, still cradling the

162

loo. Zach rushes to my side, holding my hair back and telling me it will be all right.

It will not, I think.

My romantic moment has been absolutely blooding ruined!

'I'm going to fetch you some water,' Zach says, giving my back one last rub while I feel distinctly sorry for myself. This is not how I'd seen tonight ending.

BLARRRRGGHHHHH.

Oh my god it's never-ending. I see actual pieces of oyster floating in the toilet bowl and the sight of that makes me retch again. Grim. I hear Zach padding back up the stairs and quickly flush it, trying to retain the last shred of dignity I can.

'Here,' he says. He's put ice in it. I'd thank him for being so sweet if I could find the energy. I take a grateful sip and then lie down on the bathroom floor for a bit, trying to figure out if there's anything else left to come out. After five or so minutes I realise I'm done. The sweating has stopped and I feel weak but no longer on the verge of chunder.

Zach helps me to stand up. 'Shall we get you out of those clothes?' He asks.

'That's the sort of thing I was hoping you'd say,' I joke feebly.

'There she is,' he laughs. 'Still making a joke after you've chucked your guts up.'

'Do you feel okay?' I check.

'Absolutely fine,' he says. 'I think you must have got a bad oyster. Is it inappropriate to tell you that I like your underwear right now?'

I look down at my lacy bra and pants. There's a bit of sick on the left bra-strap. *Sigh*.

'I tell you what, why don't you grab a shower while I get you some fresh clothes?'

I nod appreciatively.

* * *

163

After a warm shower, I feel better for getting cleaned up but a wave of exhaustion hits me. My hair's back to smelling like apples rather than oyster vom and as I step out of the bathroom, Zach strides in with some bathroom cleaner and starts scrubbing the loo. I'm both mortified and bowled over by his thoughtfulness.

'You really don't have to . . .'

'It's not a problem,' he says. 'I've put some comfy looking stuff on your bed.'

I pad into my bedroom and find a pair of soft cotton joggers and an oversized T-shirt there, along with another icy glass of water.

There's nothing else for it. I sit down and cry.

'Hey, what's the matter?' Zach rushes in and crouches at my feet. 'Do you need to be sick again?'

'No,' I sob. 'I'm just . . . this is so sweet of you.'

'Alice, you're not feeling very well. I'm just taking care of you.'

'Exactly!' I sniff, and we can add snot to the bodily fluids Zach has had to witness this evening.

'Being sick's the worst,' he says.

'Surely cleaning up someone else's sick is the worst?' I ask and Zach smiles. 'I think I might need to crash out now, I'm really sorry tonight didn't go to plan. Please feel free to head home.'

'I'm definitely not going to leave you when you're not feeling well,' he says. 'It's part of the job description as your boyfriend. No arguments.'

It strikes me that this is the first time in my adult life that someone has taken care of me when I felt sick. I've grown used to taking care of myself as a way of self-preservation, not letting anyone get too close for fear that it would be too claustrophobic, too involved. Too dangerous. But now, as Zach lies down next to me and gently draws circles on my forehead with his fingers, I can see that there are so many things I've been missing out on. Having him by my side when I'm feeling unwell is new, and very comforting.

Relaxed by his gentle touch and reassured by his presence I fall asleep in his arms.

Ping Pong

Zach

With bowls of yoghurt and two cups of tea balanced on a tray, I reverse through Alice's bedroom door, trying not to spill anything as I set the tray down on her bed. Sunlight streams through, casting her in an ethereal light where she's propped up in bed.

When she sees me she pulls a pillow over her face and pretends to hide.

'If you're looking for the girl who spent last night throwing up, she's not here,' she cringes. 'In fact, it never happened. Erase it from your memory!'

'Happens to the best of us,' I smile as she peeps at me over the pillow. 'How are you feeling?'

'So much better. I slept like a baby. Thanks for taking care of me, Zach.'

'It's what I'm here for.' I say, handing her a cup of tea. I've never seen her vulnerable like that before, but even when she was hurling her guts up she was trying to crack jokes minutes afterwards. She is one tough cookie. She has a couple of spoons of yoghurt and yawns.

'Want me to head to the pharmacy? I'm not sure what I could get but I bet they could offer advice.'

165

'Thank you but honestly there's no need. I'm just going to take it easy today and drink a lot of water.'

'Sounds like an excellent plan. Can I stay, keep an eye on you?'

'That's really thoughtful but I know you'd planned to get into the studio today so you should go and work on that new painting. I'll be fine, honestly. I promise I'll take it easy and I'll probably end up napping for most of the day.'

The last time I had food poisoning I'm sure I was out of action for at least a couple of days, but Alice is a force to be reckoned with. Satisfied that she's had some food and plans to rest, I kiss her goodbye and on the walk to my studio I use my time wisely, planning our next date. What I need is something that will cheer her up and put that smile back on her face. She went to loads of effort for our O date, pulling out all the stops with a romantic meal only for it to massively backfire, so it seems right that I should opt for something that I know she'll love. And given that Alice is the life and soul of a party, I figure a big group hang out could be a winner.

Later, I check in with her.

How are you feeling? Fancy being cheered up on Friday night, if you're free?

Bit bored. I hate being stuck at home! But miles better, thank you. And YES I AM FREE! Is it time for our P date? As long as it has nothing to do with Puke, I'm in 😂.

We'd better keep you away from the kitchen then 😉.

How rude.

I grin. Now it's time to execute the rest of my plan. I call up the venue and book us a table, and then scroll through my emails to find one from Natalie. She sent me a few back when her company was organising my first exhibition and I'm pretty sure I remember seeing her phone number in her email sign-off.

Bingo. I save her mobile number to my contacts and start up a new message, which feels a bit weird given this is the first time I've spoken to her without Alice around, but this is for a good cause. As soon as I've asked if she can make it Natalie sends back three thumbs up emojis and says she can't wait. Which means there's only one person left to invite.

Dylan.

Alice mentioned that he's back up in Sheffield this week and we didn't get off to the best start when we first met; there's just something about him that got my back up. But he's Alice's best mate so it's time for me to be the bigger person and make an effort, for her sake. I know that she'd love to hang out with him and things have changed since Dylan and I last met. I feel more secure in my relationship with Alice now that she's my girlfriend, so hopefully that'll help me not to overthink everything he says.

After asking Natalie to send over his number, I tap out a message to him too.

Hi Dylan, it's Zach. I'm planning a night out for Alice on Friday. Would be great to see you there if you can make it? Cheers.

The ticks go blue immediately but he doesn't reply, so I put my phone away and crack on.

Three days later I'm eating an unimpressive chicken salad for lunch in my studio when I finally hear back from Dylan.

Thanks for the invite. I always love seeing Pickle when I'm back so I'll be there.

Hmm. It's a friendly enough reply but I'm slightly annoyed nonetheless. I think it's the nickname he has for her, which feels territorial even though I know I'm being unreasonable. Not to mention the time it's taken him to reply to my message. I know he's a hotshot comedian and everything but seriously, how does it take three days to type thanks and I'll be there? I try to shake it off, knowing that Alice will be thrilled that he's coming which is the main thing, really. She's had a rough few days with being ill at the weekend and then on top of that she's had such a busy start to the week that we've barely had a chance to talk yet, let alone see each other, so I figure she'll be ready to let off some steam come Friday night.

Mind if I bring a date? It's Dylan again, obviously struck with an afterthought.

No problem, the more the merrier.

Feeling like I handled that quite well and could do with a treat after the sub-standard salad, I lock up my studio and walk to Division Street. It's a swelteringly hot day so I grab an iced coffee and a doughnut from Steam Yard, taking a picture and sending it to Alice before I demolish the lot, because I know how much she loves these.

WTF where's mine?! She replies immediately.

As it's date night on Friday we could always come back on Sat morning and get one each?

You're assuming I'll stay over? Bit presumptuous 😉

I'm wondering what to reply but she gets there first.

Joking! You had me at doughnut.

As the first to arrive, I order a round and head to our reserved table, taking a swig from my beer bottle while I look around. It's already getting busy in here and I watch a couple getting seriously competitive at their ping pong table, smiling as they get more and more into the game. I think Alice with her competitive nature is going to be in her element.

Dylan's bringing a date, which brings our group up to five, but I grab four paddles because you can't play ping pong with five people. If needs be, I'll be happy to sit out for a bit.

People are piling in after work now, poking their head into the room where all the tables are set up in the hope that there might be one free but it's fully booked already. And suddenly there's Alice, walking in arm-in-arm with Natalie.

'OMG ping pong? I'm so into this idea,' Alice grins. 'Hey, you.' She's still smiling at me as we kiss and hug and I feel a rush of adrenaline, chuffed that she's happy.

'I thought you could do with cheering up after our last date.'

'Urgh. Romance and I definitely don't go hand in hand.'

'Don't say that! Maybe we should make a no seafood rule from now on?'

'Yes,' she laughs. 'That sounds better.'

'No Dylan?' I ask as Alice and Nat drop their bags and Alice starts inspecting the paddles on our table.

'He just messaged to say he's been out with Octavia and they're running late. This one looks good!' Alice adds, holding up the newest-looking paddle. 'Not that I'm trying to find the best one for myself or anything.'

'You definitely are doing that,' Natalie points out, rolling her eyes. 'I might get a bottle of wine, anyone in?'

She heads to the bar and I try to squash the niggling annoyance that Dylan is running late.

Fifteen minutes later he's still not here and my heckles are up but Alice and Natalie don't seem fussed. They're having an in-depth discussion about Dylan's new date, Octavia, and from what I can gather neither of them are massively impressed.

'She runs an art gallery in London,' Alice says for my benefit.

'And she seems very posh and pretentious,' adds Natalie.

'There's a fair bit of posh and pretentious in the business but there are some good eggs too,' I say.

'I was hanging out with them last weekend while you guys had your O date and to me, Octavia seems cold and stand-offish. I just don't understand what Dylan sees in her, other than the fact that she's incredibly hot.'

'I think you might have answered your own question there,' Alice grins.

'How about you Nat? Still taking some time off from dating?' I ask.

'You bet your ass! I'm enjoying being one hundred per cent me at the moment, if that makes sense? I'm not diluting myself with any of the guys I've been dating. I think I prefer my own company anyway. So tonight you're getting pure Natalie juice, not from concentrate. Though I can't stay late. Early start in the morning.'

'Let's hope Dylan gets here soon, then,' I say. 'We've only got the ping pong table for an hour and the slot starts in five minutes.'

'Oh, don't worry about that,' Alice says breezily. 'He'll get here when he gets here. It's fine if we start a bit later, don't you think?'

'Sure,' I reply, my inner stickler for time-keeping having a minor panic attack.

Alice has tied her hair back with the silk scarf she found in her bag so that she could 'concentrate on annihilating me'.

'My favourite thing about you is how very charming and not at all competitive you are,' I tease. We bat back and forth, running lengths of the ping pong table as she shouts things like 'oh look, it's Banksy' and 'I'm pretty sure Margot Robbie just walked in' in an attempt to distract me.

'Nice try!'

There's a commotion by the bar and I turn my head to see that people are recognising Dylan as he arrives, some clapping him on the back and asking for selfies. He's lapping it up, so confident in himself, and I try to ignore the annoyance prickling at me. There's a broad smile across his face as he makes his way over to us, followed by a beautiful redhead with the curves of a Titian painting.

'Oi oi,' he says, giving Alice a hug first. 'Pickle, you haven't met Octavia yet. Octavia, this is my other best friend Alice . . . and her friend Zach.'

Forty-five minutes late and now he's referring to me as Alice's friend? I'm a bit pissed off. I guess calling me by my real name is a step up from No Big Deal, though, which I could see he'd put down next to Alice's name on the guestlist when we went to see his gig. I really should try to play nice for her sake.

Introductions and greetings over, Alice and Nat head to the bar for another round while Octavia looks like she's searching for the least contaminated chair to sit on, finally perching on the edge of my sofa.

'Good to see you again, mate,' Dylan pats me on the back a bit too hard.

'You too. Alice says you've had the week back up here?'

'Yeah man, it's been awesome. I wanted to introduce Octavia to my friends and family.' I'm sure that's been a blast, I think as she smiles tightly at me. 'Actually, Octavia, you might have heard of Zach. He's an artist.'

'Zach Moretti,' I say, extending my hand.

I watch her whole face change as she stares at me, like she's seeing me in a completely new light. 'Shut the front door,' she says eventually in a cut-glass accent. 'The Zach Moretti? Red Circle? Black Square?'

I nod.

'This is too much,' she says. Dylan looks distinctly put out, bristling as she slides along the sofa to sit right next to me. The smell of rich, heady perfume fills my nostrils.

'Well I never. Zach, it's a pleasure to meet you. We've just taken a few of your pieces in the gallery and they're getting a lot of interest already.' She laughs at this, a light, tinkling noise. 'I did not expect to meet the artist responsible for some of my favourite pieces in a . . .' Octavia pauses as she looks around. Alice and Nat are back at our table with the drinks now and we all watch her search for some acceptable words. 'Liddle bar slash ping pong venue up north. We can't be far from Scotland here!'

'Sheffield's in South Yorkshire,' Alice points out defensively.

'Sure, sure,' nods Octavia. 'I'm a Londoner, you know? It's all just a blur once you get past Hampstead Heath. All these liddle villages!'

I can see why Alice and Nat were having an in-depth about her earlier. I might not think much of Dylan but if he was my best friend, I'd be wary of his new date too. She's definitely a bit annoying.

'Sure, sure,' Alice bats back. 'Dylan, why don't you explain to Octavia that some brilliant, creative things happen north of the capital.'

Dylan looks uncharacteristically nervous.

'Goes without saying, Pickle,' he says. 'I'm from Sheffield for a start!'

'And Zach, too. I had no idea the provinces could produce such fantastic talent!' Octavia giggles.

The provinces. No wonder the art world gets a bad name where there are snobs like Octavia working in the industry.

'Who's for another game?' I step in before Alice puts Octavia at the top of her hit list.

Half an hour later Alice and I are watching Octavia and Natalie finish a game together.

'Natalie looks like she might shove that ping pong ball where the sun doesn't shine,' Alice chuckles.

Natalie throws her hands in the air as she wins. 'Yeah! Well done Nat,' Alice cheers.

'Thank you,' she says, taking a bow. 'And with that, I'm going to leave the couples to it. Have a fun rest of evening.'

Octavia grabs a seat next to me and Dylan challenges Alice to a quick fire round of ping pong which has them racing around the table, one batting then running to the other side to bat back. It looks quite complicated to me but that might have something to do with the fact that I'm on my fourth beer. Alice is roaring with laughter as she chases Dylan round the table and I sit back, quietly wishing I was the one she was having fun with. But that's ridiculous, I invited her friends for a reason and it's good to see her having such a good time, even if I do feel a bit left out.

Sitting next to Octavia isn't helping. She seems to have overcome her disdain for the plastic seating options and is now sitting uncomfortably close to me, causing Dylan to shoot daggers in our direction every time he looks over.

'You're very popular tonight,' he says at one point.

'What?' But he's back to ping pong with Alice and doesn't answer. She looks so happy as she plays and my old friend self-doubt creeps in. Is she ever that happy when we're together? Do I make her laugh as hard as Dylan does? I kick my foot absent-mindedly on the chair leg opposite me. I suppose that's what you get when your girlfriend's best mate tells jokes for a living.

I should have more faith in myself, I know, but the combination of beers and Dylan's evident annoyance at my existence are unsettling. Once again I'm sat on the sidelines watching other people have fun. Once again I'm left feeling like the awkward kid at school, the one who everyone thought was weird because I was so quiet. They didn't realise that I was only quiet because I was worried about what I might say and how I might come across. I spent so long racking my brains thinking of the right thing to say that I'd miss my opportunity or, worse, I'd speak too soon and then feel mortified about it.

I clear my throat, turning back to Octavia and trying to focus on her as she lists people we may have in common.

'Clara, of course you must know her? Fellow Northerners and all! She's doing brilliant things bringing art and magazines together.'

Having my ex dragged into the situation is the last thing I need. I know that Alice is working on her wedding flowers but we've agreed not to talk about it, for both of our sakes. I take another swig of beer as Dylan strides over.

'You two look like you're getting on like a house on fire,' he says.

'We've got so much in common,' Octavia pats my hand lightly.

'Have you now?' Dylan's doing a bad job at not scowling. I stand up, slightly woozy and wanting to get out of this weirdly tense atmosphere.

'You okay mate?' he says, just aggressive enough for only me to notice.

'Where's Alice?'

'Loo,' Dylan grabs a chair and I find myself sitting back down. 'So, you've been bonding over art have you?'

'Just talking about a mutual friend, Clara,' Octavia says.

'Isn't she your ex?' Dylan asks.

'How did you know—'

'Pickle told me all about it,' Dylan replies without waiting for me to finish my sentence. 'Sounds like it caused a lot of hurt.' By *it*, he means *me*. I hurt Alice when she found out that my last relationship was a messy one, that's what he's trying to say.

'I'm going to head to the bar,' I announce, not wanting to dignify Dylan's comment with a response. As I get up, he calls after me.

'We should have a game when you get back. See who's the winner after that, shall we?'

'Do you know what?' I say, turning back to face Dylan. 'The drinks can wait.'

I pick up my pint glass and tap my index finger against it. 'See? I've got a quarter of a pint left which gives me plenty of time to beat you before I get another round in.'

The smug smirk on Dylan's face turns sour and he reaches out for a couple of paddles.

'I doubt that, but I admire your confidence,' he says, pushing a paddle against my chest and stalking over to the ping pong table.

Thwack. Run. Thwack. Run. Lunge. Thwack. Run.

Beads of sweat are moving down my hairline and I'm concentrating so hard that the headache is not getting any better.

'Nice shot,' Dylan says as I take the point. 'You're not as bad as I thought.'

I take a pointed sip of beer. 'Don't sound so surprised.'

Thwack.

'I thought artists were too busy brooding over landscapes to keep fit.'

'Low blow!' laughs Alice, watching us from the side with Octavia.

'Yeah, that's a sweeping generalisation, *mate*. You're not bad either but then you've probably got the time and the money to spend every day in the gym,' I retort.

'I have, actually.'

Thwack.

Dylan sends the ball back over to me so fast that I miss it.

'Why don't we focus on the game,' I suggest, trying to calm down.

'Good idea. You've had a busy evening talking about your ex with Octavia.'

Alice's ears prick up, confusion written across her face.

'Really?' She asks.

'No, that's not what happened at all,' I answer, feeling the injustice of Dylan's words so keenly that my blood boils. That self-entitled fuck is deliberately messing things up. 'You're the one who can't stop talking about my past relationships. What's that all about? Ulterior motive?'

THWACK. The game is mine.

I serve again, fast and hard.

'What kind of ulterior motive?' Dylan pants as he runs to make the shot.

'Trying to put Alice off me?'

Dylan laughs. 'Just protecting my best friend actually.'

I stop playing now. 'What does she need protecting from?' I ask.

'You, mate. Dangerous.'

What the hell? I'm seriously angry now but I don't get the chance to reply because Alice has stood up and she looks *furious*.

'What is wrong with you two?' She shouts, slamming her hand down in the middle of the ping pong table.

Dylan puts his paddle down and takes one last swig of beer, catching my eye triumphantly.

'We should probably go,' he says. 'See you soon, Pickle. Zach.'

* * *

175

I'm still hot from the game, patches of sweat blooming under my T-shirt and my head swirling with the effects of the beer.

Alice has sat back down at our table, her arms folded across her chest.

'What was that all about?' she asks.

In my hot, drunken, angry state I find myself unable to find the words to ease her worries and I already hate myself for it.

'He's obviously in love with you,' I say.

'What?' She almost laughs at that and I find myself getting more het up.

'Please don't laugh at me. Dylan's done enough of that already. I've spent the whole night feeling like the dork at school being rounded on by the popular kid.'

'Dylan is *not* in love with me,' she says firmly. 'I'm really sorry that you've felt awkward tonight Zach, I never want to make you feel that way. You have been acting weird, though . . .'

I try to sort through my swirling thoughts.

'Why did you tell him about Clara?' I ask eventually.

'Why wouldn't I? He's my best mate and I needed some advice.'

'I get that, it's just that now he obviously hates me.'

'He doesn't hate you!'

'He made it his mission to put me on the spot this evening. I invited him out tonight because I wanted to show you that I was making an effort with him and he's gone out of his way to make me feel like a dick.'

'I don't think that's true.'

'That's how I see it. I thought it was pretty rude when he turned up late and you just shrugged it off like it wasn't a problem.'

'Oh my god, why are we arguing about Dylan's poor time keeping?' Alice shoots her hands up, exasperated. 'He's always been like that, Zach. And it's not really that big of a deal is it?'

'It's not just that. He thinks I'm dangerous, Alice. What the hell? He's clearly made assumptions about me that aren't fair. Yes, I made mistakes in the past but I would never deliberately,

176

knowingly, hurt anyone. That's not who I am. But Dylan doesn't see that. I understand that he's protective of you, I just wish you'd thought twice before telling him about my past because now he's got a reason to make you question things.'

'It's not my fault that your last relationship was a huge mess, Zach,' Alice says, and I feel myself recoil. That stung.

'I'm just saying . . .'

'That I shouldn't talk to my friends about you?'

'Well, no . . .'

'Because they have been by my side for my entire life and I trust them implicitly.'

'Well then I'm fucked then, aren't I? Because Dylan has already made his mind up about me.'

'And what about you? Seems like you've made your mind up about him, too. He's never on time and you don't like that. He's confident and it seems to me like he makes you feel insecure. And he's protective of me and you don't like that.' Alice is listing the problems on her fingers and my head is spinning.

This is spiralling out of control, fast.

'I felt backed into a corner by him and it would have been nice to have your support.'

Alice shakes her head. 'I don't know what to say to that. I thought I was supporting you but that's clearly not the case. You know, I've always avoided relationships because I don't want this kind of drama in my life. I don't want to be the person arguing with my boyfriend in a public. I don't want to feel angry and hurt and confused.'

I rub my forehead, hating that tonight has soured so badly and that I'm a bit too pissed to think straight.

'Can we just call it quits for the night?' I suggest.

Alice grabs her bag from her seat, her brows still knitted in obvious anger.

'I think we should call it quits, full stop. Sorry Zach, but I'm done.'

Quiz Night

Alice

I wake up thirsty and blissfully memory-free, but in the few seconds it takes to reach for my glass of water, reminders of what happened last night come flooding back. I definitely wasn't as pissed as Zach but my brain's decided to drip feed the flashbacks anyway. Dylan and Zach acting like a pair of teenage idiots. Zach getting incredibly stressed out over what I thought were little things. And then the kicker. Us breaking up.

Last night I pressed eject on the best thing that has happened to me in years.

Too hot and bothered to lie in bed, I kick off the duvet and push my bedroom window open as far as it will go, hoping to let some cool air in but it's stiflingly hot already. Idly picking my phone up, I try to numb my mind with an Instagram scroll but even social media's conspiring against me today. The first post I see is from my favourite café, sharing a picture of today's batch of doughnuts alongside an iced coffee. Zach had suggested we could go there together this morning and I'd teased him for being presumptuous, assuming that he'd get to stay over after our P date. The stark contrast between yesterday, full of excitement for a weekend with my boyfriend, and today, sad, angry and now completely boyfriend bereft, is a painful one.

I need to take my mind off this. There's only one thing for it.

Twenty minutes later and I'm at the allotment, a satisfying pile of weeds next to me as I work my way through the soil. It's the kind of thankless task I've been putting off for ages but if there was ever a day for weeding, this is it.

'No handsome helper today?' ViVi asks, her head popping over the fence as I drop another weed onto the pile.

'Um . . .' The weight of what's happened threatens to spill over again and I find myself lost for words. I catch ViVi's eye, her face growing concerned as she watches me, and I realise that mine has crumpled.

'I'm coming round,' she says decisively, bustling through the little gate onto my patch. I pull a few more weeds out as ViVi announces she's making us a brew, before returning from my potting shed with two mugs. She unfolds the deckchairs and motions for me to sit down.

I can feel the sun on my face as I do what I'm told, my fingers exploring the cracks in the mug, my eyes shut tight. I can hear ViVi pottering around and feel comforted by her presence. My mind wanders back to the last time I sat like this in my deckchair, with Zach by my side. He'd listened so patiently as I'd unloaded a whole load of emotional baggage onto him that day.

'Oh love, you're crying,' ViVi says, handing me a hanky.

'Urgh, sorry,' I reply, swatting at a tear. 'I'm not normally a crier. I just split up with my boyfriend.'

'I'm so sorry,' she says kindly. 'You know there is nothing wrong with a good cry. Just get it all out!'

So I do. ViVi sits down next to me while my tea goes cold and the tears stream down my face. Eventually, I blow my nose on her hanky and try a smile. 'You're right. I do feel better.'

'Would you like to chat about it?'

'Hmm, I'm not sure I can face it right now. I think I'd prefer to bury my head in the sand for a bit longer.'

'There's nothing gardening can't fix,' she beams. 'However if you do any more weeding you won't have any soil left. What about a bit of watering instead?'

'Will you stay?' I ask.

'Of course, love! I'm here all morning. Shall we put some music on and have a little sing along? Though Gerry from two plots down still has my radio, he's meant to be fixing it but between you and me, I suspect he's made it worse and now he's playing for time.'

'That's a problem I can solve,' I smile, heading into the potting shed and firing up my stereo. 'What do you fancy listening to?'

Ten minutes later, ViVi and I are singing along to some sixties classics. Every now and then she chuckles, recounting a story from the decade, and I listen, happy not to be processing anything more than ViVi's penchant for beehives and Twiggy eyeliner right now.

The following morning I find Natalie sitting with her legs crossed under her, a laptop resting on her lap, when I walk downstairs.

'If it isn't the lesser spotted Alice,' she says. 'I haven't seen you all weekend.'

I slump down next to her. 'I spent most of yesterday at the allotment and then when I got back I . . . um, took a Pot Noodle to bed and called it a night.'

'A Pot Noodle? Couldn't you have at least upgraded to those Itsu ones you can get from the supermarket?' Nat nudges me to let me know that she's joking and then takes a deep breath. 'So . . . wallowing in bed with instant noodles, huh? I take it Friday night's ping pong date didn't improve after I left?'

I shrug. 'I don't think I'm quite ready to say it out loud just yet.'

'How about I tell you some good news and *then* we talk about it?'

'Deal. What's the good news?'

'You know Rustlings Lodge?'

180

'The chicest hotel in all of Yorkshire?'

Natalie beams and points her thumbs towards her chest. 'I've been sweet-talking their marketing manager and she's agreed to put you and I on their roster for wedding suppliers.'

'What? Seriously?!'

'Yes! I've organised a corporate thing there before and when I went on a recce, it was all set up for a wedding. The space looked amazing but our company could do it So. Much. Better. So I went back and pitched our tushes off and they were sold.'

'NATALIE! That's amazing. I know we'd agreed that you'd handle meetings and bring in new business because that's your area of expertise but honestly, I hadn't realised it would happen so quickly.'

'I know! And on that note, I just want to make it super clear that I'll keep you completely up to speed with all of this going forward. This meeting was all very last minute . . . They called me yesterday morning and I did knock on your bedroom door, but when there was no reply I figured you and Zach were probably sleeping off a late night.'

'I must have already gone to the allotment.'

Natalie looks at me with concern. 'I guess so.'

'Well, thanks Nat. I'm so proud of you!'

'I'm so proud of *us*. We'll need to get our website sorted asap so that potential clients can find us, and I was thinking that we should organise a shoot to show what we can do. Your flowers, my events planning, etc. We'll also need business cards printed and to come up with an actual name for our company . . .'

'So quite a lot then,' I laugh, my spirits lifting. 'I'm so ready for this. Shall we spend today working on it? It's not like I have any other plans.' That was meant to sound easy and breezy but I don't think I nailed it. Nat's giving me a sympathetic look.

'Alice, shall we talk about Zach now?'

'It's over,' I say, forcing my finger though a hole I've found in the hem of my T-shirt. How did that get there?

She snaps her laptop shut and pulls me in for a hug.

'I'm fine,' I insist. 'I temporarily let a boy come along and side-track me and now I'm back on track thank you very much. You know me. Work. Friends. Those are the things I thrive on, right? I'm *fine*.'

'So you're fine then?'

'FINE. I opened myself up to a relationship and now my heart hurts. I knew this would happen.'

'What happened after I left ping pong? Yes Octavia was snooty but I thought everyone was having a good time?'

I fill her in on Zach and Dylan's drunken jibes over the ping pong table and our stupid, stupid fight which I think started because of time-keeping? How angry Zach was that I'd confided in Dylan, how he suggested Dylan was in love with me, how awful it was to watch them clash. 'Ultimately, it was a huge drunken mess and I bailed.'

Nat sucks in her breath.

'Jeez. Have you spoken to Zach since?'

'Nope.'

'Do you want to?'

I shuffle on the sofa, kicking my feet out in front of me as I think it through.

'Dunno,' I puff. 'When I woke up yesterday I felt his absence so keenly that it was almost like a physical pain and that hasn't gone away. The idea that I won't see him again makes me feel desperately sad, but what's the alternative? Besides, I've told him it's over so I guess that's that.'

'You know what, you don't need to make your mind up right now. How about we get stuck into some work on the business and you just let it sit for a bit?'

'That sounds like a very wise idea,' I say, relieved. Work, I can do.

Working alongside my best friend is just the tonic I need. After the weekend's debrief we've spent our evenings getting our heads together, brainstorming ideas for the brand and working on a website.

I'm sifting through photos on my computer, looking at all the weddings I've worked on and pulling out my favourite pictures to use on the new website when Natalie sits down opposite me, pushing a plate of spaghetti bolognese in my direction.

'What would I do without you?' I smile, twirling some onto my fork.

'Possibly be suffering from some kind of nutrient deficiency,' she suggests. 'I've seen the amount of instant noodle packets in the bin this week, Al. What would your mum say?'

'She would not be thrilled.'

'Exactly. It's all very well throwing yourself into our new venture but you are going to have to face up to things at some point. Have you heard from Zach?'

I shake my head. 'He hasn't messaged but I did made it brutally clear that we were over.'

'But is that what you actually want? Because it seems to me like you're pretending to be all right when deep down, you care way more about this than you're letting on. I've seen you checking your phone and staring off into space.'

'I think I'm just really confused,' I admit. 'I ought to feel relieved that it's over but the truth is, I don't. I liked Zach and I miss him. I feel like I'm grieving for what we had together and if I let myself dwell on it I feel sad and cross and not in very good headspace at all.'

'So you're just going to paper over the cracks by working even harder than usual?'

I shrug, dusting some parmesan onto my food.

'We've spent all our spare time planning and working on the new business. I know I need a break so why don't we go out tonight?'

I shovel hot forkfuls of pasta into my mouth, surprised at how hungry I am.

'Tonight?' I say eventually.

'Yes,' she says, polishing off some salad.

'Tonight was meant to be my next date with Zach.'

'All the more reason to get you out of the house, then,' Nat replies, clearing our dishes away.

'I got some Mr Kiplings on the way home earlier . . .'

'Oh no you don't. You're not binning me off in preference of a couple of cherry bakewells, babes. Come on!'

Dismayed, I cast one last look at my outfit before finding myself being bundled out of the door.

Natalie is clearly trying to torture me. She's dragged me to the exact pub I'd planned to meet Zach at for what would have been our Q date. The only difference is that I am wearing an extremely baggy old man's jumper pulled over the same T-shirt with the hole in I've been wearing all week, rather than a cute date outfit. I've made the hole even bigger now. Oh, and did I mention that my lewk is completed by a pair of leggings?

I take a sip of unspecified white wine and resolve not to let myself feel too despondent about the situation. Just push those emotions down! That's definitely the best way to deal with things, I think as I grab a quiz sheet.

'How about Cool Story, Brew?' I ask. 'For a team name.'

'Why don't you ask him?' Nat's nodding behind me and I spin round.

Zach's here.

His hair's wet from the rain and he's walking towards our table. Where I am sat.

Zach.

My heart starts to beat quicker and my brain fires out questions so quickly that I struggle to keep up with them. *Am I happy to see him?* Yes. *Why am I happy to see him HAVE I NOT LEARNED MY LESSON YET?* Shrugs. *Why am I dressed like I've just got out of bed?* That's not important right now.

'Hi,' he says nervously, looking at me through thick, dark lashes. 'I didn't know if you'd want to see me or not. I can go, if you'd prefer?'

'Um.'

Why have I lost the ability to construct sentences? I flit from Zach to Natalie.

'I may have messaged him,' she whispers, already scrambling out of her seat. 'WILL YOU LOOK AT THE TIME! I've got to get back for . . . that programme I've been watching. Totally forgot it was on tonight!' I narrow my eyes. 'Zach, why don't you sit here and take my place.'

'Is that okay, Alice?' he asks. He looks so anxious and hopeful that my initial shock turns to something else. I think it's hope.

'Sure,' I say.

'Excellent,' Natalie is actually clapping now, looking like she's just masterminded a genius plan. 'Bye Al, bye Zach.'

Bye Zach. Is that what I want to say to him, too? I've never even had a long-term boyfriend to break up with before. The thought of not seeing him, or laughing with him, or jogging through woods with him makes my head heavy. I don't want that. But what's the other option?

Zach sits down opposite me, fidgeting with the table salt.

'I'm so sorry,' he's suddenly saying, meeting my gaze. 'I behaved unbelievably badly on our last date and I know that I've messed things up. I've missed you . . .'

'You haven't been in touch since.'

Zach's eyes search the room as he collects his thoughts. 'I've wanted to, so much. But you were so cross that night and I knew you'd need space.'

'And yet you're here now,' I point out.

He looks completely defeated, I realise, and my fingers yearn to reach out and touch his.

But the problem is that this week, while I've been throwing myself into work and picking a hole in my T-shirt, I've realised something. That the main reason I bolted is because I'm worried I can't trust Zach.

'I am here now,' he confirms. 'You mean so much to me Alice. I had to try.'

I'm reminded of something I said to myself a while ago.

Don't let him be the one who gets away.

'Argh,' I say, resting my head in my hands. 'There seems to be too much to deal with, Zach. You made assumptions about me and Dylan and I did not like that. He's my best friend. Why does there have to be a subtext to a male–female friendship? Our friendship is purely platonic, always has been.'

'That night at ping pong was the perfect storm of me feeling inadequate and jealousy rearing his ugly head. I feel really bad about it so I reached out to apologise to him.'

That's something, I think. 'I hope he apologised too? He didn't exactly cover himself in glory, either.'

'Well, sort of. I know now that he's just being protective of you as his friend.'

'He always has been. The day after we found out that mum's illness was terminal, Dylan's mum drove us to the seaside for the day to try and take my mind off things. We ate fish and chips on the beach even though the wind was blowing sand in our food and I just cried and cried. He was a constant support through all the tears and he's fiercely guarded me ever since. I think . . .' I pause.

The pub quiz has started. Zach's listening intently, an unmistakable glint of hope in his eyes, and I feel torn right down the centre of me as the realisation hits.

'I think Dylan is wary of you because he knows I am,' I blurt out. Blunt as ever. I wince as I watch Zach compute this. He's back to wearing all black tonight, looking exactly like the boy I met at the art gallery.

'Why are you wary of me?' he whispers.

I can feel tears prickling and I blink hard.

'Is it because you don't need me? I'm not part of your plan?' He's hunched over, leaning his forearms on his legs now.

'You definitely aren't part of my plan,' I smile softly though he's not looking at me. His head's hung low.

'Okay,' he says eventually, looking up at me sadly. 'Okay.'

'I'm wary of you because of your past,' I blurt out. 'The relationship with a woman who was already seeing someone else? I know she lied to you about it but you said yourself that the warning signs were there and you pretty much ignored them. You wanted to believe her when she told you it was over with James, so you did. I really feel for you Zach, but still . . . it's not great, is it?'

Zach looks like he's been punched. He pulls off his glasses, sets them on the table and pinches his nose. I've seen him do it time and again when he's anxious or nervous. Now he looks full of sorrow and the fact that my words have done that to him makes me feel awful. But it's the truth.

'Fuck,' he says, shaking his head. 'I really wish I could unpick that whole strand of my life. I thought you and I had got to the point where we'd dealt with it together and were moving past it but it's really hard to do that when my ex keeps cropping back up. You're working on her wedding flowers. Octavia brought her up at ping pong. Dylan seems furious with me for having a past, full stop. The thing is, Alice, there's nothing I can do about Clara now. I regret it all so much but more than anything, I wish I hadn't caused you this pain.'

'You're right. We had dealt with it and I thought we were moving forward, too. But then that night at ping pong . . . I hated seeing you and Dylan fight like that. I know you were angry with me for confiding in him but he's my best friend so that will never change.'

'I know that.'

'And I think I made you feel insecure and I hate that too.'

'That wasn't you, that was Dylan. He's such a big personality and I just panicked that I can't make you laugh like he can.'

I raise my eyes at that. 'He's a comedian, Zach,' I say with a

187

small smile. 'He's been cracking jokes since we were kids. But you make me happy . . .' I pull up short.

'You're crying,' Zach whispers.

I swipe at the tears drizzling down my cheeks.

'I feel, argh, I don't know. Confused. I hate the idea that when we're together, you're not sure of yourself. I know you crave stability and a proper home,' I say, thinking about all that Zach has told me about his parents' divorce. 'I worry that I'm not right for you. That I can't give you what you really want.'

'Alice, what I really want is *you*. You're right, I can be insecure but that's not on you, that's on me. It's something I'm working on and our last date was a massive slip-up in that respect. The whole night was just a ridiculous clash of stuff that doesn't really matter, I don't think. Yes, my last relationship was messy and I shouldn't have taken Clara's word for it, but I only realised that she was still seeing her ex long after we'd broken up. I was foolish but I'd never deliberately hurt anyone like that.'

His words hang in the air and I lean back in my chair, contemplating all that's been said while the quiz master rattles off questions in the background. It's the oddest soundtrack to our heart to heart. Zach's hunched over his pint, staring into the amber liquid like he'll find the answers in there. Maybe if I'd had a serious relationship in the past, I'd be able to figure this out more easily? Maybe I wouldn't feel like I'm swimming against the tide. I'm exhausted from all the questions that my mind keeps firing at me but if I sift through the daunting feeling that I'm opening myself up to something new for the first time since Mum died, I know that these concerns are just my defence mechanism kicking back in. Because even though it's only been a few days, being apart has made it feel like longer and I've missed Zach. I love spending time with him. And my gut instinct tells me that I do not want that to end.

'We all have a past, right?' I say eventually.

'I'd like to make a case for the past not mattering so much. It's the present that we should be focusing on.'

188

'You are quite maddeningly wise sometimes.'

He looks at me, eyes wide with hope.

'Does that mean . . .?'

'I chatted to my dad about you a while back,' I say, spinning Mum's ring around my finger absent-mindedly. 'He asked me a couple of questions and one of them was if my life feels better with you in it. The thing is, Zach, it does. I've missed you.'

'I've missed you too,' he says, coming round to my side of the table and kneeling down next to me.

'But the problem is, I don't know if I can trust you. Or myself. The closer we get, the more I panic that I'm going to hurt you because I'm always on the edge of running away.'

'I can do something about the first problem, if you'll let me? Let me prove that you can trust me on our next date?'

I laugh at that. 'Have you had an R date in mind all this time?'

'It's just come to me,' he says with a look full of promise. 'I haven't dared hope until now.'

'I like hope. Hope is good. It's optimistic and full of possibility.'

'Just like you,' Zach says.

Feeling my reservations drop down a notch, I let myself breathe in properly for the first time since Zach got here.

'I've missed you,' I say simply. He crouches by my chair, kissing me oh so softly on the lips and it feels right.

'I've missed you so much,' he replies, a huge smile reaching across his face as he sits back down.

'There's just one problem. There's no way we can win this quiz because we've missed half the questions already and I do not like to lose.'

Zach laughs and I revel in the sound, jubilant that we seem to be getting back on track. 'Shall we have a go at the last half? Maybe you can explain who was in charge of calling us Cool Story, Brew while we're at it.'

'That was all Natalie,' I fib. It's suddenly dawned on me that I'm now on a *date* with Zach wearing a baggy jumper and faded leggings, the look completed by a pair of once white Birkenstocks. He sips at his beer, listening intently to the quiz master as we try to catch up, and I realise it doesn't matter.

'Not to brag, but I am really quite good at quizzes,' Zach catches my eye.

'Well then I'm very glad you're back on my team,' I grin, grabbing his hand as Janet, the gravelly voiced quiz-master welcomes us back into the game.

Rock Climbing

Zach

I've fallen into classic Zach mode of overthinking the crap out of things as I drive around to Alice's house but I know it's just down to nerves. Will it go back to feeling like us again, or will we be treading carefully around each other? It feels like so long since we last had a proper fun date. One that hasn't ended in one of us being ill, or breaking up or having an awkward conversation, that is. Today I am desperate to make things right between us.

I ring the doorbell and wait.

'Hey,' she smiles.

'Hey,' I reply, deciding to go in for a kiss right when she leans up to kiss my cheek, so I end up brushing my mouth on her chin instead.

Stop being awkward, Zach.

I shake my head.

'Shall we try that again?' she suggests.

This time we're in sync, sharing a soft kiss on her doorstep. I take a deep breath, feeling comforted by the scent of her shampoo. We stay there for a while, arms wrapped around each other, enjoying the feeling of being together again.

'Want to come in?'

'I'd love that.' I'm chuffed to see my artwork still hanging above her fireplace as we walk through the house.

'You didn't chuck that on a bonfire after the last disastrous few dates, then?' I say, feeling bold.

'Nah,' laughs Alice. 'Figured I could sell it to fund my doughnut obsession instead.'

'Ouch,' I grin, bolstered by the fact that we've easily fallen back into our stride. 'Now we're going to have to do something about your outfit before we leave for our R date.'

'What's wrong with it?' asks Alice, looking down at her blue dress. I recognise it from our bookshop date back in the very early days of us.

'Nothing, you look beautiful, but it might not be practical enough for what I have in mind today.'

'Practical?' Alice raises an eyebrow. 'Does that explain why you're dressed like you're about to do a HIIT class?'

'Exactly. Think sportswear.'

'I'll go and get changed then,' she groans, looking at me suspiciously.

Alice is giving me that you've-got-to-be-kidding-me look again. After she changed into her lilac yoga outfit we drove out to the Peaks and now we're at our date destination, a twenty minute walk from the car park. She's craning her neck up towards the top of a crag, hands shading her eyes against the morning sun.

'Dare I ask why you've brought me to this giant rockface?' Her eyes flit to the mat I'm carrying on my back. 'Or why you've carried a mattress all this way. My only hope is that it's so we can spend the day having sex in the great outdoors.'

'That's your only hope?'

'Sounds good though, doesn't it?'

'Well, yeah, definitely.' In fact, now she's made that sugges-tion I'm struggling to think of anything else. 'Though I'm not sure they'd approve?' I nod towards a couple in their fifties

192

who've just turned up and are setting up camp at the next rocky outcrop.

'Spoilsport,' she tuts. 'So what are we doing?'

'We're going rock climbing. After all that's happened lately, I think we both feel like we could work on our trust issues and I thought this could be perfect way to give it a go. I want to show you that I've got you, Alice.'

She looks at me like she's half touched and half terrified.

'It's okay, I promise,' I say, reaching my arm around her back and turning us both to look at the crag we'll be climbing. 'The technical term for what we're doing today is bouldering. Loads of people come here to practice getting their steps right before moving on to climbing the big rocks.'

'That *is* a big rock,' Alice harrumphs, collapsing on the mat I've just laid on the ground and slapping a hand across her forehead.

'Don't panic,' I scoop her back up again. 'It'll be fun.'

'Fun? That thing is higher than Everest!'

'Not *quite*,' I moderate. 'Mount Everest is the highest mountain above sea level on earth.'

'Well then this one's probably second highest,' she says, hands on hips.

I clear my throat. 'Couple of things. Everest is a mountain and this is a crag. And from memory, Everest is roughly 8,800 metres high while this crag is maybe three meters off the ground.'

'All right Captain Zach the Brainiac,' she grins, putting on a geeky voice. 'It's still a lot bigger than me.'

'That's true,' I concede. 'But the good news is, I'm big into rock climbing and I will not let any harm come to you during this massive ascent.'

She pouts. 'You're teasing me.'

'Only a little bit. Honestly I'm completely happy if you'd rather not. When I first started out climbing I'd do crags like this with Raff and I remember them feeling really daunting at the time so I do understand.'

'Are you saying you climb bigger land masses than this, normally?'

I spin her round to face an actual peak. 'Yep, that sort of thing.'

'Holy shit. Don't you need ropes and stuff for that?'

'Ropes, a harness, chalk . . . all the gear.'

'What's the chalk for? So you can draw a big smiley face halfway up?'

'Ha, not quite, though maybe I'll try that next time. The chalk's to keep your hands dry. Bouldering the little rocks like this is the best way to start learning how to find your feet and climb. Plus you don't need any equipment.'

Alice spins back to our crag. 'The things I do for you.'

Finding her first grip and hoisting herself up, Alice clings to the crag with a happy smile on her face. 'I'm doing it!'

'Yes you are!'

'How far am I off the ground? I don't dare look down.'

'Um, about two or three inches?'

'Oh. What now?'

'Have a look round for your next foothold, find somewhere to grip and push up again.'

'There's one! I'm going for it. Oh my god, I'm going for it! How high am I now?'

'Gotta be nine inches by now,' I say.

'There's a joke in there somewhere. I'm sure I'd find it, if only I weren't in the middle of a life-threatening date with my maniac boyfriend.'

I grin to myself at that. Hearing Alice call me her boyfriend reassures me that we *can* put what happened in the past and move forward together. Her panicking on the mini-break, me acting like a twat at ping pong. I keep my eyes fixed on her as she makes her ascent, watching like a hawk to make sure she feels safe and calling out praise as she goes. I remember feeling all over the place when I first started climbing and massively admire her willingness to give it a go.

'Hate to brag but I think I'm a natural at this,' Alice announces.

'You're doing brilliantly. You've got to be halfway up by now.'

'Really?'

Alice looks elated. Then she looks down.

First rule of climbing . . . don't look down.

'SHITTING HELL ZACH,' she shouts. 'I'm so high up.'

Her knuckles grip tighter and the blood drains from her face. I realise that she's starting to panic so I try to reassure her.

'You're doing really well. Keep it up.'

'I can't,' Alice yells, panic etched across her face. 'I'm too far off the ground. What am I supposed to do?'

'Exactly what you've just been doing,' I encourage. 'Find a foothold. Ease yourself up. Take it nice and slowly.'

'But what if I fall? I can't do this.'

There's genuine fear written on her face now and I leap into action, scaling up the steeper route so I can scramble to her side.

'Deep breaths,' I instruct. 'You're doing great. Here, lean on me for a bit.'

'Won't we both fall?'

'I've got a strong hold,' I say, wrapping my arm around her waist for support. With my help she lets go of one handhold and rests her upper body against me.

'I'm scared,' she whispers.

'I've got you.' I hold her gaze and rub my thumb across the side of her body until I sense her starting to calm. 'Now, we've got two options. Option one: carry on climbing to the top. Option two: climb back down. Either way, if you fall (which you won't) the mat is there to protect you.'

She puffs air out of her mouth. 'Gawwwwwd. What about option three: stay here forever. Or option four: go back in time and use the mat for outdoor sex as I initially suggested, rather than for landing on with several broken limbs after I tumble down this GIANT ROCKFACE.'

'The jokes are back,' I grin. 'Which means you can do this. Do you trust me?'

She stares me straight in the eyes as if she's searching in them for her answer. I feel like she's sifting through all that we've been through, all of my baggage. Eventually she nods. 'I'm starting to.'

In my head I'm doing a Chandler from *Friends* dance but obviously I don't tell Alice this. I still haven't recovered from the fact that she knows I used to love Point Romance and the Spice Girls, so I think a secret *Friends* addiction may just be the final nail in my cool coffin.

'Let's make it happen then.' I ease her hand back towards the crag and track her steps with mine, pointing out each new foothold as I spot it for her. She's breathing fast at first, completely silent with concentration and nerves. Slowly but surely, we make our way to the top of the crag.

'I can see the top!' She yells.

'One more step and you'll be over the edge.'

'I'm going to put my foot here?'

'Looks good to me. See, you don't even need my help now.'

She pauses. 'I JUST LOOKED DOWN.'

'Stop doing that!'

'I think I've developed vertigo?'

'One more step and you'll have reached the summit.'

With one last burst of energy she scrambles over the top, me in hot pursuit. I find her lying like a starfish on the grass. I lie next to her, our fingers touching, enjoying the rush of endorphins as I stare up at the airplane trails criss-crossing the sky.

Alice is the first to sit up, pulling herself into a cross-legged position. A smile spreads across the whole of her face, eyes bright with the effort.

'That was incredible! Sorry I swore at you a lot.'

196

'Did you?'

'You didn't hear?'

'Nope.'

'Right. Well I definitely didn't call you a dastardly bastard or anything,' she grins. 'Only dainty words of love fell from my lips as I feared for my life.'

Dainty words of *love*?

I'm not sure if today could get any better. She definitely just used the 'l' word. I know well enough by now not to make a big deal about it so I carry on watching the sky, my heart quietly on fire. For her to even talk about that kind of stuff is a massive deal and it gives me hope that one day, *one day*, she might feel that way about me. I watch Alice jump up to survey the peaks around us, looking like a conqueror with her legs stretched wide, her hair whipping madly in the wind.

'Top of the morning to ya!' she calls over to the couple in their fifties who've reached the top of the next crag along. They wave their Thermos flasks at her.

'Are you Irish now?' I hoot.

'I do not know where that came from,' she giggles, pulling me up to stand and wrapping her arms around my waist. 'It's invigorating up here.'

'I think so too.'

'There's just one small problem,' she says, biting her lip and looking up at me.

'I brought snacks, don't worry.'

'Not that,' she laughs. 'Though, thank god, I'm starving. The problem I'm talking about is our descent. I'm not sure I'm brave enough to climb back down again.'

'Then I have good news for you.' I spin us both round, away from the edge, towards a gently sloping path.

'THERE'S A PATH? Why didn't we just walk up that in the first place?!'

'Because that wouldn't have been rock climbing, would it?

Besides, I very much enjoyed the view as I climbed up behind you,' I wink.

She places both hands on my chest and gives me a playful push back towards the edge.

'So what you're saying is, we've spent the morning risking my life scaling the world's second highest mountain . . .'

'Still just a crag . . .'

'Scaling this behemoth,' she presses on. 'And all because you wanted to admire my ass?'

'It wasn't the *only* reason,' I grin.

'I'm afraid that puts you right at the top of my hitlist, Zach Moretti. Your entire life now hinges on the calibre of those snacks you mentioned.'

Unzipping my backpack, I pull out a bottle of water, a couple of Snickers and some Real McCoys.

She bites her lip as she considers the offerings.

'You're safe,' she grins, ripping open the crisps.

Reaching out to hold her hand, we fall into the kind of comfortable silence that reassures me that she's feeling at ease with me again, just like I am with her. All I can think about is how happy I am to be here with her. Not long ago, I spent most of my time hunting for the next thing as if they were targets to hit. Girlfriend, house, marriage, kids. It strikes me that right now, I'm content to just be. How could I not enjoy the simple pleasures of eating a Snickers out in the wild with my girlfriend?

'You looked a bit like Tarzan climbing up that rock after me,' Alice points out.

'I'll take that,' I laugh, giving her a squeeze.

'MY ARMS!' she wails, stopping to rub them.

'You'll be feeling it for a few days,' I warn.

'Rock climbing,' she says in an astonished voice. 'Who'd have thought it. I would never have tried it if we hadn't met.'

'I think it's fair to say that we've both done a few things we wouldn't necessarily have tried if we hadn't met.'

Alice nods. 'I'm always up for new adventures but there's something about you, Zach. I've never been fussed about *sharing* the adventures with a boy before.' We skirt down towards the car park and she looks off towards the cars, lost in thought. 'Maybe I am starting to believe in l . . . stuff.'

'Le stuff? Is that French?' I tease, mostly because if I let myself dwell on her last sentence too long Chandler's dance might come out in real life and nobody needs to see that. She was definitely about to say love, I'm sure of it.

'Shut up,' she punches me in the side.

'You old romantic.'

'You know what I mean, though? I feel like I've grown in ways I never expected this summer. Sort of . . . allowing more stuff in?'

'I do know. I was just thinking how my own outlook on life seems to be readjusting.'

Alice pulls a lip balm out of her rucksack and smooths some onto her lips, making them shine. 'Mmm. Me too,' she nods. 'Hard to explain, really. One thing's for sure. I'm definitely happy.'

'Same,' I grin, and she kisses me with those soft lips. I may not have my dream future all lined up, but what I do have is worth so much more than that. A brilliant, beautiful girlfriend who makes my whole world brighter. Maybe I don't need promises of a happily ever after, after all.

Supermoon

Alice

'S is for sex, surely? Oodles of it. A whole weekend of ripping each other's clothes off. It will forever be known as the weekend of a thousand orgasms,' Natalie's looking lusty as she leans towards me. I push my laptop back and let my mind wander for a minute.

'So . . .?' She prods, all thoughts of work clearly abandoned. 'Are you going to share details of your make-up sex with me or what? Come on! Huge fight. Big split. Reunion followed by cute climbing date. That is surely the recipe for an absolute bonk fest?'

'You're spot on,' I laugh. 'But Nat, are you okay?'

'Yeah yeah, fine,' she clicks her fingers dismissively. 'Ever since going on this man sabbatical I find myself craving details of other people's sex lives. You know Betty, from the bakery?'

'The sixty-year-old with an unfailing commitment to blue eyeshadow?'

'Still bonks her husband daily. Isn't that sweet?'

'Gosh. May I ask how you know this?' I fold my arms.

'We just got chatting when I went to buy buns,' she shrugs. 'So . . .'

'Do you think it's time for you to start dating again?'

'Nah. Too much faff. What I need is a purely physical partner who will occasionally take me out for dinner, like, once a month. Most men are so needy.'

'Natalie, you have transformed.'

She bites the end of the pencil she was using to make notes. We're working on branding for our new company which we've now named The Hitch, focusing on eco-friendly weddings using seasonal flowers and local, independent providers. I'm buzzing with ideas and it feels like setting up my flower shop all over again, only this time with Nat's events knowledge and the help of a certain artist I'm dating. Zach has been brilliant with the branding side of things and I'm so happy with our new logo.

'I think we've both changed, actually,' Nat says. 'Even though you seem to be refusing to throw me any details of your make-up sexathon, I can see that you're super happy right now.'

'I am,' I agree. 'I've realised that having Zach around doesn't mean I have to give up on my own freedom, you know? It's not like I've lost my identity, I've just gained a whole other person to share experiences with.'

'Whereas I am way better at being on my own than I thought,' Nat says. 'I'm not defined by the person I'm dating any more and now I have the time to throw myself into new challenges like our business.'

'Speaking of which, this *is* meant to be a work meeting,' I point out, shuffling the stack of handwritten notes in front of me.

'Fine,' she sighs. 'Though may I just add that I think Zach sounds like a keeper.'

'You might be right. You know he knows the words to pretty much all songs from the noughties? Let me show you.'

I pull out my phone and send Zach a Justin Timberlake lyric.

He taps back instantly with the next line of the song.

Nat roars. 'He looks like he spent his teenage years listening to David Bowie and wanting to be Serge Gainsbourg and yet there's a little bit of mainstream hiding under his arty exterior.'

I grin. 'I love that about him.'

201

Natalie raises her eyebrows and I'm left thinking how easily that last sentence came out.

'Did you just say the L word?' She asks.

I roll my pencil backwards and forwards on the table, deep in thought. 'I've felt this almost physical pull towards him, even from the first day we met. So, maybe, yeah. Whatever life throws at us we seem to end up orbiting round each other.'

'So what you're saying is he makes you feel out of this world?' Natalie jokes.

That's when the perfect idea for our next date pops into my head.

My heart flutters when the doorbell rings on Saturday night and I open it to find Zach leaning against the doorway. I'm so excited for tonight and also a little bit nervous. It feels like the right time to tell Zach how I feel, mostly because the thoughts have been taking up most of my headspace for days now, and I think I have the ideal date to say what I need to say.

'Hello, you.'

'Hello YOU!' I press my body up against his and inhale that familiar citrus scent. He leans back to look at me and I feel a bit giddy.

'I brought a coat and hat as instructed.'

'Excellent,' I nod, pulling him inside. You'd be forgiven for thinking that autumn has started early this year, what with August being pretty grey and rainy so far.

'Are you going to tell me then?' He asks, that wry smile curling at his lips.

I clap. I'm quite excited about this one. As I run into the kitchen to grab my stuff I call out: 'Supermoon.'

'Superman?' Zach shouts after me excitedly. I walk back in to find him delightedly saying the words 'comic convention' to himself and my heart melts.

'Sorry, no. Super MOON. If there had been a Superman thing in town then obviously we'd be going to it.'

Zach coughs. 'Yeah, no, that's *fine*. I definitely wouldn't be fussed about going to a comic convention anyway,' he says, talking in his deepest voice and pretending to deny his cute thing for superheroes.

'No, for sure, what with you being so utterly cool and all that.'

'Exactly,' he laughs. 'So, what does a supermoon date involve?'

'Prepare to be amazed, Zach.' My stomach fizzes as I grab his hand and we head outside.

We straighten up the picnic blanket before folding down onto it and I hand Zach a tin of gin and tonic from the stash in my bag.

'It might be a bit fizzy from the walk . . .' but my warning comes too late. Gin and tonic explodes out of the can and into Zach's face, spritzing his wild dark hair with supermarket booze.

'Argh!' He laughs, fumbling for a tissue. 'My glasses are covered.'

I ease his specs off and give them a clean while he deals with the rest. Zach looks so sweet without his glasses on. They're a permanent part of his style but when we wake up together in the mornings, I love to see him without them on. All short-sighted and ever so slightly vulnerable, which is probably a weird thing to like about my boyfriend? He's just ever so slightly less polished at times like this, and ever so slightly less intimidatingly handsome.

'You'll be needing these. Spectacles for tonight's spectacle,' I hand them back and try not to laugh too hard at my own joke.

'Sex spectacle?' he suggests.

'What is wrong with everyone at the moment?' I titter. 'I don't have a one track mind, you know?'

'No,' he nods. 'Maybe two tracks.'

I reach back into my rucksack and pull out the fish and chips we grabbed on our way up to the top of Meersbrook Park. I hand one paper bag to Zach and unwrap the second, the tang of salt and vinegar filling my nostrils. By the time the sun sets there's a definite chill in the air, a warm cloudless day having given way to a crisp night. We're lying like sardines in a tin, tucked up next to each other on our backs as we watch the stars come out.

'The good news is that I'm an expert astrologer,' Zach announces.

'Really?'

'Yup. Can you see the very bright star up to the left, above those trees?'

'The red-ish one?'

'That's . . . Mars.'

'What's with the suspicious pause?' I ask, snuggling in next to him.

'Nothing.'

'Also Mars is not a star,' I point out.

'All right! I *might* be trying to consult the star-gazing app I just downloaded.'

'You're cheating!'

'No, just, er, enriching?'

'My mum always used to tell me a story about how the moon was made of cheese and I spent most of my childhood wanting to eat it.'

'Sounds very much like you,' he laughs.

'The moon's bloody massive tonight though, isn't it? Apparently there are only a few of these a year. They happen when a full moon is at its closest point to earth.'

'It's stunning,' Zach says, lifting his arms behind his head. I curl in next to him, resting my head in the pit of his arm. 'This explains why you're wearing a jumper with stars all over it,' he grins, turning to look at me.

'You know I love a theme,' I reply.

'This is nice, Alice. Really nice.'

'This is my favourite park in Sheffield. You get such great views out over the city. It's amazing on bonfire night and when it snows in the winter, people bring their skis and ski down there,' I say, pointing at the steepest hill.

'You know, I haven't been to a bonfire night in years.'

'What? Why not?' I pull my gaze away from the city below and turn to him.

'Tiny's not big into fireworks so I usually spend the night dog-sitting while Raff and Ellie take Sienna and Francesca to a big display. I'm sure he'd be all right by himself for the evening but I like to keep an eye on him and I know Raff appreciates it.'

'That's really thoughtful of you. But the twins are five, so are you telling me you haven't seen a firework in all that time?' I'm incredulous. I love a firework.

'They only started going out when my nieces were two or three so it's not been *that* long,' he's laughing at my reaction.

'Well this year will be different.'

'It will?'

'Yes. I absolutely insist that we spend bonfire night together.' I hold up a finger to let him know there's more to come. 'I know what you're about to say. We can still go and dog sit Tiny. But I am telling you right now that I will be bringing sparklers and a tiny Catherine wheel and there will also be mulled wine, okay?'

Zach's looking at me intently.

'What?'

'Nothing,' he smiles to himself.

'You definitely have to tell me now,' I press.

He takes a sip from his can. 'It's just that bonfire night is in November,' he says slowly.

'Oh, well done.' I tease. 'Can you do all the days of the week, too?'

'I can indeed, and I can tell the time too,' Zach retorts, spinning over to my side of the blanket and kissing me hard. His lips are salty.

'I must make a mental note to poke fun at you more,' I murmur.

'Please don't, I'm not sure my ego can take it.'

'But if it gets me kisses like that . . .'

'That kiss had nothing to do with your relentless teasing,' he smiles.

'Oh?'

'For someone who told me I wouldn't make it past our third

205

date, it struck me that you've just casually mentioned making future plans with me.'

That did come out quite easily, didn't it?

He turns onto his side so we're both facing each other, propping his head up with one arm. 'I'm just surprised to hear you talking about us making plans for later in the year, that's all,' he adds, watching me nervously. 'It makes me happy.'

I absent-mindedly bite a nail. 'I guess I do have previous when it comes to my aversion to forward planning.'

'Just a bit,' he smiles. 'And I would never want to push you.'

'A few months ago I thought having stuff planned out was boring at best and risky at worst. When Mum died, she and Dad had just booked a holiday for the three of us. She was so excited about it . . . We all were. It's one of the things that really stood out during that time, having to cancel the holiday.' I shake my head at the memories. 'Dad tried to sort a refund out over email but the travel company called up when he was out one morning so I picked up. The travel operative kept saying they needed a death certificate as proof before they could issue a refund and I remember just crying down the line. Like, certificate did not seem like the right word to use . . .'

Zach grabs my hand in sympathy and I take a deep breath.

'I think that's why I'm more of a spur of the moment type of person. And then you see all these couples who have dates for stuff in the future. Like, we'll get engaged on our two-year anniversary and we'll be married the year after that. All that sort of stuff, you know? It always just seemed so . . . predictable.'

I look over at Zach. He's watching, listening.

'But with you I'm starting to think that it would be nice to have some things to look forward to. I'm really happy to be here with you, Zach.'

A huge smile has lit up his face in the moonlight.

'What?' I grin.

'That may be the most romantic thing you've ever said to me,' he smiles.

I laugh. 'It's probably the most romantic thing I've said to anyone.'

'I think the moon is smiling at us,' Zach says, and I stare out at it for a while, making out eyes and a lopsided grin.

'Do you think it approves?'

'Of us? No doubt,' Zach smiles. 'We've come a long way since we first met, Alice. We've had so much fun and a couple of hurdles along the way but I don't think there's been a better date than this. I feel so lucky to have this beautiful moon shining overhead, my beautiful girlfriend curled up next to me . . .'

'You charmer,' I tease, feeling my stomach do somersaults as I snuggle further into Zach. He turns to look at me, our eyes trained on each other in the moonlight. And that's when I know it's time.

'Zach?'

'Alice?'

'I think I'm starting to fall in love with you.'

Zach scoops me into his arms, covering my face in kisses and stopping every few minutes to look at me, this incredulous look on his face.

'I think you know that I love you already,' he murmurs.

The supermoon shines bright overhead as we kiss under the glistening stars.

Train Trip

Zach

Alice is falling in love with me. *Alice is falling in love with me.* I keep repeating that phrase in my head as if I need to remind myself that it's true. I imagine this is what it must feel like if you win the lottery, the constant buzz that something really incredible has just happened. Even the stuff that usually annoys me is water off a duck's back, like needing to remember my pin code when I've spent a few quid over the contactless limit, or my alarm going off when I'm in the middle of a deep sleep. Which is exactly what happens this morning.

I reach out to hit snooze, painfully aware that it's not even light outside yet when I remember that today is the start of our T date. Showered and dressed in record time, I check my phone as I walk to the train station and find a message from Natalie.

All going like clockwork here, the birthday girl is excited and confused!

Today is Alice's thirtieth birthday and I've been quietly planning a special date to celebrate for almost a month now, roping Natalie in to help me out with the logistics. It's been really tough to keep it a secret. The amount of times I've wanted to blurt it out to Alice, even though I know she loves surprises. And then there was the situation after that disastrous ping pong date, where

208

I thought I'd have to request a refund and cancel the whole thing but something told me that we could work it out so I'm glad I had a rare moment of confidence and hope, and I'm grateful I listened to myself that day. Everything between us is better than ever and I'm really glad I can show her how much I love her with this surprise.

Now Nat's confirmed they're on their way and I feel myself relaxing into my plans.

The earliest commuters have started trickling into the station, hands wrapped around coffee cups, while I flick through a newspaper. I'm reading an article about jet pack paramedics when the station doors slide open again, allowing the bite of cool early morning air inside. Followed by Alice. My heart leaps.

Natalie trails alongside her, pulling a wheelie suitcase which has a cluster of helium balloons attached to it. I notice that Alice also has one around tied around her wrist and laugh.

'What *are* you up to?' She grins as she gets closer.

'Happy birthday, beautiful,' I reply.

'Ta daaa!' Nat gestures with magician hands. 'May I present the birthday girl. It took a bit of persuading to get her up at such an hour on her auspicious day but in the end I bribed her with balloons.'

'I may be officially thirty today but I will always love a balloon,' Alice chuckles.

'Thank you, Natalie,' I say, grateful to her for executing the plan perfectly.

Natalie wafts my thanks away with a wave. 'Right, I'm going to leave you lovebirds to it. Might get back into bed to be honest. Have fun!'

I turn back to Alice, looking bemused as she stands there in a green T-shirt tucked into slim white trousers on this chilly September morning. She runs her hands up her arms and shivers so I circle my arms around her for warmth.

209

'I hope there's a jumper in there,' she points towards her suitcase. 'Natalie was so bossy this morning. She insisted that I spent a full twenty minutes in the bathroom, putting a timer on my phone and everything, and when I was finally allowed back into my bedroom she'd packed all my clothes and was pushing me out the house. I didn't have a chance to grab any layers!'

Top marks, Natalie, I think as I pull off my own jumper and ease it over Alice's shoulders. It swamps her but she snuggles gratefully into the warmth before jumping up and down excitedly. 'Come on then! I'm guessing that we're at Sheffield train station at the break of day because our T date is train based?'

'Correct.'

'Where are we off to?'

I wrap my arm around her shoulders and point to the departures board.

'A birthday trip to London?'

'Come with me,' I grin.

I feel a bit bad, letting Alice tick off all the things she's excited about doing in London, and resist the temptation to tell her everything now, reminding myself that I spent ages planning today out for a reason and that she'll love it even more if I keep the suspense building for a little bit longer.

'Obviously Columbia Road Flower Market, too,' she's saying. 'I mean, that's the place to go for flowers in London. I've never been before so I'd love to do that if we have time?'

The train's pulling into St Pancras now and Alice is looking at me expectantly.

'We might not make it to Columbia Road,' I say as gently as possible.

'Okay,' she nods, trying not to look disappointed. 'I'd only be taking pictures for Instagram anyway.'

'There will be lots of things to take pictures of, I promise.'

'You're being so mysterious today. I like it!'

I laugh, wheeling our suitcases off the train as Alice practically skips through the turnstiles.

'How about the champagne bar, to start?' I suggest.

'Seriously?' she says, stopping short of stepping onto the escalators down to the main station.

'Well, it is your thirtieth birthday. And it's five o'clock somewhere,' I add, pretending to check the time.

Minutes later we're sat at a high table with flutes of fizzing champagne in front of us.

'Champagne for breakfast. Zach, you're spoiling me,' Alice says, her eyes bright.

'Would you like some facts to go with your champagne?'

'Always, you know I love a fact, especially if it's wine related.'

'This is the longest champagne bar in Europe.'

'It is long,' she muses, looking up and down the bar, which runs almost the entire length of the platform. A train to Paris has just pulled in behind us and Alice spins round to watch passengers getting off.

'You can find another fact in there, if you'd like,' I say, pushing an envelope towards her. She looks at me, full of curiosity, as she picks it up and peels it open.

There's a birthday card inside and as she opens it to read it, a pair of tickets drop onto the table.

'What are they?' She asks.

'Why don't you take a look?'

Alice places the card on the table and picks them up.

'WE'RE GOING ON THE EUROSTAR?'

Her excitement seeps into me and I laugh as she shouts out a stream of enthusiastic phrases.

'SERIOUSLY? YOU'RE TAKING ME TO FRANCE?'

She still hasn't stopped shouting by the time we've drained our drinks and I lead the way to the Eurostar check-in.

* * *

211

By the time our train pulls into Paris, Alice has her face pressed up against the train window in delight. She looks slightly less enthusiastic when I tell her we're getting on another train as we arrive at the Gare du Nord.

'Um, okay,' she says, pretending to use the balloon attached to her wrist as a pillow as we stand on the concourse. 'Train to London, yes. Train to Paris, yes. But another train? Have you taken this train date too literally, Zach? I'd love to get out and see some of Paris before we head back to England.'

'I'm afraid Paris is off the cards today. However . . .' I pause, laughing to myself as I watch Alice perking up. 'We will see some of France soon, I promise.'

She rearranges the Happy Birthday tiara she's been wearing ever since St Pancras and follows me as we head underground. Cramming a birthday girl, four helium balloons and a well-packed suitcase onto the bustling metro isn't the easiest and we're both roaring with laughter as we make it into the carriage just in time. In fact, making any connection with Alice isn't simple. At Gare de Lyons she gets so distracted by a large display of profiteroles in a bakery window that once again we find ourselves scrambling onto our train with seconds to lose.

Countless rounds of Uno later and our destination is finally revealed.

'*Prochaine arrête, Avignon centre.*'

'This is us,' I say.

'We're getting off at Avignon?' Alice asks.

'Have you been before?'

She shakes her head. 'And are we staying the night?'

I laugh. 'I wasn't actually going to ask you to spend your entire birthday on a train. We're here for a couple of nights.'

'But what about work?'

'Natalie's got it all sorted with Eve,' I explain. 'Apparently Eve was more than happy to take charge for the weekend and she said it was about time you took some time off, too.'

'So you've been in cahoots with Natalie and Eve?'

'Just wanted to plan something special for you.'

Alice sits back in her seat, a smile curling at her lips. 'You incorrigible romantic,' she says. 'A surprise birthday trip to France?'

'Are you happy?'

'Very. I can't believe you've planned all of this, Zach. I'm so impressed. I had no idea and Natalie is usually rubbish at keeping secrets, too,' she laughs.

Alice has been racing around our hotel room since we checked in, sampling all the little products in the bathroom, rifling through the minibar and throwing herself onto the bed to "check the bounce". It's like going on holiday with a puppy on crack.

I lean against the bathroom door, watching her unzip her suitcase to find out what Natalie packed for her. On the top of her clothes is a tissue paper parcel wrapped in ribbon with a little envelope attached and she flashes me a look as she goes to open it.

'That has nothing to do with me,' I say.

'The card says, "YOU'RE WELCOME",' Alice tells me, looking suspicious. Then she opens the parcel and pulls out something black, lacy and extremely sexy-looking.

'Oh my.'

'Are you sure this has nothing to do with you?' She raises her eyebrows and holds it against herself.

'Promise. It looks like a . . . sexy swimming costume?'

'It's a body,' Alice grins, folding it gently into a drawer. 'Natalie must have packed it. She's been taking an OTT interest in my underwear recently.'

I clear my throat, unsure what to say.

'Oh look, a room service menu!' Alice says, sitting at a little desk and turning it over in her hands.

'Given that I've made you spend your entire thirtieth birthday on a train, maybe room service and some more champagne could be the perfect end to the day.'

'You read my mind. Burgers and fries? But maybe . . .' She pauses, looking me straight in the eye. 'A shower together first?'

I follow her into the bathroom like a shot.

'Now *this* is how you should spend you birthday,' she says later, as we stand by the window in the hotel's towelling robes, our arms wrapped around each other as we look out over the city.

The next morning, after an indulgent breakfast in bed which feels like a scene from the romantic comedies I'm definitely not into, we finally leave the hotel and make our way to the Palais des Papes.

'It dates back to the fourteenth century and was once the residency of the popes, apparently,' I say, pulling out facts from my guide book. 'It's a huge Gothic building.'

'I think this might be it,' Alice says, turning a narrow corner which opens out into a vast square, the enormous palace looming large in the background.

'I think you might be right.'

Before we head inside, Alice insists on trawling the stalls selling trinkets out front. She buys three lavender soaps, a stack of beaded bracelets and now she's inexplicably picking up a tiny Virgin Mary.

'I'm getting this too,' she announces. I must look confused because she adds: 'I thought your Nonna might like it?' Alice catches my eye and I am completely touched by her thoughtfulness.

The heat picks up by mid-morning, the cobbled streets of the city shining under the warm September sun, so we stop to grab a coffee and waffles, watching the world roll by. Alice's sunglasses are neon pink and she's wearing a sleeveless blue gingham dress. I feel like the luckiest man in France right now.

I check the time and tip some Euros on top of our bill. 'Ready for your next train?'

'I thought we were staying here another night?' She asks, crestfallen.

'We are. I'm talking about this . . .' I turn to point at the little silver train arriving bang on time in the sun-dappled square.

Alice's mouth makes an o shape.

'Har har. Very funny.'

'I'm not joking!'

'You want me to get on that tiny train? Isn't that for children?'

I laugh. 'It's called a Petit Train. As you can see it runs on wheels rather than tracks and it's a great way to see the city, apparently. You're the first to admit that you love a theme so I thought we'd keep the train one going for a bit longer.'

'I do love a theme,' she says cautiously. 'But I don't love public humiliation. Look at that little tinker toy . . . We're going to end up looking like a right pair of geeks!'

'I see,' I say with a smile, folding my arms.

'What?'

'Sounds very much to me like the introvert and the extrovert have suddenly exchanged roles.'

She purses her lips. 'Not wanting to go on that dork-mobile doesn't make me an introvert.'

'You're embarrassed!'

'I am not.'

'You're worried about how you'll look.'

She gives me a side eye. 'Okay fine, I am a bit. What's your point?'

'Just suggesting that we're all different, that's all. I might not like singing and dancing in public but I am happy to hop on this tiny train . . .'

She sighs, taking the last bite of her chantilly-topped waffle. 'I hate it when you're right.'

'Well, well, well,' I pretend to gloat. 'Can I have that quote printed on my next business cards?'

'Those business cards are the reason we're in this predicament in the first place,' she pulls her purse out of her bag and opens it up, handing me the card I gave her when we first met. Touched that she's kept it, I flip it over to read the note I scrawled on the back.

A-Z. Call me.

'I can't believe you still have this,' I say, remembering feeling so nervous writing it, back then. This clever, confident woman had just stormed straight into my life and I didn't ever want her to leave it. It's unreal to think that we're here, now, twenty dates in and she's showing this secret, romantic side to herself that I never knew existed.

'I can be sentimental occasionally,' she says with a coy smile, taking the note back and sliding it into her purse. She carries it around with her. I'm so touched that I reach out for her hand, pulling her towards me for a kiss.

Alice's initial mortification wears off so fast that she's soon waving at passers-by from her spot on the Petit Train. Turns out she's remembered how to say 'it's my birthday' in French and even though her birthday was yesterday, she's been trotting out the phrase to anyone who'll listen. A sweet little French kid on the row behind us wishes her happy birthday and Alice is *thrilled*.

I love that she's loving it.

We weave through the tightly packed streets at quite a pace, which makes me think that our train driver may be breaking the tiny speed limit. The tannoy points out landmarks in English and French and Alice grabs my hand every time she sees something of interest, which seems to be mostly patisserie based.

'Zach, this place is divine,' Alice says later as we walk through the cobbled courtyard of our hotel. Jazz hums in the background and the smell of lavender drifts up from endless planters. 'It must have cost you a fortune.'

The truth is it wasn't cheap, but work's been going really well for me lately. A couple of big sales and another new commission mean I'm feeling more financially stable than I have in a long time, and it feels good to be able to do stuff like this with someone I love.

'Come on,' I say, grabbing her hand and leading her back up to our room. 'I made dinner reservations so we should get ready.'

'Let's hope Natalie chose something suitable,' she winces rummaging through her suitcase. She emerges from the bathroom half an hour later looking so beautiful my breath catches in my throat. She's changed into a long, navy dress with thin straps which delicately drapes from her frame. Star-shaped gold earrings hang from her ears and she's pulled her hair up into a loose bun, a few curls still cascading down past her shoulders.

'Wow.'

'Wow yourself,' she grins, looking me up and down. 'You've put a shirt on!'

I wasn't sure when I put the navy suit I'd packed on while Alice was in the shower. The white shirt felt quite formal though I've undone a button and I'm wearing it with trainers. She walks straight up to me and slips one hand inside my shirt, undoing one more button.

'You said a while back that you thought I might look good in a suit and as this is a special occasion . . .'

Alice looks me up and down appraisingly.

'I can confirm that Past Me was right, you look very sexy.'

As we walk back out of the hotel and into the night, I catch a glimpse of us in the large mirror in the foyer.

'We scrub up all right, don't we?' Alice says at our reflection.

'You look stunning, birthday girl.'

The glasses on our wicker table are filled with a crisp white wine and Alice is chatting happily as she takes pictures on her phone.

'This is the fanciest restaurant I've ever been too,' she says when she puts her phone down. 'Look at us Zach, about to eat haute cuisine . . . in France!'

I love how happy she seems as she skewers an olive, not quite able to take my eyes off her and feeling so lucky to be here.

'I've never done this before,' I admit. 'Plan a surprise trip away for a girlfriend, I mean.'

Her eyes linger on me as I talk. 'Seriously? That surprises me.'

'Why's that?'

'You're such a romantic person, Zach. You told me as much when we first met, remember?' She puts on a deep voice and says: 'I love love.'

I grin. 'Is that your impression of me?'

'Good, wasn't it?'

'Well . . .' I smile, pulling a face. 'You're right, I did say that and I suppose I am a romantic person but the truth is, I've never found someone who I've wanted to share big adventures like this with. I've been on holidays with exes but nothing that's felt like this.' I pause, not wanting to get in too deep because I know how Alice can feel about that. 'Having the alphabet dates to work around has made it all more fun, too. I wanted your thirtieth to be special and first I was thinking about places beginning with T . . .'

'I hear Twickenham is nice at this time of year,' she jokes.

'Ah, damn, I missed a trick there,' I grin. 'When I saw that the Eurostar came all the way down here, I thought, let's do it.'

'I don't think I'll ever forget the time my boyfriend took me on a whole heap of trains for my birthday,' she winks. 'Obviously I'm teasing you. Avignon is so beautiful and honestly, this weekend means so much, Zach. I've never been on holiday with a boyfriend before, full stop.'

'I guess there's a lot of things we hadn't done until we met each other. Going to an eighties disco, for example.'

Alice laughs. 'Going on a 10k run. I should have known back then that I liked you.'

'Oh?' I say, chuffed.

'I can't think of anyone else I'd agree to run around Sheffield with.'

'Well now it's my turn to feel honoured. We've done a lot of cool stuff together and I just want that to continue, to be honest.'

'We have, haven't we? I think we've both been thrown out of our comfort zones and surprised the heck out of ourselves in the

218

process. My biggest surprise has been how much I like you. How much you make me want to try new things with you.'

I look out across the restaurant, feeling bowled over by what she's saying. 'Thank you. Shall we have a toast. To . . . us?'

'To us,' she says, raising her glass to mine.

Over mains, Alice tells me that she's been giving my spirit animal some thought for a while now.

'My what?'

'Your spirit animal. People see them in lots of different ways, for some a spirit animal can be a sort of talisman that guides you through life.'

I set my cutlery down. This sounds intense.

'And for others it's more of a fun metaphor for your personality in animal form. So, like, if there's someone you don't like they could be a snake, or something.'

'Okay,' I nod. 'I think I follow. So have you figured out mine?'

'A panda,' she beams.

'Because . . . I have an affinity with bamboo?'

She laughs. 'Because you're gentle and emotional but you also have strength. And you like to climb.'

'Hmm. A panda. I'll come back to that one but first let me have a think about your spirit animal. God, no pressure, you've been mulling this one over for a while.'

'And we're drinking tonight . . .'

'Exactly! Unfair advantage to you,' I laugh. 'So many animals.'

Alice sits back as I think it over, a smile on her face.

'I've got it.'

'Oh?'

'Hummingbird.'

Alice looks distinctly unimpressed. 'A tiny little bird? I was hoping you'd go for something a bit more vital and strong. Like a lioness or a jaguar.'

'Hear me out,' I grin. 'I watched a nature programme about

219

hummingbirds a while back. They might look delicate but they're also fiercely independent and playful, and let's not forget the most important Alice-like element.'

'What's that? They love flowers too?' She laughs.

'I hadn't actually thought of that one. I meant that they're only a couple of inches big but they can fly for thousands of miles.'

'So I'm small but I can go the distance? It's not the most romantic analogy I've ever heard, Zach,' she teases.

'I mean they're resilient, like you.'

She's quiet for a minute. 'That is quite sweet,' she concedes.

'Better than being a panda,' I point out.

'Come one, pandas are adorable.'

Our plates are cleared away and we're well into the second bottle when Alice gives me a look.

'I know this place is fancy, but do you think we could get away with a little drinking game while we wait for our puddings?' She stage whispers.

'Absolutely,' I laugh.

'Never have I ever. Drink if you have,' she suggests. 'I'll start. Never have I ever worn a black lacy body out for dinner.' Her eyes flick down to her chest rendering me temporarily paralysed with lust.

We both drink.

'What?!' She laughs. '*You* have worn a lace body out for dinner too?'

'It was a long time ago, in my defence,' I explain. 'We got caught up in the usual Freshers stuff at uni and got dressed up one night, which ended in me in McDonalds wearing black lace.'

'I think it could be a good look for you,' Alice giggles.

I find myself blushing so I take another turn. 'Never have I ever skived off school.'

Alice drinks. 'You never skived?' She asks.

'It wasn't especially easy at boarding school. I was deliberately late for Latin once, though.'

220

'Ooh you rebel,' she teases. 'Me and Dylan used to skip a fair bit which I'm not very proud of now. We'd go and sit in the skate park and pretend to be Avril Lavigne.'

'I bet Dylan made a great Avril.'

'My favourite fact about Avril was that she willingly married a man called Deryck Whibley. I mean, that must have been love.'

My heart's a beating drum by the time we get back to our room, arms wrapped around each other. I feel like the luckiest human on the planet to have Alice by my side. As soon as we've shut the door she slides the straps of her dress down and lets it fall to the ground.

She stands there in that black lacy underwear and I walk towards her, realising that there's nothing more I want from life than to be in this hotel room with her right here, right now.

Later, as Alice pads back into the bedroom in her robe, she folds herself into my arms.

'Now *that* was the best birthday present,' she jokes.

I watch as she pulls her hair up into a bun, her cheeks still flushed from an incredible end to the night. She turns back to me with a smile and I wrap my arms further around her body, wanting to stay like this for the rest of my life.

'I love you, Zach,' she whispers into my chest.

The girl who made it crystal clear that she didn't believe in dating when we first met has told me she loves me again. She could say it a thousand times and I will never take it for granted.

'I love you too,' I reply.

Unplugged

Alice

'Happy belated birthday my love!' Dad cheers. 'Come on through! I've got a surprise cake and some of those party popper things, too.'

I chuckle to myself as I head inside. Dad's idea of a surprise is to tell you about it repeatedly, several times before the event, so that by the time the surprise is happening you will be distinctly unsurprised. It's one of the many endearing things about him.

'SURPRISE!' He shouts, letting off the party poppers as I walk into the living room.

'What a great surprise!' I reply obligingly as he waves towards the cake.

'Oh hang on, I need to light the candles.'

'I'll go back out,' I say, closing the door.

Seconds later I'm called back in to find Dad proudly holding the cake in his hands, candles blazing on top of it as he sings 'Happy Birthday' to me. I cut us both a slice and hand one to Dad.

'How was the trip with Zach?'

'Really lovely. He was so thoughtful and had planned one activity after another. I had no idea where we were going until we arrived in Avignon!'

'Sounds like a lovely getaway.'

'It *was*. He'd gone to so much effort to make it special and we didn't stop laughing the entire time.'

Dad nods approvingly. 'I'd love to meet him when you feel ready.'

I shovel in a mouthful of cake. Introducing your boyfriend to your dad feels like a big step, even more so than meeting my friends for the first time, but as I scoff another forkful of lemon drizzle – my fave – I realise that the thought hasn't had me choking on cake crumbs like it would have in the past. Pre-Zach, even the idea of having a boyfriend was totally alien to me. And yet now, I actually think I'd quite like Dad to meet him.

'Okay, sounds good.'

Dad heads into the kitchen and I plonk down on our old pink sofa, sitting just how Mum used to, with my knees together and my legs tucked up to one side. It used to feel strange coming back here when I was at uni. I missed our old home so much but really, it wasn't home I missed, it was Mum. Slowly Dad and I filled his new house with our favourite things that Mum had collected over the years, plus some renegade choices of our own. He's particularly partial to a drinks trolley he found in Sheffield's Antiques Quarter which I'm pretty sure Mum would have vetoed, and we laugh about it every time it's in use.

Dad potters through with it now, resplendent with a bottle of Harvey's Bristol Cream and a bowl of Mini Cheddars.

'Drinks from the trolley?' He grins. A birthday sherry has been a tradition for as long as I can remember.

As we sip our sherries I notice that Dad's a bit fidgety. 'Are we still on for pie and mash this week?' I ask. Dad and I head to his local pub for pie and mash night every other Tuesday and it's a long-standing highlight for me.

He munches on a snack before pausing and looking a bit mystified. 'Well . . . yes,' he says, picking up one of Mum's cushions and having a good look at it before sending his eyes skyward.

'Dad?' I'm worried now.

'I thought I might bring a plus one.'

I chuckle with relief, amused that Dad thinks an extra person for pie and mash constitutes a plus one like we're attending a wedding.

'Who's the VIP? I haven't seen Frank or Chris in a while.'

Dad coughs.

'Er, not one of the chaps. A lady friend of mine,' he blushes.

'A lady friend?' I'm caught by surprise, watching him bob his head up and down.

'Okay,' I say, taking a quick sip of sherry and stuffing in a fistful of crisps. 'Are you trying to tell me that you're seeing someone, Dad?'

Dad gives the cushion a good flumph.

'Well, yes, I suppose I am.' He looks so incredibly nervous that I make a gargantuan effort to swallow all the Mini Cheddars asap and rush over to give him a cuddle. Only all the snacks make my throat very dry and I splutter.

'Are you crying?' he asks.

'Mouth full,' I cough. 'Not crying.'

We sit on the sofa in silence for a while, me knocking back sherry in an attempt to clear my throat while waiting for Dad to say something. As I slurp he busies himself stacking snacks into a crumby pile on his arm rest.

'So . . .' I prompt after an age.

'Oof,' he says, wiping a tear from his eye.

'Oh Dad! Don't be sad. Why are you sad?'

'I'm not sad, love. I'm happy. It's just all a bit much. She's called Gloria and we met at the golf club. She decided to take up golf as a way to destress after her divorce. Her ex was a bit of a scoundrel by all accounts. Gloria said she was taking great joy in pretending the golf ball was her ex-husband's head.'

I laugh. Gloria sounds great.

'That was a couple of months ago and I suppose you could say we're dating now. I've wanted to tell you but I didn't know how you'd react.'

224

'I'm happy for you, Dad!'

He looks down at his hands.

'No one will ever replace your mum, you know.'

I feel tears threaten behind my own eyes and blink them back.

'I know that, Daddy,' I say softly. 'You deserve to be happy and I'm honestly thrilled for you. This is the first time you've mentioned a partner to me since Mum died so we've all waited long enough,' I laugh. 'Tell me more about Gloria?'

'I think you'll get on swimmingly,' he says shyly and my heart swells for him. 'She loves gardening too so you've got that in common, and she's a bit of a firecracker. We went salsa-dancing the other day. She's got such a zest for life, just like your mu—' Dad cuts himself off.

'Dad, it's all right,' I reassure him. 'Mum will always be the bloody best, that's a stone cold fact. But it's okay to find joy with someone else, too. I can't wait to meet her on pie and mash night.'

'You could bring Zach, too?'

I waver at this. I'm definitely up for Zach meeting my dad but this week? Is it a bit soon still? Dad picks up on it straight away.

'Life's short, Alice. You've made some fantastic friends for yourself over the years and now it sounds like you have a found a partner who is making you very happy, too. I'm happy for you, love.'

I've been thinking about what Dad said ever since and something hasn't quite been sitting right. It was the fantastic friends comment, I think. Because the thing is, I haven't properly spoken to Dylan since we went out on that hideous ping pong night. Other than the collage of photos of us from our youth which he messaged me on my birthday, we've both been unusually quiet with each other and there's stuff that needs to be said.

I decide to bite the bullet and dial his number.

'Pickle! It's been a while.'

'I know. Have you got a minute?'

'Sure,' he says, and I can hear him walking to a quieter spot wherever he is.

'Just thought it was time we had a chat after . . .'

'After I acted like a dick when we last hung out?'

'Exactly.'

'I've been meaning to call but . . .'

'But you're a bit useless?'

'Ouch! Though you're probably right. Listen, Alice, I'm sorry about all that. The beer definitely didn't help but that's no excuse, I think I went a bit overboard on the whole protective best friend thing.'

'You made Zach feel bad for stuff that he and I had already had a private conversation about, and then we ended up dragging it all back up again and having a massive row. I was so upset and angry about all the drama that I ended up drunkenly breaking up with him.'

'Fuck, Alice, I didn't realise that. Nat told me that things hadn't been great but . . .'

'So why didn't you call me?'

I hear him sigh down the phone. 'I didn't know what to say. I thought I was looking out for you. You've always said that you're not into relationships and ever since Zach's been on the scene you've been all . . . confused about your emotions.'

'That's because this is all new to me! What I need is for you to support me through it, not make things worse by picking fights with him and behaving like a dickhead.'

'I thought I was supporting you by reminding you of the decisions you made after your mum died.'

'I get that but Dylan, people change. I feel like I've grown recently and yes, you're right, I have been confused but I've also been having the time of my life with Zach. I could really do without you trying to piss on that.'

'Okay, well, I'm sorry. It's good to hear that he makes you happy. Zach and I are obviously quite different . . .'

'You're not wrong there,' I chuckle.

'Maybe we need to spend some more time together, figure each other out a bit more.'

'I think so. You're both so important to me and I need you both to make an effort for my sake.'

'Understood. I promise I won't go into overdrive next time I see him, okay. Even I know I can be a bit much sometimes.'

'Understatement of the year,' I stage whisper.

'All right! So, sounds like your birthday was good?'

'Amazing,' I grin, relieved to have spoken my mind to Dylan and eager to get things back to normal with us. 'So, big news. Dad's got a girlfriend!'

'Good for Geoff! You get some!'

'Um, can we not? I'm very happy for him but I don't need to hear you encouraging my own father to "get some" thanks very much.'

Dylan laughs at that.

'Seriously though, are you okay about it?'

'Completely. It's a really nice feeling to think that Dad has a companion. I've been worried about him being lonely. How about you?'

'Yeah, you know me, all good in the hood.'

'You defo can't get away with saying that, Dyl. Listen, I'm going to be OOO for the next twenty-four hours.'

'OOO? What's that? Are you trying to tell me you're spending the next twenty-four hours getting some too?'

'It means Out Of Office, Grandad. As in, officially offline.'

'I think we can all agree that the abbreviations have got out of hand now. What if I have an SOS? Abandoned by my best friend, FML.'

'Har har. I'm going now.'

'TBH IDK Alice, what's a guy supposed to do IRL without you? LOL ROFL.'

'You're a fool. Speak to you soon, okay?'

Laughing, I hang up and then switch my phone off. Off!

* * *

Zach opens the front door just a fraction and peers out.

'I wasn't expecting you until later,' he says, reaching out and pulling me inside before shutting the door. It's quite dark in his hallway and I blink as my eyes adjust to the lack of light. Zach is wearing a pair of joggers and an old T-shirt covered in paint.

'Surprise!' I grin, enjoying the view of Zach off-duty. 'Our date starts now. Unless you're busy?'

'I am actually,' he says, flashing me that smile and leading me upstairs.

We sidestep an old rolled-up carpet on the landing and head up to the top floor. It's much brighter up here, with natural light flooding through from the huge windows in the roof.

'This has been a room of doom for too long. Full of my unfinished work, boxes of crap and cat wee-stained carpet thanks to the last owners. I ripped the carpet up when I finished work the other day and found these,' he says, tapping the old wooden floorboards with his foot. 'I've been working on it since.'

'It looks incredible already.'

He grins. 'Wanna help me finish the floor? Or do we need to be somewhere for our U date? Because I'm definitely going to need a shower first.'

'Right here is where we need to be and hell yes I'd like to help. Do I get a go on that sander?'

'Yes ma'am. I've got some spare gloves, too.'

I'm whizzing round with the floorboard sander like Carole Smillie in *Changing Rooms* while Zach neatens up the edges by hand.

'I had no idea you were into DIY,' he laughs, watching me.

'Me neither. It's quite satisfying though, isn't it?' I waft the T-shirt I borrowed from Zach before I started sanding, hot from the effort.

'I need to get a picture of this,' Zach says, reaching into his pocket and pulling out his phone. 'Don't think I've ever seen you wearing so few colours.'

I look down at the outfit I borrowed from him before I started helping out. Grey joggers, grey T-shirt.

'I'm like fifty shades of grey,' I laugh.

'You did manage to keep your fluorescent yellow hair bobble in, though.'

'What's a DIY outfit without a scrunchie to add colour?' I say, sneezing from all the dust we've kicked up before striking a pose. I know this is going to sound ridiculous but one of the many perks of having Zach in my life is that he captures brilliant pictures of us. He has one on his screen saver of me at the film festival we went to and it's the most flattering picture ever. I love scrolling through his camera roll sometimes, smiling at the snapshots of our time together. Zach holds his phone up to take a photo now and . . .

Hang on.

'NO! Put that away!' I say, suddenly remembering.

'What do you mean, no? You look adorable.'

I rush to bat the phone out of his hand and stuff it into the pocket of the joggers I've borrowed.

'Thank you for the compliment but our U date has already begun.'

'It has?' Zach looks around the his empty top floor, ever so slightly underwhelmed.

'U for unplugged. We're going off grid for the next twenty-four hours. I know I can be on my phone a lot. Mostly it's work but sometimes I just find myself scrolling for no reason and the next thing I know it's the end of the day and I've racked up a frankly unacceptable screen time tally.'

Zach's eyes crease up with a smile as I talk.

'You mean like when we're watching a real-life drama on TV and you insist on Googling it before we've finished the programme because you're too impatient to wait and see what happens?'

'Exactly.'

'Or when we go out for dinner and your phone eats before we do?'

'Ha ha, yes.'

'Or when . . .'

'I think we've had plenty of examples now, thanks. We can all agree that I'm on my phone a fair bit and for the next twenty-four hours, it's going to be you and me. No distractions.'

'How *will* we fill our time?' he jokes, his voice low.

'I'm glad you asked that. Follow me.'

Downstairs in the hallway is the bag I dumped when I arrived and I grab it now, opening it up so Zach can look inside.

'Board games?'

'Bingo! I've brought loads because there is strictly no TV allowed on an unplugged date.'

Zach rubs his hands together. 'All right then, but do you promise not to get grumpy when you lose?'

'What do you mean, *when* I lose?'

'I'm very good at board games.'

'Oh you just wait, sucker!'

It feels strange not reaching for my phone every ten minutes. I'll pick it up with no purpose, lighting up the screen to check the time and then getting lost down a social media rabbit hole. Or constantly checking messages to make sure I've replied to clients and feel totally on top of work at the flower shop. Plus I've been so excited about the new venture with Nat that I feel like I'm on my phone even more than usual at the moment.

Ordinarily my fingers would automatically have grabbed for my phone while Zach sets our first game up, seeing it as downtime I could mindlessly fill with something unnecessary like a time lapse video of someone having their eyelashes tinted, but I'd have missed this very cute scene if my phone was on. We're playing Jamaica first and while Zach lines up a row of miniature pirate ships and stacks up piles of bounty, he's also muttering pirate phrases to himself.

'Fire in the hole!'

A smile spreads across my face as I settle into a spot opposite him on the living room floor, pouring red wine into glasses and feeling hella cosy.

It gets very competitive very quickly and when I realise that Zach is on course to win the game, I default to trash-talking.

'You scallywag!'

'Very pirate appropriate. You scurvy dog,' Zach grins.

Quick, think of more nautical curses Alice! 'You . . . poop deck.' Hmm.

Zach's laughing now. 'You landlubber.'

'What's that mean? I can't even google it because our phones are banned.'

'It means you're a lily-livered land-dweller who can't cope with the seas.'

'Oh now you're for it. Just because you're winning doesn't mean you have to gloat!'

'You started this! I'm going to the loo, please try not to cheat while I'm gone.'

I consider cheating for the entire time Zach's away but manage to have a word with myself. When he walks back in the first thing I notice is that he's fashioned an eye patch out of loo roll over one of his glasses lenses and I almost spit my wine out from laughing so hard.

'Oh. My. Days,' I say between gulps of laughter.

'Ahoy me hearty,' he says with a flourish. 'Did you cheat?'

'No I did not! Like your eye patch.'

'Thanks,' Zach grins, rubbing his hands together. 'Prepare to lose, Alice!'

As we get back into the game, uninterrupted by the world, I realise that in spite of my attempts to thwart his winning streak, I'd actually be happy not to win right now. With Zach, it feels like taking part is the most fun. So when I do lose, and when Zach spends an unacceptable time gloating, I pour us both an on-theme rum and immerse myself in the feeling that I'm extremely happy in his company.

'Shall I cook?' I ask, realising that it's getting late and we've only consumed alcohol on our U date so far.

Zach fails to disguise a nervous frown.

'OMG it was *one oyster,*' I laugh, pretending to be affronted. 'Besides, I brought food.'

'Well then why don't I cook it while you clear the game away?'

'Fine,' I say. 'I was going to make a mushroom stroganoff and I've put all the ingredients in your fridge already.'

I linger in Zach's living room while he cooks, absorbing all the things in his house which I so rarely get to see. The patches of sample paint colours he's painted above the radiator. The framed poster above his sofa which looks like a picture of Mount Fuji. We spend most of the time at mine but I enjoy being in his space, and finding out more about him from the trinkets scattered around the house.

'Dinner's up,' he shouts, calling me into the kitchen where he's lit candles on the table and pulled up a couple of mismatched dining chairs. 'I have big plans for this place,' he says, watching me take it in. 'It's just a matter of getting it all done.'

'Well, you know who to call when you need some more DIY doing,' I grin.

We sit opposite each other, scooping up forkfuls of rice and chatting easily about life, fully absorbed in each other's company and feeling seriously content to be having a lazy weekend together.

If this is what my thirties is going to look like, I'm pretty sure I'll enjoy it.

Volunteering

Zach

As the tube creaks and grinds towards my stop, I replay the voice note from Alice through my earbuds. 'You've got this! I'm so proud of you.' She's my own personal pep-talk. Being the centre of attention is never going to be my favourite part of the job but as I make my way to the gallery in Whitechapel, I realise I feel much more confident today than I did before my exhibition at the start of the summer. How much of that has to do with Alice and how much is down to me? She's pushed me and challenged me in ways I'd never expected but I know that a lot it has come from me, too. I feel capable of this, today, in the same way that I feel capable of so much now.

Octavia pulls open the door before I have a chance to knock and hugs me like we're long-lost siblings, a cloud of her perfume filling the air.

'Welcome to Goldbury's, we're thrilled to have you. Safe journey down from Sheffield?'

'Thanks Octavia, I really appreciate this.'

I suck in a breath as I look around the gallery. With its polished wooden floors and spotlights suspended from the ceiling, throwing light onto the art on the all-white walls, it feels intimidating. At the back of the long, narrow room is a makeshift stage with a couple of soft chairs centred around a microphone stand. I feel a rush of pride as I see my own art hanging around the stage. Here, in a respected art gallery in London, is *my stuff*. It's exactly what I've dreamed of since I was a kid, lying flat on the beach near Nonna's house, drawing pictures in the sand.

I wasn't in the best headspace when Octavia got in touch shortly after we met at that ping pong date. Alice had ended things and I was all over the place, but I knew what Octavia was suggesting would be a brilliant boost for my career. I'd said yes, determined to throw myself into focusing on work. Now that I'm actually here, so much has changed. Alice and I are good. *Great.* And while she's back in Sheffield working her butt off with Natalie tonight, I'm here in London doing a 'meet the artist' event at Octavia's gallery. Octavia's currently shouting 'THINK OF THE AESTHETICS' at a couple of gallery staff as they set out seats around the stage while her PA, Iris, shows me into the staff kitchen out back.

'Don't mind Octavia, she can be a bit . . .' Iris raises her eyebrows instead of finishing her sentence, her comforting Mancunian lilt putting me at ease.

I grin. 'She can a bit, can't she? How long have you worked here?'

'Since I graduated two years ago,' she says, handing me a cup of tea. 'I studied art at Camberwell and Octavia came along to my year's grad show, that's how I got to know her. I would love to be in your position one day, my own art on display in a place like this.'

'So you work here during the day and paint in your spare time?'

'Yeah. I'm at the point where I'm panicking, like, will my work ever be good enough or will I end up working a job like this forever?'

'I can relate. I used to work at a coffee shop and paint in the crap light of my flatshare as soon as I finished work.'

'Did you really? I'm a bit scared that I'll never get to where I want to be, you know?'

'Try not to put yourself under too much pressure. If it helps, I'd be happy to take a look at your work? Maybe help connect you with some other up and coming artists?'

'Seriously? I'd be honoured.'

'I know what it's like to feel nervous about what's around the corner,' I say, handing her my card.

Octavia bustles in, grabs a red lipstick from her bag and announces that guests have started to arrive. 'You're drinking tea? Iris, there's champagne on the gallery floor.'

Iris looks panicked and I step in, saying: 'There's never a bad time for a brew.'

'Honestly, you're just like Dylan. You can take the boy out of Yorkshire . . .' Octavia rolls her eyes. 'How are the nerves?'

'Surprisingly okay.'

'Excellent. Let me run you through the plans. I'll make a liddle introduction first and then you'll join me on stage and I'll invite questions from the audience. After the Q&A we'll move on to a more informal meet and greet, just the usual mingling and chatting. You know the drill. We've got fifty guests coming tonight, big names from the art industry, clients here at the gallery and some of your fans. It's going to be a boon!'

A 'boon'? Iris and I exchange bemused glances.

'Are we ready?'

I set my mug of tea down and a bit splashes over the edges onto the kitchen counter. Am I ready? The nerves are there, just waiting to take over, but I remember what Alice said and steady myself with a deep breath.

'Ready,' I nod.

The evening is filled with interesting questions which I manage to answer without faltering, thank god. Back at my first exhibition I felt like an imposter, a guy who'd lucked out on making a career out of his passion somehow through chance. Now I see that it was all down to hard work and, even though I know there will still be days when I doubt myself and my talent, I *am* a success and I should be proud of myself. I'm still buzzing with the energy of the room and, as daunting as it was, there were some funny moments too. During the Q&A one guest asked a completely non-related question about what I like to do in my spare time and we started down an Agatha Christie rabbit hole which Octavia finally managed to steer back towards the art. I found myself not wanting to leave as the final guests said their goodbyes.

'That was amazing,' trills Octavia, her heels tap-tapping as she walks back into the kitchen with Iris following close behind. 'Zach, I've sold three of your pieces tonight. Three!'

'Wow, yeah, that is awesome,' I say, bowled over.

Octavia hands us all a glass of champagne and the three of us are taking a sip when Dylan strides into the gallery. We haven't seen each other since that disastrous ping pong night and I tense up instinctively.

'The man of the hour,' he says, clapping me on the back. 'How did it go?'

'Good thanks.'

'Listen man, I'm sorry again about all that . . .'

'Yeah, me too,' I reply. 'Shall we just draw a line under it?'

'I'd like that. Octavia and I are heading out for drinks now, do you guys want to come?' He asks me and Iris.

'I've got a friend's birthday thing,' Iris says, grabbing her bag.

'Thanks for the invite but I can't tonight,' I say. 'There's only one person I want to celebrate with now. 'Another time though? Would be good to hang out. Maybe next time you're in Sheffield we could meet up with Alice?'

Dylan nods and as we shake hands, it feels like we're both making an effort to move on from what happened. We're never going to be best mates, that much is obvious, but I'm hopeful that we'll be able to hang out in the same space, for Alice's sake.

* * *

'TENTERHOOKS! I've been on tenterhooks, Zach! How did it go?' I can hear Alice's excitement and anticipation when I call her later that night.

'Really, really well,' I say, my voice still shaky with adrenaline. 'We sold some paintings and I wasn't even that fazed by the question and answer bit.'

'YASSSSS. I knew it! You legend. I'm so proud of you!'

I bask in that for a bit, lying on the bed of my hotel room for the night.

'How was Octavia?' Alice asks, a hint of distaste in her voice.

'Same as last time . . . very posh and she's got a strange way of pronouncing things. There was a table set up with drinks and snacks and she kept calling hummus "ho-mousse".'

Alice laughs.

'She was cool, actually, and I'm grateful to her for hosting this thing tonight. She's already said she'll stock more of my work in the gallery. And Dylan turned up at the end, too.'

'Oh?'

'It was all right, Alice. We might never be best buddies but I think we'll get along just fine. We've agreed to draw a line under all of it.'

'Phew. I'm really pleased, Zach.'

'Yeah, me too. So, back to us. I've had an idea for our V date and it's inspired by you. Are you free at the weekend?'

'I'm intrigued! And yes, I'm free.'

Alice is helping me pile art supplies into the back of Gerty, who's heaving under the weight of it all.

'I cannot figure it out,' she says as she shoves the last of the rolls of paper into the boot. 'We're clearly doing something arty. But why do we need so much stuff? And what relevant word begins with a V? Van Gogh?'

I love the fact that our dates are still such a source of fun for the two of us, the mystery of what's happening next keeping us both on our toes. We hop in the car and pull up at my studio, dragging all the extra kit I've bought into the middle of the room. When I figured out what I wanted to do today, I realised I was woefully low on supplies and took the opportunity to pick up a load more stuff.

Alice's guesses are getting wilder.

'V for vegetarian? Apparently cauliflower steaks are all the rage. You basically just slice up a cauliflower into thick pieces and then pretend it's meat.'

'Nope,' I laugh.

'Videos? I'm sure Dad has some old VHS thingies but how would we play them?'

I shake my head.

'Violin?'

'How about I put you out of your misery? Today we're volunteering.'

Alice folds her arms. 'Here in your studio? Does that mean I'm volunteering to help you work for the day? I know you're busy Zach, but you can mix your own paint up.'

'So quick to judge.' I step closer to her, kissing her on the forehead. 'Back when we went to your allotment for our G date, you told me all about volunteering with a gardening group when you were at uni. You explained how it had helped you to deal with your mum and how rewarding it was to see other people benefit from your efforts.'

Alice nods.

'That really stuck with me,' I carry on. 'I remember thinking how brilliant you were for taking your own tough times and channelling them into something so positive. Recently I've been wondering about some volunteering opportunities for myself, only I didn't really know where to start. Then last weekend in London, I met a young artist who's working at Octavia's gallery and panicking that she'll never get to where she wants to be . . . turning her passion into a career. It made me think of me and you and how lucky we are to be doing what we love, but how much we've both fought to get here . . .'

'God yeah, I remember being in my early twenties and having zero clue if the flower shop would work, if I'd ever make money again, if I'd have to give up on my goals and do something different.'

'Exactly! That time of your life can be really daunting and it's not just an early twenties thing. Life constantly throws challenges at us. Look at Raff. To me, he has it all – the family, the house – but he's still looking at people like us who don't have the same kind of responsibilities like kids and, uh, stuff . . .'

'And he's envious?'

'Sort of. I think there's a grass is greener thing going on for most people.'

'I totally agree.'

'So today I'm running my first art therapy workshop. We're going to set up the studio so that people can come along and get creative in any way they'd like, giving them the chance to get some headspace and do something that hopefully takes them away from their concerns for a couple of hours.'

Alice gives me a side-on look.

'Seriously? I love that idea, Zach. I take it I'm the headline artist in residence for the day?' she teases.

'Oh, sure,' I say, pretending to hide the fliers I made last weekend which have my name at the top. 'These read: "ART SPACE, come get creative and get away from it all with renowned artist Alice O'Neill. She may even help you make a papier-mâché 'moon'".'

Alice laughs. 'Right, well I'd better get ready for my starring role.'

Twenty-six people have come to the workshop and I have to say I'm pretty chuffed with the turnout, given how quickly I pulled it together. I've been leaving fliers at cafés, colleges, old people's homes and charities and now my studio is full of people looking nervously around, wondering what to expect.

'Hello, everyone, and welcome,' I say, standing up on a chair to get everyone's attention. 'It's brilliant to see so many people here today. The main aim is for you to relax and enjoy yourselves, take your mind off any worries and just have fun. There are loads of materials over in the corner, please help yourself and get creative in any way you want. I'm on hand if you'd like any tips or advice but also, you can ignore me too! Today is a no pressure day. This is Alice who's helping out as well, and we're both happy to chat.'

Alice waves and I walk everyone around the studio, pointing out where they can help themselves to drinks and snacks and grabbing them all a chair. Soon enough the room is filled with the buzz of concentration from some and happy chatter from others, as Alice and I work our way around everyone, listening to stories or proffering biscuits.

I get chatting to Dexter, a teenager whose parents are desperate for him to follow in the family business while he wants to go to uni and study art. Then Tricia, who has brought her elderly father Eric. He has dementia and she's hoping a day of drawing will bring him one of life's simple joys. And a solicitor called Jacqueline who 'just needs a fucking break', she says.

'Dexter says he wants to draw you naked,' Alice says later, her paint smock splattered with colour.

'Oh . . .' I stumble. 'Um . . .'

'Don't worry,' she laughs. 'I've told him it's not that sort of art class. It's made me think, though. Maybe there's something we can really do with this.'

'You want me to set up a life drawing class next? Because I'm not sure that's quite my thing.'

'I meant this workshop. Just look around you, Zach.'

I follow her gaze around the room, watching people from all different walks of life getting stuck into creating something. Eric's face is lit up in animation as he shares a joke with Jacqueline, Tricia looking on with a huge smile on her face. A guy called Bryn who's in the middle of a break-up is drawing a picture of his dream holiday and says he plans to travel there on his own, his first solo trip in six years.

'Everyone is getting something different out of this. Just look how happy they are. Maybe we could contact an art therapist, or a charity, or something like that? You could make it more structured and really make a difference here, Zach.'

'That's a great idea.'

'It's like when I'm gardening, I'm always reminded that there's joy to be found even in challenging times.'

'When Fran and Sienna were born they were premature and needed to spend a few weeks in intensive care. That was so hard for Raff and Ellie. I remember visiting them in hospital and thinking about all the other children who were spending time there, how frightening it must be for them to be away from home in somewhere so clinical. Maybe I could contact some hospitals, too, and donate artwork to the children's wards?'

Alice beams at me. 'I think that's a lovely idea.'

Later, as we're saying goodbye to the last of today's attendees, Tricia rushes over and clasps both of my hands in hers.

'Dad loved that so much. Thank you. Seeing him engage in something that doesn't frighten him, or remind him that he's not totally with it these days, has been wonderful.'

Alice nudges me as we pack up. 'That was really sweet. I feel all warm and glowy inside.'

'Yeah, me too. I wasn't sure how I'd feel, opening up my studio to so many people. Glowy is definitely the right word for it. Shall we celebrate with some food in town?'

'You had me at celebrate.'

Together we wind our way through Sheffield's city centre, settling on burritos and carrying them into the Peace Gardens. We find an empty bench by the water fountain in front of the town hall and sit in easy silence as we eat, me demolishing a pulled pork burrito while Alice scoffs a beef brisket version in record time.

241

I think of all the stories I've heard today, all the people on the cusp of change, and I know that I'm in the same boat. Watching the water splash close to our feet as we eat, I realise that I'm content with Alice. All my life I've been searching for what Raff has and yet ever since I've met Alice, I've found there's so much more to life than those things. I know she doesn't want marriage or kids. Or at least, not yet. And the truth is, I still do. But right now, the most important thing in my life is having Alice by my side. Maybe my future doesn't look so certain after all, but as long as Alice is in it, I don't think I mind that.

Wine Tasting

Alice

TGIF I think to myself as I shut up the flower shop and dash home to get ready for date night. It's been another busy week with long days in the shop as well as working on The Hitch with Nat each night. The hope, the excitement and the nerves of setting up a new business jangle constantly in my mind, jostling for space. I'm used to being busy but even I've questioned whether I've gone too far this time and bitten off more than I can chew. To summarise, I am ready for a wine or three, not to mention some time with Zach. I'm more grateful than ever that I have his support when I'm super busy, and for the fact that he manages to keep me level when I'm trying to juggle a thousand things.

I arrive at the bar to find him stood outside in a light-weight jumper tonight. My whole body feels like it's breathing a sigh of relief at the sight of him, like a beacon, and I bound over.

'I'm guessing it's W for wine tasting,' he smiles, pointing towards a sign by the entrance. It reads 'WINE TASTING, 7 p.m.'.

'Well done you,' I grin, realising how good it feels to see him again. Our volunteering was very sweet and noble etcetera but I'm secretly pleased to have him all to myself today for purely selfish purposes. I rest my head against his chest and breath in his citrus scent. Once inside we're shown to our table and Zach listens intently as our wine expert leads us through the instructions for tonight's tasting like the adorable geek that he is.

As we work our way through 'the world of wines' our glasses are filled with a small measure of each and we sniff, sip and discuss each one.

'I like them all,' I giggle after the third mini tipple. Our sommelier Andre is heading back over to our table and I'm learning that he really approves of creative ways to describe the smells and tastes.

'This one smells like a warm summer's breeze,' I say confidently.

'Very good,' Andre nods in his clipped South African accent.

I flash Zach a look and he smiles back, looking impressed. I don't think he's twigged that I'm winging it. He jots down *warm summer breeze* on the notepad we've been given and I feel another rush of affection towards him. As we move through the continents, Zach and I settle into the kind of easy chat that, I'm learning, comes with a long-for-me relationship. I'm breaking into new territory with Zach and the months we've spent together are really clocking up.

'Notes of wildebeest.'

'Sorry, what?' Zach looks confused.

'This Argentinian Malbec. I'm getting strong wildebeest vibes.'

'Speaking of wildebeest, my nieces turn six soon and I have no idea what to get them.'

'You can't compare your nieces to wildebeest!'

'They *are* wild.'

'I love that about them. Kids can be kind of boring these days but Fran and Sienna are full of energy. Such little personalities already.'

'Like someone else I know.'

'So now you're calling *me* a wildebeest?' I laugh, pretending to look affronted.

'Isn't wildebeest a plural? What's one wildebeest called?'

We both wrestle with this for a bit.

Andre clears his throat next to us. 'Wildebeest is both the singular and plural noun,' he says, before moving on to another group.

Zach leans across the table. 'So, if you had to pick, which of your exes could be a murderer?'

'What?' I splutter, flecks of Malbec decorating the white table-cloth. Oops.

'I was reading a feature in one of those real life magazines . . .'

'Let me stop you there,' I titter. 'How did you find yourself reading a real life magazine?' Zach's eyes crinkle as he jots down *notes of wildebeest* followed by a question mark. I think he's growing suspicious of my wine musings.

'I was at the hairdressers the other day and there was a bit of a queue and one thing led to another,' he explains.

I laugh. 'Makes sense. Do continue.'

'I read an article about a woman whose ex-boyfriend had gone on to kill someone. He's in prison now and she was saying how she had never suspected he could be capable of that while they were together. Isn't that weird?'

'Christ, yes. Imagine.'

'So I'm wondering which of your exes could fall into the I-can't-believe-he's-a-murderer category.'

'And to think that just moments ago we were discussing glitter pens for six-year-olds,' I chuckle. My mind scrolls back through previous flings like a rolodex. 'Hmm. I never got to know any of them that well but I did go out with a guy who insisted on having his pasta sauce served in a separate bowl at dinner . . .'

'As an Italian, I can confirm that is truly murderous behaviour.'

'And then there was Pete, who measured his biceps every day to check for progress. Something to do with gains?'

'I already don't like him.'

'Yeah but, you know, none of them lasted. I dumped one guy when I found out his most-used emoji wasn't the crying-with-laughter one.'

245

Zach laughs. 'Wow. I've always known I'm incredibly lucky to get beyond date three with you and now you've proved it.'

'Date W. That's twenty-three dates! An absolute PB for me,' I say, incredulous, as Andre arrives with a splash of German Riesling.

'This Riesling brings tropical notes on the nose,' he informs us.

Zach has a sniff. 'Absolutely,' he nods, flashing me a look that tells me he's cottoned on to my game. 'I'm getting mango and pineapple. Watermelon and coconut. Sun cream and a ninety-nine with a flake.'

Andre looks less pleased with Zach's final two observations and moves over to a couple of middle-aged men who seem to be taking the tasting far more seriously.

'Do you get ninety-nines with a flake in the tropics?' I giggle.

'I let the seaside theme go too far,' Zach laughs.

'I'd love an ice cream,' I admit, stomach rumbling on cue. I'm feeling quite tipsy now.

'Didn't you eat before we got here?'

'Nope,' I chuckle.

The good news is I'm definitely not drunk. Nope. I'm as sober as a judge, if, for example, said judge was coming to the end of a booze cruise around the Mediterranean Sea. It's that lovely kind of drunk, though. The one where you feel all soppy and so filled up with love it's like someone's attached you to a helium canister.

Helium. Like the birthday balloons when Zach took me to Avignon. God that was sweet, wasn't it? Veeeeerrrrrrryyyyyyy romantic.

Discreetly, I disguise a hiccup with another sip of . . . what is this?

'It's an English sparkling wine.'

I jump. Andre is standing right next to me and I hadn't noticed.

'Perhaps now is a good time to remind everyone here that the spit buckets on your table are there for a purpose,' he says loudly.

I stick my hand in the air.

'Yes?' Andre says.

'What if you've liked all the wines and haven't spat any out?'

He coughs. 'It's not about whether you like the wines or not. It's about sampling them all and spitting them *all* back out again.' Oh. 'Did anyone else fail to pay attention during my introduction to the session?'

A few hands shoot up. Andre looks very displeased. 'We'll be needing more jugs of water, then,' he tuts, striding off to the bar.

'I do feel quite tipsy,' I whisper to one of the two Zachs sat opposite me. Who's the other guy? A stunt double, I deduce eventually.

'Shall we get you some food?'

'Could we just try this sparkling wine first? I do like bubbles.'

'Okay, but then we have to get you something to eat.'

I bob my head up and down in agreement.

'You are lovely,' I say.

'Oh?' Zach grins.

'Looking after me. So thoughtful. A really good guy. Like a great boyfriend.'

'Well, I'm definitely your boyfriend and it's very sweet of you to say the rest.'

'You *are* my boyfriend,' I nod. The notion that I'm about to dive off a cliff and into a pool of emotions hits me and I start giggling because my feet are already dangling off the edge. There's no going back now.

'I like that fact,' I announce.

'That's good news.'

'Yes,' I agree, leaning in conspiratorially. 'I like that you're my boyfriend and a whole lot more about you, too. I know we're different in many ways, but people are complex aren't they?' I click my fingers in the air, searching through a fog of wine to find the words for my poignant and heart-felt speech. 'We're not chalk and cheese, actually.'

247

'I didn't say that we were,' he replies, amused.

'We're more chalk-ish and cheese-ish.' Yes, that's it. This is going very well. I'm feeling so profound today so I should definitely put my eloquent streak to good use and tell Zach how I'm feeling. 'I like that you're not as full on as me. I like that you can be shy but also strong. I like that you are kind and caring. I like that you listen without judgement and that you don't mind when I relentlessly tease you and that I can be my whole self around you and actually now that I think about it I like that I've become more of a whole self since we met. That's not all down to you obviously because I've done a bloody good job of seeing myself in a new light this summer. I've been able to open up about my mum and I've helped Natalie through her break-up and I've set up another bloody business like an absolute champion too. So what I'm saying is, I'm great. And so are you.'

Another hiccup. Not so well disguised.

'I've figured something out. We've all got flaws, haven't we? For a while I thought your past was a reason for me not to trust you, and then I realised that I should stop looking for reasons. Why actively seek something out when there's been nothing to worry me in *our* relationship? Besides, I can't just pick and choose the best bits of life – the easiest, simplest bits – because if I did that with you I'd have missed out on all of these amazing experiences we've had together. And maybe your best bits are because of what you've been through?'

'Which bits are you talking about?'

'You know! You're lovely and thoughtful and sometimes shy and your heart is always on your sleeve. You wouldn't be who you are now if you hadn't been through the tough times. Same for me. Ever since Mum died I've been trying to move on from my grief. I'd built up barriers to stop myself from feeling that sad, ever again. And now look at us! My barriers are down and I'm actually very happy and I don't think you ever do move on from grief, anyway. You move forward with it. I am happy moving forward with you because I really like you a lot.

'That doesn't mean I've changed, though,' I say, sweeping my arm across the table in demonstration of change. 'I'm not sure I'll ever want marriage or kids. But I can see a future with you. One that goes beyond an alphabet's worth of dates. To conclude, I'm yours if you'll have me.'

HICCUP.

No doubt Zach is bowled over by my display of affection, I think, realising that now is probably the time to lean in for a kiss. I rest my elbows on the table and lean forward, meeting Zach's gaze.

He's put his wallet on the table, a sure sign that he wants to leave, which I am one hundred per cent sure is because he wants to take me home after all the super cute things I've just been saying to him.

'Let's get you some food,' he says.

Sensible lad.

'Food first!' I agree with a wink.

A hot bowl of noodles and three vegetable gyoza later and I'm feeling much less drunk but quite confused. Zach steered me to Wagamamas after our wine tasting and since we sat down to eat, I sense that he's deliberately kept the conversation trained on day to day stuff. He hasn't once mentioned my romantic outpouring and I get the impression that I said something wrong, but what? Zach *loves* talking about his feelings!

I spear another dumpling with my chopsticks and munch thoughtfully. It's possible that I was just being drunk and waffly. Maybe that's the kind of conversation he'd prefer to have when I'm sober?

OH MY GOD of course that's it!

I necked a whole load of wines before telling him how I felt and now he's probably wondering how accurate I was being. Alice, you buffoon!

'I meant all of it,' I say later, as we sit in the back of a taxi on our way back to mine, Sheffield city flying past our windows.

'Thanks Alice,' he says.

'Thanks? Is that all I get?'

He turns to me in the half-light with a frown across his face. 'What do you want me to say?'

'I dunno. I thought you might be a bit more appreciative, that's all.'

Zach sighs. 'Look, it's getting late and I don't want to ruin a nice night.'

'Why would you ruin it? What's up?'

The cab pulls up outside my house and we step out, my mind spinning in confusion as I search for my keys. Inside, we shrug off our coats and kick off our shoes in an awkward silence, the helium balloon levels of happy I'd felt earlier now falling completely flat.

I'm about to speak when Zach beats me to it.

'I'm beat. Mind if I head up to bed?'

'Go for it,' I reply. Looks like we're calling it night, then.

I'm awake before Zach so I inch quietly out of bed, padding downstairs to make us some tea. Now that I'm one hundred per cent sober, I'm still not sure quite what went wrong but I'm guessing my boozy declaration of love just hit the wrong note, somehow.

'Morning,' I say, setting a mug of tea down next to Zach as he stirs. 'Look, I found our wine notes from last night in my bag.'

I hand him the piece of paper as he pulls on his glasses. 'I'd forgotten about the Barolo which we decided tasted like "recently turned soil",' I add with a laugh.

Zach yawns and stretches and doesn't laugh back.

'Do you want to talk about it?' I ask eventually.

'I worry that if I say what I want to say, it will push you away.'

I sit down on the bed next to him.

'Why would it push me away?'

Zach sighs. 'Because it's a future thing. Our future.'

'Zach, I know I was drunk last night but I'm pretty sure I said I wanted a future with you. I wish you didn't feel like you were treading on eggshells around me all the time.'

'I don't feel like that all the time.'

'Some of the time?'

'Well, yeah. In the early days of us I didn't want to scare you off, so I made a conscious effort not to put too much pressure on you. And now we're at this point where I really fucking love you and . . .'

'You still feel like I might do a runner?' I suggest.

'No, that's not what I mean. I think you and I are really solid right now. It's just that there's no getting away from the fact that we want different things in life. Alice, I loved all of the things you said to me last night. I feel so happy that you feel that way about me, and that you want to talk about it. The problem is that I still want to have a family of my own and you made it pretty clear last night that you don't see that for yourself. So are we just going to bump along together until we realise that we can't make each other truly happy? You don't want kids. I do. Surely that we seem to want different things is a bit of an alarm bell?'

I push back, the enormity of what he's just laid bare hanging between us like a thunder cloud.

'It doesn't have to be an alarm bell, Zach.'

'I love you so much, Alice. I would love to spend my life with you if we could and it made me so happy to hear you talking about our future too. I just don't want us to get to a point where we're in too deep and then find ourselves hating each other because we want different things from life.'

'I love you too! Zach, I'm not saying I definitely don't want to have a baby one day. I just haven't made my mind up yet. There's so much that I thought I didn't want at the start of this year, like a relationship, and yet here we are. You're the best thing that's happened to me. But, look, I understand what you're saying and

I don't want to get your hopes up. If you need a definite decision on that right now then . . .'

My voice cracks. I can't believe we're here now. I hate that I'm causing him pain but I will not make promises I can't keep.

'Alice, I want you more than I want anything else,' he says, reaching out for my hand. 'If it came down to it, I'd chose you over having a family any day.'

'But you shouldn't have to. We should all have the chance to get exactly what we want out of life,' I say sadly.

'Argh, please don't be sad. I'm sorry.'

'You've nothing to be sorry about.'

'I've messed up another date.'

'No, you've been honest with me. That's important. I don't want to lose you Zach but I don't want to make you unhappy, either.'

'That's it, though. You don't make me unhappy. I've never been happier.'

I nestle into his chest, screwing my eyes tightly shut and hoping beyond hope that this isn't going to be it for us.

'You know what? Every time we've hit a hurdle in our relationship, we've dealt with it together. We've worked a way around it. I have faith that we'll be able to work out a solution to these big questions if and when we get to them.'

'We are pretty good at navigating a shit storm,' I laugh. 'Listen, Zach, it's not a definite no from me on the babies thing, okay? I just don't know right now.'

'It's not a definite yes from me, either. I thought it was but the most important thing is that we're happy.'

I tip my head up to look at him, his hair still mussed up from sleep.

'I think we're going to be okay,' I whisper.

X Marks the Spot

Zach

'Are we in another SOS kind of situation?' Ellie asks, handing me a trolley and clipping her shopping list in place. She messaged earlier to say she was coming into town to do a big supermarket shop before the girls' birthday party and I seized at the chance to get some advice from my best friend.

'It's not like we had a big fight or a massive freak-out,' I say as we steer through the shop. 'Things with Alice feel much more stable these days, I think. I'm just worried that we want different things out of life. On our last date she reminded me that she doesn't think she wants kids and, well, you know how I feel about being a dad one day.'

Ellie nods as we head towards the crisp aisle.

'And why do you want to be a dad?'

'Um, I just do?'

'Right. Well, I understand that. I "just did" want to be a mum, too. It's not all sweetness and light though. It's hard work. There are days when you would do anything to have a lie-in, an uninterrupted night's sleep, or only yourself to worry about. Becoming a parent is like doubling your anxiety overnight.'

'Or trebling in your case.'

'Only a maniac would have two in one go,' she laughs. 'The

minute the girls arrived I realised that there were these two little lives that were completely reliant on me. As a parent everything you do, every decision you make, will have an impact on them too.'

'Bloody hell.'

'It can feel overwhelming at times. But it's also the best thing in the world. Watching your child light up just because you put the tap on, or they saw a bubble, or someone made a funny noise. You see the world through their brand new eyes and honestly, it's a joy. Dinosaurs or unicorns?'

'Huh?'

'For their cakes?' She says, pointing at the celebration cakes.

'One of each?'

'Good call. Don't tell Nonna I cheated with shop-bought cakes?'

'My lips are sealed. So you're saying that parenting is the best and worst job, all rolled into one?'

'Spot on,' she agrees as we move on to the booze section. I assume from the amount of prosecco she loads into the trolley that there will be a lot of thirsty parents at Fran and Sienna's birthday party. 'I think it's important that you and Alice are talking about this stuff now, Zach. You want to be able to be open and honest with each other about what you'd like out of life now, before you both get hurt.'

'It's the unknown that makes me nervous.'

'You do like a plan,' Ellie grins.

'Neither of us is dead set on having kids or not having kids, or at least that's the impression I get from Alice. I think she's spent so long thinking that even a relationship wasn't for her that suddenly being with me and having these discussions is a lot to handle. She's never considered starting a family before. But also, I completely respect her decision and I don't want to be the one to make her question things. So should I question myself instead?'

'I don't think so. In my opinion, if one of you felt completely one way or the other then you should probably get out of the relationship now, even though it would be incredibly painful to

254

do so because it's obvious how much you love each other. But as it stands, there's room for manoeuvre in your future. I believe that you and Alice can carve out a path that you're both happy with.'

'Honestly?'

'You're both kind, considerate people and you have a mutual respect for each other. I really think you'll find a way. Now how about you stop procrastinating and hand me that box of Italian red wine up there?'

'More booze?' I balk.

Ellie looks at me. 'All children's parties are basically just an excuse for parents to get pissed while their kids run riot in somebody else's house. I need as much as we can fit in the boot.'

Talking to Ellie always helps me to feel more at ease with the way things are going and a couple of days later I'm ready, if a little nervous, for my next date with Alice. I've been running through the day, thinking over every last detail and wondering what she'll say at the end of it all. If it's even a good idea at all given what happened on our last date. But my gut's telling me to go for it.

I knock on her door and Natalie opens it.

'Hello Mr Mystery. I've just spoken to Alice and she's not due back for another hour or so.'

'Thank you for checking,' I reply gratefully. 'I need a bit of time to set up.'

'So, what *are* you up to?'

'It's a surprise for Alice.'

'Do you want me out of the way?'

'I could actually do with some help if you don't mind? I brought coffees with me.'

'Consider me bribed,' she laughs. 'Honestly Zach, you didn't need to.'

'I just wanted to say thanks. You really helped me out with that trip to France for Alice's birthday.'

Natalie takes her coffee and we head inside. 'It was nothing.

255

Alice was there for me when I split up with Jake and I love her to the moon and back. I can see that you do too, so basically, you're in my good books.'

'That's good to hear,' I laugh.

'So, how can I help?'

I talk her through my idea, watching her reaction carefully. Natalie knows Alice better than anybody and I would love to get her seal of approval for this X date idea of mine.

'HOLY SHIT,' she shouts at me when I've finished. 'This is big.'

'I know. Do you think she'll like it? Or is it too big?'

'I think she's going to be totally bowled over by your romantic gesture.'

I wince. 'Alice isn't into romance.'

Natalie looks at me disapprovingly as I sit down at the kitchen table with my own coffee cup.

'Correction, Alice *wasn't* into romance. Still isn't, probably. But she is into you. She loves you!'

'She told you that?' I ask, surprised.

'Obviously. Now it sounds like we've got a lot of work to do before she gets back.' Natalie checks her watch and moves into planner mode.

Ninety minutes later Alice bursts through the front door shouting 'I'm getting married!'

What?

I shoot a panicked look at Nat, who's helping me tuck little notes into envelopes in the living room. She wrinkles up her face and heads into the hallway. 'What are you banging on about?'

I listen as Alice kicks off her shoes. 'Me and Eve. Totally getting hitched. We've got a really tricky bride on our hands at the moment. You know Zach's ex? So awkward! She's been very exacting about the details, which is fine, but when we met this morning she pulled such a sour face when I showed her my initial designs that I wanted to scream a bit. DON'T YOU KNOW HOW

LONG I'VE BEEN WORKING ON THESE FOR? Anyway, Eve stepped in just in time and I think we're all back on track now. So I'm marrying her.'

'Hmm. What will Zach say?' Nat asks.

'He'll get over it,' Alice laughs.

I pop my head around the living room door. 'I'm not sure about that.'

'You're here,' Alice smiles widely. 'Hello! Why are you here?'

'I was hoping to start our X date early but if I've been usurped by Eve I can always . . .' I start moving towards the door with a smile on my face.

'Stay!' She laughs, stretching her body across the hallway to stop me. 'I'll tell Eve I've got cold feet.'

'I'd appreciate that,' I grin, my stomach flipping as I realise what's about to happen. We both turn to see Natalie clasping her hands at her heart, looking at us like a proud mother watching her kid win a prize at school.

'Why are you being weird?' Alice asks.

'Oh you know me, too much caffeine in the morning and I'm basically bonkers,' she breezes, pulling on some black boots and a puffer jacket. 'Right, I'm off on a solo date to the cinema because *that's* how much I like my own company these days! Have fun.'

Alice spins around to me, her hair piled high and a pair of rainbow earrings sparkling in her ears.

'I've been wondering about this one,' she says after we kiss. 'Not much begins with X. Can I guess?'

'Go ahead.'

'Actually, I've already come up with a list of things I don't want to do today.'

Oh hell.

Alice holds up a hand and starts ticking things off with her fingers. 'X-Box,' she frowns. 'I'm not big into gaming. But I don't think you are either?'

257

'Nope.'

'Also X-Men. We've already done a filmy date. Though I know you're into comics and I will make an allowance for doubling up if Hugh Jackman's involved.'

I smile. 'No again.'

'Okay, well that's ruled out the two things I didn't fancy.'

'And the things you did?'

'I wondered if we might be going to Exeter, but that's not strictly an X.'

'You know I'm a stickler for the rules.'

Alice nods. 'So then I settled on X-rated.'

It takes me a moment or two to compose myself.

'Let's not rule that one out for later,' I say, my voice gruff. 'Follow me.'

In the kitchen is a piece of art I've been working on, propped up on an easel I brought over from my studio this morning. I'd been playing around with fonts and hand-drew this X, layering on bold colours in the background. It's pretty different to my usual stuff but I saw how much fun people had when I opened up my art studio for the workshop a while back. It kind of took me back to how painting felt when I was little, just messing around with colours for fun without any of the pressure to create my next big piece.

Alice rushes over to it, her hands tracing the letter. Then she spots the envelope propped up in the fold of the wooden easel, her name written on it. She glances over at me, her eyes filled with excitement as she tears it open. '*X marks the spot,*' she reads out. '*Follow the clues until you find another X.* A treasure hunt! Oh my god YES. I love this already. Will there be food at the end?'

'From now on, I'm saying nothing more. Turn the card for the first clue.'

Alice claps her hands together before reading the clue.

'*One: I love your XXXX for life.*' She frowns. 'As in, me, Alice?

My quadruple X for life. Okaaay.' She drums her fingers on the kitchen table as she thinks.

'ZEST,' she shouts after a while. 'Is it zest?'

I press my lips shut.

She rushes over to the cutlery drawer and rifles around for the lemon zester, finding no second clue. Then she spins around, her eyes lighting on the fruit bowl in the corner. 'Aha!' She races over, spotting a lemon with a card attached to it.

I grin to myself as she impatiently tears at the paper. I knew she'd get stuck straight in.

'*Two: You are a breath of XXXXX air*. Fresh. Easy! Right.' Competitive doesn't cover it. It's like watching a human whirlwind taking part in the Crystal Maze. Alice takes the stairs two at a time and I stand at the bottom with a smile on my face. I can hear her rummaging through a cupboard and after a while she leaps back onto the landing, proudly proffering an air freshener.

'But there's no clue,' she frowns.

'That's because you haven't got it right.'

Alice pouts. 'A breath of fresh air. It's definitely fresh.' She looks down at me for confirmation and I can't help but give a tiny nod. 'So what else is fresh?' Alice runs downstairs and tries the cupboard where she keeps her fabric softener. 'Nothing there.' She pokes her head out of the back door on the hunt for fresh air, to no avail.

'Argh,' she huffs. 'Hang on, what about Saskia?' Struck with another idea, she's back up the stairs and I follow her into her bedroom.

'You remembered!' She says, full of glee as she spots a card tucked into the snake plant by her bed.

'How could I forget about Saskia?' I laugh, remembering the time Alice had given me a very thorough lecture on the benefits of having air purifying plants to freshen your home. The fact that she'd named her snake plant Saskia had made me feel incredibly fond of her.

Alice darts around the house, congratulating herself every time she gets one right and harrumphing when she finds a tricky clue. She guesses clue number three immediately, '*Zach's most embarrassing secret*', and heads straight to her bookshelf where she finds a stack of Point Romance books waiting for her. '*Clue four: You dress like a XXXXXXX*' sees her rummaging through her wardrobe before finally heading out into the courtyard to find a rainbow balloon attached to clue five. '*We can't travel anywhere without XXXXXX.*' She loops the balloon string around her waist like a belt and heads back into the kitchen, on the hunt for snacks.

There, in amongst the Hula Hoops, is clue six.

'*Your most precious item.*'

Alice frowns. 'Mum's ring, without a doubt,' she says, looking down at the gold band on her middle finger. 'But I'm already wearing it.' I raise an eyebrow mysteriously. She looks ever-so-slightly nervous now as she heads back upstairs, cracking jokes about keeping fit on the way up. Alice keeps her mum's wedding ring in its original box, taking it off every night before bed and storing it carefully next to her while she sleeps.

I lean against the doorframe as she spots the clue I've left there.

She spins back to me.

'Zach . . . I . . .'

'Just open it,' I smile.

'Argh, Zach, please don't . . .'

'Trust me?'

She opens the ring box.

'It's empty,' she says, looking like she's just dodged a bullet.

'I know that,' I say as Alice gingerly picks up the envelope underneath. She's more careful this time.

'It's another clue,' she says, turning surprised eyes towards me.

'Isn't that the point of a treasure hunt?'

'Well, yes,' she says, flopping down on to end of her bed. 'I had rather wondered if you were about to . . .'

'About to . . .'

'Propose?'

'To the woman who's not sure if she wants to get married?' I say, sitting down next to her and watching her intently. I can't help but feel a pang of disappointment that she looks so relieved, but I have to remind myself that we're not ready for that kind of commitment yet.

She looks at me, her eyes saying 'phew', and I'm hit by a fresh bout of nerves. I know it's too soon for marriage proposals but seeing her reaction has me wondering if my plan for today's treasure hunt is going to be pushing us too far, as well?

'I was slightly panicking for a minute there,' she smiles.

I wrap my arm around her and kiss the soft, apple-smelling hair on the top of her head. 'It was a bit of a red herring if I'm honest. I just wanted to throw you off the scent.'

'Oh my god!' she says, play-punching me on the arm.

'How about you follow the rest of the clues. That X isn't going to find itself.'

Back in the living room, Alice has followed her nose to the laptop I've set up and is pressing play on a playlist I've made called 'Our A-Z Soundtrack'. The sun's starting to set and a rich orange light is pitching in through the window. The final clue is peeking out from under my laptop but she's not opened it yet. Music fills the room and Alice turns to me, her green eyes alight. 'Shall we dance?'

She takes my hand and I pull her in close as we sway around the room, moving to the songs that take me back to the specific moments in time that frame our relationship. The eighties tunes where I couldn't take my eyes off her at the disco, but felt like I wasn't enough for her and ended up leaving early. The duet we sang at karaoke where I started to realise that maybe it wasn't as black and white as I'd thought it was, after all. The songs I'd spent ages painstakingly selecting for our first trips out in Gerty because I was so desperate to show her how cool I was, when ironically I suspect she prefers the Point Romance-loving, comic-drawing geek I really am, anyway.

After our wine tasting date I'd felt those all-too-familiar prickles of insecurity coming back. Not that they'd gone anywhere, really, I've just got better at managing them. Because I've thrown a lot of stuff at her to deal with since we first met. Why had she stayed this long? Surely it was a matter of time before she upped and left? I look down at her now, her face lit up with happiness, and I realise that something's lifted. The fear that she might realise what a dork I am and give up. That worry that she might remember her no-love rule and leave. Because, of course, that might still happen. No one knows what's just around the corner. But with Alice's help, I've learned to appreciate what's right here in front of me. And tonight, the most beautiful sunbeam of a woman is trying to get me to attempt body-popping.

After a couple of semi-successful attempts, Alice is roaring with laughter.

'I forgot the last clue!' She says, eyes dropping back to the laptop.

'Ah, yes. Would you mind waiting here for five minutes while I put the finishing touches on it. No looking! No cheating.'

'*Clue eight: Your XXXXXXX make my heart pop.* A seven letter word? Bloody hell, Zach. Is it filthy?' I'm back in the living room and Alice is trying out some potential words, counting their letters on her fingers. 'Hmm. Can't think of anything boob or butt related.' She leans back on the sofa, the Sweet Valley High theme tune currently playing from the laptop.

'Flowers? Is it flowers? Though why would they make your heart pop. I mean I know I'm good at my job and everything.'

'Want more of a clue?'

'Wouldn't that be cheating?'

'What, like when you jabbed me in the ribs on our jogging date so you could overtake me?'

Alice chortles. 'All right then.'

'Look at the last word of the clue.'

'Pop. What pops? Pringles?'

'That's eight letters.' I shake my head.

'Pop pop pop. Pop ya collar, ha ha, good old Usher. Ooh, wait, pop a cork. Is it bubbles?'

I click my fingers. 'Bingo! I actually wanted to go for effervescence but that felt a bit too long so you got bubbles instead. Well done. Now, where to find some?'

But Alice has already raced out of the room.

Alice gasps as she steps into her kitchen, now lit with candles on every surface. I spent the last five minutes hanging up polaroid pictures of us in here and attaching an X-shaped balloon to a bottle of fizz in the middle of her kitchen table, two of her mum's champagne saucers next to it.

She looks at me, eyes filled with curiosity.

'I found the X,' she says, suddenly ever-so-slightly shy as she points towards the balloon.

'Congratulations,' I say, heart halfway up my throat as the nerves take hold.

'Is that the English sparkling wine I drank most of at our wine tasting date?'

'You said you liked it.'

'I did.' She bounds over to the balloon and I steel myself. Alice's eyes are on me as spots the key I've attached to the bottom of the balloon.

'What's this?'

'It's a key to, um, my house. I wanted to . . .'

'Oh Zach that's so sweet,' Alice interrupts. 'So now I can pop round without having to ring the bell.'

No! That's not it.

'Actually I . . .'

But Alice is on a roll. 'I could get you one cut for here too, if

263

you'd like? I'd have to check with Natalie first but I'm sure she wouldn't mind.'

Fuck. I thought I'd been really clear but she's misunderstood. Hastily I take the envelope I'd left underneath the key and slide it into my pocket while she's not looking. She seems so happy with just having a key to let herself in, I can't bring myself to ask her what I really wanted to.

Alice turns back to me and kisses me deeply on the lips before pulling back with a big smile on her face. 'This feels like a big step for us.'

Then she pauses. 'Sorry to kill the mood but would you mind pouring us the drinks while I nip to the loo? All that running around! I'll be back in two mins.'

Alice dashes upstairs and I find myself standing in the kitchen at a loss, the envelope I quickly stuffed into my pocket now making its presence known. I pull it out, the last envelope in her scavenger hunt and the one she'll never get to see.

Inside is my handwritten note and a butterscotch yellow keychain which I had embossed with *A-Z*.

Alice, will you make my house a home and move in with me?

It's too late to explain what the scavenger hunt was really about now. Alice thinks having a key to my house is a big step so there's no way I can ask her to move in with me. I tear at the casing on the champagne bottle, gutted that my plans for tonight have gone wrong. Maybe I was wrong. Maybe we're on completely different pages, after all. Once again I find myself moving at a million miles an hour while Alice is still idling happily in her own time zone.

'Are you okay?' She asks, walking back into the kitchen to find me grumpily wrangling with the wine bottle. 'Here, let me.'

She takes it from my hand and pops the cork, laughing with delight as sparkling wine fizzes out and over her fingers.

'I can't believe you gave me a key and trust me to let myself in,' she beams. 'To us?'

264

I watch her eyes light up as she holds a drink out for me. It's not what I thought we'd be toasting to but I find myself raising my glass anyway.

'To us,' I agree.

Yoga

Alice

I went for tie-dye harem pants and a maroon T-shirt with the words 'You Had Me At Namaste' written on it for today's date. Not my usual choice, I'll admit, but I thought it would be fun to try some actual yoga and not just the sit at home, eating cake on my yoga mat with Natalie type. Besides, Zach loves exercising and he's seemed a bit distracted all week so I thought this would help him de-stress.

He's standing outside the studio when I arrive and I can see him do a double take of my ensemble.

'Hey,' I beam, reaching up to kiss him.

He smiles down at me but there's something missing. His usual spark. I was utterly touched by the treasure hunt he'd set up for our last date but he's seemed a little bit lacklustre ever since and I can't for the life of my figure out why.

'I'm guessing we're doing yoga?'

'Ten points! Was it the invitation to join me at a yoga studio that gave you your first clue? Maybe I should do a scavenger hunt for you next time.'

'Always teasing,' he says with a smile.

'Come on, let's go and stretch it out. I know you've been stressed with all the house renovations you're doing on top of everything else, so I thought yoga could be a great way to unwind.'

Our instructor is called Ocean, a wiry, red-haired man with a South Yorkshire accent which leads me to the conclusion that Ocean may not be his actual name. He's definitely big into water, though. The sound of crashing waves floats from the studio's sound system and Ocean is wearing a pair of cropped but baggy blue shorts with a nautical print on them. And nothing else. Once the room has filled, he rolls out his mat at the front and switches off the sounds of the sea.

'Heyyyyyyyyy,' he says in a soft, lilting voice, motioning for us all to sit down. 'Welcome. Today we'll be practising with no music so that we can completely tune into our own bodies.'

Oh no. Please don't let me fart. I've only done two classes at this studio before and let's just say that I learned an important lesson about why you should never do group yoga after a cannellini bean wrap for lunch. At least that time there'd been background noise so I could look around accusingly, hoping no one could pinpoint me as the source.

'During today's flow we'll focus on our upper bodies. Easing from one movement to the next. No jamming or forcing, just letting ourselves flowwwwww.'

Zach shoots me a look.

I bite my lip.

We start with our legs crossed and our palms at our hearts and I try very hard to listen to Ocean as he talks about clearing our minds. Mine is totally clear, I think. Absolutely empty. Did I use the last of the milk this morning? I should get some on the way home. No, focus on the flow. Did I lock up the flower shop last night?

'Anyone find their minds wandering?' Ocean asks and I realise he's now standing right next to my mat.

I shake my head serenely.

'Now to breathing,' he says, taking a deep breath in through his nose and exhaling with an extremely loud AHHHHH sound through his mouth.

'Inhale,' he instructs and the sound of about fifteen people breathing in fills the room.

'Exhale AHHH.'

We all attempt a tiny ahh.

'Louder,' instructs Ocean.

'AHHH.'

'LOUDER.' Ocean practically barks this, losing his seascape voice for a second, and I jolt one eye open. After breathing in, I see Zach opening his mouth wide and I follow suit, trying not to giggle.

'ARRRRRRGGGHHHHHHHH.' We all but shout as we breathe out, tittering to ourselves.

Bridge pose isn't going so well for Zach. I can hear his bones creaking as he tries to push himself up, wobbling for a second before collapsing back down on his back.

'This is very undignified,' he whispers over to me.

I love how much he's trying.

Ocean pads over to Zach, crouching down until his bum practically hits the floor. So bendy, I marvel. 'Looks like we have a yoga newbie here,' he says. 'What other sports do you do?'

'I'm a runner and I do a lot of rock climbing,' Zach replies.

'Oh dear, oh dear. Verrrrryyyyy tight,' says Ocean, running a hand across Zach's broad shoulders. 'Let's try some simpler stretches for you, try to ease out those muscles.'

After that, the entire class is basically ignored while Ocean pervs on my boyfriend. Zach looks mildly flattered and quite a bit embarrassed as Ocean leads him up to the front, positioning their mats together so he can demonstrate to the rest of the class how to get a flat back.

'Going back to basics is super important, even for seasoned

268

yogis,' he says, bending Zach over and running a hand down his spine. I try hard not to snort. By the end of the session, Zach's been handed a leaflet and instructed to attend every week from now on. His cheeks are adorably pink as he finally extracts himself from ohms with Ocean and when we're back out on the street, we both burst into laughter.

'Well, at least I know that if it all goes tits up with you I've got options,' he says.

I jab him in the side.

'Hey! I actually don't think it will go tits up, thanks very much. And if it does, you are not leaving me for a yoga instructor called Ocean. Deal?'

'How about I'm not leaving you, full stop?'

My heart flutters as I take the hand he's extended and we shake on it.

We head out for breakfast at Tamper in town afterwards and as we read through the menu I find myself wondering how many people are drawn to Zach like Ocean was, like I am. He's the roaring fire on a freezing cold night that you just want to inch closer and closer towards. And yet he doesn't seem to realise it.

'What can I get for you guys?' asks a member of staff.

In an ideal world I'd be following up yoga with some kind of smoothie bowl or maybe some avocado on toast but, let's face it, that's just not what I'm about. I opt for their version of a full English while Zach chooses the salt beef benedict.

'Sounds good,' I smile at him when our menus have been cleared away. 'So, how did you find the class?'

Zach stretches his arms behind his head. 'I'll be feeling it tomorrow.'

'Me too. My calves are going to be on fire after all those downward dogs.'

Zach nods, unwrapping his cutlery from the napkin and looking around the busy café. It's packed in here already, filled with people catching up over a lazy weekend brunch or fuelling themselves before a day of shopping in town. And Zach and I . . . who don't seem to have much to say to each other.

Our coffees arrive and I start up an overenthusiastic conversation with the person who brought our drinks until she's called away to another table.

I look at Zach. He catches my eye and looks away.

'What's going on?' I ask.

'Nothing, you?'

'Nothing! You've been quiet all day . . .'

'I guess I'm a bit preoccupied,' he shrugs.

'You know you can talk to me about stuff. Is there anything I can help with?'

Zach sighs and stares off into the distance.

'Am *I* the problem?' I ask.

'No, Alice, you're not the problem at all.'

He's interrupted by the arrival of our food. My breakfast is so huge it barely fits on the table and I'm starving but I can't bring myself to start eating. Zach is definitely being off and it's making me worried.

'What is it then?' I ask as Zach takes a slow sip of coffee.

'That treasure hunt last week? It didn't end how I'd planned it to end,' he says, picking up his cutlery and piercing a poached egg. Yolk runs down and into a pool around the toasted muffin.

'You mean you had something else in mind?' I ask, racking my brains as to what that might be.

'Well, yeah. I didn't mean for the key to be just an open invitation for you to come round whenever. I would love for you to come around whenever, obviously. But it was going to be more than that.'

'In what way?'

'I was going to ask you to move in with me, Alice.'

My breath catches in my throat. The plate of food I'd been so looking forward to devouring is now the last thing on my mind.

'You want me to move in with you?'

'Yes. But then you were talking about what a big step it was to have a key to my place and I froze. I didn't know what to do. So I hid the last envelope and just went along with it.'

'I feel like an idiot. I just assumed it was a key for, like, getting into the house more easily?' I scratch my forehead uneasily, feeling stupid for jumping to the wrong conclusions. Things had been going so well between us, too. 'I had no idea that's what you had planned.'

Zach runs a hand through his dark, wild hair and gives me an awkward look.

'I think that's the problem,' he says. 'Will we ever want the same things?'

I lean back in my chair, suddenly exhausted.

'I want you,' I say simply.

'Is that enough, though?'

'I will never be the person with the five year plan, Zach. I don't have the kind of agenda so many other people do. I can't tell you where we will be in the future and I hate that that hurts you, but I just can't make any promises right now. I love you. Surely that's all we need to know.'

Zach breaks eye contact and looks down at his breakfast. I do the same.

'I actually need to head off,' he says.

'But we haven't finished breakfast,' I point out, noticing how downcast he looks and feeling like I could cry.

'Have some for me?' he suggests with forced joviality as he gets up to leave.

Zucchini

Zach

All that's left to do is unpack a box of books and fix a few paintings to the freshly painted walls. It's been a long time in the making but I'm so close to feeling like my house is now a home. I thought I'd be elated walking around here now that the renovations are finally finished. And I do, in a sense. I'm proud of how it looks and for all of the hard work I've put in but there's an Alice-shaped piece of the jigsaw missing in here. I'm so annoyed with myself for bringing up the moving in thing after yoga yesterday. She didn't need to know that I was planning to ask her to live with me and I went and told her anyway. How many times do I need to remind myself that Alice likes to move at a slow pace? How many more times will I put my foot in it? I was so frustrated with myself that I had to get out of there.

The morning passes with all of the little jobs I've been putting off. Unloading the dishwasher. Sticking a load in the washing machine. Unpeeling masking tape from the skirting board in my living room. Finally, I'm ripping open the box of books and about to stack my bookshelf when the doorbell rings. I go to answer it, vaguely wondering whether it's the toaster I ordered online arriving early. I'm pretty hungry so a slice of buttered toast wouldn't go amiss.

A crisp, autumnal breeze blows in through the front door and I wrap my arms around myself as I stare outside to find no one there. The only thing on my doorstep is a familiar-looking plant. I kneel down to take a closer look.

'Saskia?' I say out loud, before glancing up and down the street. What will the neighbours think if they see me talking to a plant? It does look a lot like Alice's favourite plant but it can't be.

Can it?

Then Alice steps into my vision. She's pulled a hat down over her long, wavy hair and the fluffy pompom on top wobbles as she moves onto my doorstep.

'Were you hiding?' I ask tentatively.

'Maybe,' she says. 'After your sharp exit yesterday I wasn't sure if you'd want to see me again . . .'

'I will always want to see you again.'

'That's good, because now that you've finished work on your house and all, I thought I'd bring you a housewarming gift.' She points towards the plant she's standing next to.

'That's really kind of you. Did you clone Saskia?'

'That *is* Saskia!'

'What will you do without her?'

Alice rubs her hands together for warmth before her eyes meet mine. That instant connection I've felt with her all along ignites once again, like a switch being turned on.

'Well wherever Saskia goes, I go. So ask me again, Zach.'

She's jigging about on the doorstep, trying to stay warm while a smile lights up her face.

Ask her again? She can't mean . . .?

It's worth a shot.

I train my eyes on hers, nerves jangling. 'Alice, will you move in with me?'

She laughs. 'YES. I would love nothing more than that, Zach.'

In an instant I pull her into my arms, breathing her in and feeling like I might explode with happiness. She said yes.

273

'You didn't think I would just give you Saskia did you? We're a package deal,' Alice says, the pompom tickling my chin as she looks up at me. She pulls the hat off her head and stuffs it into her bag, turning to face me and we kiss right there on the doorstep of my house, which now feels exactly like the home I'd hoped it would be.

Alice is running her fingers across every surface of our home, stopping now and then to make comments about how different things look since the last time she saw it. It reminds me of our second date at the bookshop, when I watched her flick through the pages of the books we were looking at. That same curiosity, interest, zest for life. All of the things I've come to love so much about her.

'So this is *our* mantelpiece, huh?' she says, pausing in the living room with her eyes wide.

I nod in confirmation, still buzzing from the news that this incredible woman will be moving in with me. She moves into the kitchen.

'And this is *our* fridge?'

'Correct,' I laugh.

She opens it up and gives me a look. 'I'm obviously going to need to be in charge of filling it.'

'You can be in charge of whatever you'd like,' I say.

'That's good, because there's no way I'm living in a house where the only comestibles appear to be parmesan cheese, a ready-made pizza and a four-pack of beer.'

I hold my hands up. 'In my defence, I did not know you would be coming here today. If I had the fridge would be filled with your favourite things.'

'You are my favourite thing,' Alice smiles, shutting the fridge door and stepping into the middle of the kitchen. 'The house looks really good, Zach.'

'Would you like a proper tour? The bathroom's finished and my . . . our bedroom is painted now, too.'

'I would like a proper tour. Do you have a tour guide hat?'

'I'm afraid not, ma'am,' I say, doffing an imaginary cap instead.

'Here,' she says, pulling her bobble hat down onto my head and failing not to laugh when it barely fits. Before I have time to protest, she's grabbed her phone, opened the camera and is ordering me to smile. Then she doubles over in a fit of laughter after examining the picture.

'I'm not sure pompom hats are my thing,' I object.

'You look like a Smurf.'

'Exactly.'

'A really cute Smurf,' she says, reaching her arms around my back. I circle mine around her body and we stand together for a moment, eyes locked, promise in the air.

'Alice, I am very keen to give you a tour of our bedroom now.'

'Is that a euphemism?'

'Very much so. But I am going to insist on taking this hat off first.'

She grins at me, standing on tiptoes to remove it. 'Fine, but I should let you know that I fully intend to have that photo printed, turned into a magnet and stuck on our fridge. Just as a reminder of the time we decided to live together and when you looked like a Smurf.' She fake-whispers the last bit and I reach for her hands, curling them behind my back again.

'Something tells me that the fridge isn't the only thing you'll be in charge of once we're living together,' I say, knowing full well that Alice will breathe life into every single aspect of our home when she moves in.

'How about that tour, then?'

'These . . . are . . . the . . . stairs . . .' I say, punctuating each word with a kiss as I lead her up to our bedroom and open the door. 'This . . . is . . . the . . . new . . . door which, actually, I found in a scrap yard and reclaimed myself—'

'Zach,' she interrupts, pulling her yellow jumper over her head. 'I don't think now is the time for renovation chat?'

She's peeling off more clothes as she backs into our bedroom, until she's standing butt naked at the foot of the bed.

'Agreed,' I say, following suit.

I'd say 90 per cent of the day is spent in bed, punctuated only by trips to the kitchen to fetch drinks. I'm very hot, very happy and absolutely knackered by the time Alice has finished with me.

She's lying on her front, circling her fingers on my chest, when both of our stomachs rumble in tandem.

'Shall we order in?' I suggest.

'You read my mind,' she grins, flicking through Deliveroo. 'I've worked up quite an appetite.'

An hour later I'm trying to look like the kind of guy who knows how to handle chopsticks as we get stuck into a sushi platter, spearing maki rolls and dipping them in soy sauce.

'So we should probably plan this out properly,' says Alice, looking like she's surprised herself by using the words 'we' and 'plan' in the same sentence. 'Now that we're going to live together and all.'

'That sounds very sensible.'

'I've been thinking about it. Obviously there's my house to deal with and I want to make sure Nat feels totally comfortable with everything, too, so I'll need to have a chat with her. But I was thinking maybe I could chat to my landlady and see if she'll transfer the rental over to Natalie's name? That way Nat doesn't face any upheaval. She's had enough of that already since things with Jake ended.'

I nod. 'That sounds good. As long as Nat's happy, I can't see that there'd be a problem in transferring the rental agreement.'

'And then I'll just have to pack.'

'Gerty and I will be at your service to move everything over.'

'The house came furnished so it's not like there's any massive stuff to move.'

'And Saskia's already here . . .'

'Exactly! I just need to get boxes and stuff and then, I guess I could have everything packed within a week?'

I reach out to hold her hand. 'As soon as you're ready.'

The next morning, I wake up before Alice and watch her stir, stretching under the duvet in our bedroom. It still doesn't feel quite real, like I can't quite believe that this beautiful, brilliant woman has agreed to move in with me.

'Good morning Zach,' she murmurs. 'Good morning Saskia.'

The houseplant has taken up residency in the corner of my bedroom, which was one of the few things we managed to achieve yesterday other than having a lot of sex, eating sushi and coming up with a few plans. It was the perfect day.

'I've been thinking,' I say, kissing her good morning. 'We should mark this momentous occasion. How about we do something to celebrate you officially moving in next weekend? We could combine it with our next alphabet date.'

'Sounds really good. I'd better go and talk to Natalie,' she says, reluctantly inching towards the shower. I grab hold of her hand and bring her back into my arms.

'Could it wait a little longer?'

Later that week, I take a break from heaving another round of boxes into the house and look at Alice. It's Friday night and there's still at least one more car-load to bring over before she officially moves in tomorrow.

'I don't want to be rude but I did not expect you to have so much stuff. We might actually need to find a bigger house to fit all your clothes in though I am impressed with how quickly you've managed to pack all this.'

'I can be very efficient when I want to,' she says. 'And pipe down, I have a perfectly normal amount of stuff.'

'You try saying that after you've carried boxes with things like 'Memories', 'Summer Sandals' and 'Misc. Scarves' written on them up two flights of stairs. How can you even fill a box with miscellaneous scarves?'

'You can never have too many. You're not regretting asking me to move in already, are you?'

'Never. Are you regretting saying yes?'

'Nope. Though it was a bit presumptuous of you to have A-Z stamped into the key fob when we'd only got to our X date . . .'

'Oh really? I decided it was high time to take a chance on you.'

'*You're* taking a chance on *me*? Please. It's definitely the other way around,' Alice says, nudging me in the ribs.

'I just asked a girl known as The Bolter to move in with me . . .'

'How did you know about that nickname?' She says, looking mortified.

'Dylan mentioned it a while back.'

'God he's an idiot. It's true though, they did used to call me that. I have never been in a relationship where I've wanted to stay before.'

I clear my throat. 'I'm not sure I properly apologised for what happened after yoga a couple of weeks ago.'

'When you ran off after breakfast?'

'I was overthinking the key misunderstanding and I let it get to me but seeing you here on my doorstep last weekend put my mind at rest, once and for all.'

'Funnily enough, turning up on your doorstep did the same for me,' she says. 'It felt so right. How about we agree not to make any more of a habit of bolting?' Alice suggests, wrapping her arms around me.

'I am more than happy with that.'

She pulls a photo frame out of her bag, carefully wrapped in tissue paper. I've seen it countless times by her bed at her house. A photo of Alice as a little girl with her mum and dad, sitting high up on a cliff, their hair whipping around their faces and their cheeks pink. Her mum is holding onto a flower crown, which Alice told me she made for her that windy day on a family holiday in Cornwall. The three of them are bunched up together on a rock, squinting into the bright sunshine, their faces creased with laughter. 'Do you mind if I put this in your . . . our bedroom?'

'Of course not. Are you okay?'

'Just missing Mum,' she shrugs. 'I always get like this when something big happens. Like when I got the keys to my flower shop. I will always want to be able to share these big, brilliant moments with my mum, so they will always be tinged with sadness.'

I scoop her up in my arms and kiss her gently on the forehead.

'Do you think she'd approve of us moving in together?' I ask after a pause.

Alice turns to look straight at me, a smile curling at her lips. 'Approve? She'd be beyond thrilled, Zach. She'd probably be baking us cakes and suggesting furniture options for the house. Mum always said that love was the most important thing.'

The next morning I'm awake far earlier than usual, adrenaline coursing through my veins from the minute I blink my eyes open. Today's the day. This is the last time I'll be waking up in this house by myself. The last time I'll roll over to see an empty side of the bed. The last time I'll get first dibs on the shower, no doubt. I count down the minutes until it's an acceptable time to drive over to Alice's, relishing the fact that this is the last of these journeys I'll make before she officially moves in.

I pull up outside her house and Alice flings the door open, bounding over to me.

'Today's the day. Come in for coffee?' She asks, her words tripping out even faster than usual.

Inside, Natalie hands me a box of bubble wrapped vases with a theatrical scowl on her face, then turns to Alice. 'You will obviously be coming back to hang out with me, like, seven nights a week, right?'

'For sure. Well, maybe one?' Alice says.

'Oh I see. You spent the start of the summer encouraging me to stand on my own two feet and now you've had the audacity to go totally off-brand and get a boyfriend, I get left behind? This is all your fault, Zach.'

I set the box down and hold my hands up.

'You leave him out of it,' Alice laughs. 'And as if you're getting left behind. You're finally making some sensible choices.'

'You're right,' Nat grins. 'Boys were clouding my vision and I am so good on my own, now. As for you? Shutting love out was clouding your vision. You two are too cute together. You deserve to be completely happy.'

'The funny thing is, I thought I already was. But Zach's brought this whole other level to my life. I'm ready for this, now,' Alice says, grabbing my hand. 'Part of it is thanks to you, Zach, and a lot of it is how I've grown as a person, under my own steam. I finally feel ready to let some new stuff in and to be brave. I thought romance was the last thing I needed but with Zach in my life, it feels as essential as oxygen.'

If I could bottle the things Alice just said, I would.

Natalie pretends to throw up. 'Jesus guys, I'm still here you know? How about you wait 'til you get back to your own pad before you go all Ed Sheeran on me?'

'Shall we, then? Head home?' Alice asks me.

'I'd love that.'

We pull up outside my house and I race out of the car so that I can open the door for Alice.

'So chivalrous,' she laughs.

'You know what's next?'

'Don't tell me, you're going to insist on carrying me over the threshold.'

'That's exactly right.'

'Oh hell no. It's not the nineteen fifties any more, Zach.'

'I am well aware of that,' I grin. 'But you know how I love

a romcom and this the perfect opportunity for a romantic moment . . ?'

She covers her face with her hands. 'Okay fine.'

I scoop her into my arms, kicking the passenger door shut with my foot and carrying her towards the house as she gets the giggles.

'People can see,' she snorts.

Turns out it's not so easy carrying the woman of your dreams into your new home when your house is locked and you can't find your keys. I have to set her down, jog back to Gerty to find the house keys and then run back to her.

This time she leaps up and we're both roaring with laughter as I carry her inside.

'Welcome home,' I say before I notice the flowers. They are everywhere.

'I picked some of my favourites,' Alice beams, watching my reaction. 'I gave Eve my house key and she snuck in while we finished up packing. I thought it would be nice to make everywhere look super cosy before our date tonight.'

'That's really thoughtful of you,' I say, kissing her. 'I've a little gift for you too.'

I lead her through to the living room and hand her a leather-bound sketchbook. She takes it out of my hands and opens it up. On every page is a pencil sketch I've done after each of our alphabet dates. Alice traces her fingers across the trailing ivy on page one, laughing at the memory of how we first met, when I'd wondered why a guest at my first art exhibition spent most of the night taking pictures of the plants by the toilets. The pastries we ate on our second date. A sketch of her face lighting up with laughter at the comedy gig we went to.

'Zach, did you draw these after every single one of our dates?' she asks quietly.

'I figured pretty early on that I wanted a memento from every day I spent with you. It became a bit like writing a diary for me, sitting down and sketching out my favourite memory after each date. It kept the spirit of our dates going for even longer for me. Like keeping a little piece of you with me the whole time.'

'I'm speechless.'

She moves slowly through each one. The sunrise on our dog walk, the glitterball from our eighties disco, the picnic at the film festival and Alice sat in the deckchair at her allotment on our gardening date. She pauses at happy hour, where I'd meant to draw a cocktail but gone kind of abstract in my fury that I'd ballsed things up. She lingers over a drawing of the supermoon, with us stood in front of it at the top of the park.

'One of my favourite dates,' I say.

'You've captured the whole date perfectly,' she smiles.

Then she laughs as she comes to a drawing of her tucked up in bed after our oyster date. 'I'm very grateful you didn't capture any other scenes from that night.' There's the rock we climbed, the panda and the hummingbird we decided were our spirit animals in Avignon . . .

Alice's voice catches in her throat. 'These are so beautiful. Each and every one. Though you haven't done one for Z yet.'

'That's because our Z date hasn't happened! Date night is tonight,' I point out, touched that she likes the sketches.

'Well,' she says, closing the book and laying it carefully down on the coffee table. 'You're absolutely right. Though I do wonder what we're going to be doing that's Z related, unless you're copping out and calling it a Zach date.'

'I had no intentions of doing that. Why don't you leave me to it for a bit, make yourself feel at home? Date starts at seven.'

I've watched Nonna cook this recipe so many times over the years. When Raff and I were kids we'd fight over whose turn it was to grate the parmesan and measure out the vermouth. Then we'd sit out on the terrace, still warm from another Italian summer's day, and if we were lucky Nonna would pour us each a little glass of wine to go with our meal. I smile as I slice up the courgettes now, a mountain of freshly grated parmesan in the bowl next to me. I cannot wait to share this with Alice.

Bang on seven o'clock, she appears in the kitchen wearing that shining blue silk dress she wore for her birthday in Avignon. She looks beautiful, like a midnight sky.

'That's a lot of courgettes for two people,' she points out.

'Or as we Italians like to say, zucchini . . .'

'Aha, our Z date! Zach's famous zucchini pasta? The one Ellie and Raf served at their wedding?'

I nod, chuffed that she's remembered.

'Well then, I'm honoured. And quite hungry. When are we eating?'

'In about half an hour,' I say, incredibly content to be cooking my girlfriend this special dish in our home together.

'Perfect. That gives me time to get my Halloween display on. Remember those pumpkin seeds you sowed at my allotment? They actually grew.'

'There's no need to sound so surprised!'

Alice straightens her face up. 'I harvested them earlier this week. Look.' She holds up a bag filled with pumpkins of different shapes and sizes. 'I'm going to paint some and dot them around the fireplace.' She tips the pumpkins onto the kitchen table and gets to work, while I chop, slice and steam my way through dinner prep. Every now and then I take a forkful over to Alice to try, which she eats appreciatively while asking my opinion on the pumpkin colour scheme.

Together we lay the dining table, covering it in a navy blue table cloth which Alice decides works perfectly with her newly painted pumpkins.

'Dinner's up,' I call, bringing out a massive bowl of zucchini pasta and serving some onto our plates. Alice sprinkles on parmesan and makes appreciative 'yum' noises.

'A toast,' I say, standing up and popping the cork on a bottle of champagne. 'Alice, you danced into my life at the start of the summer and set my heart on fire. It's been blazing ever since. Never have I met a woman so stubborn, so competitive and so completely and utterly wonderful. You've challenged me every step of the way, even down to my taste in pastries.'

Alice laughs.

'You are so full of life, so fun to spend time with and I am grateful every day that you took a chance on me. You didn't have to navigate my insecurities, but you did and now look where we are. My house would never have been filled with such love if it weren't for you. Thank you for the last twenty-six dates. Here's to many more.'

Alice gets up, looking almost bashful at this outpouring of love.

'I know there will still be hurdles to cross for us together,' she says. 'But I also know that we will make the decisions together, as a couple. I'm happier now than I have ever been. It felt like a huge risk, taking a chance on love, and I don't think the fear that my heart may yet get broken will ever go away. But I feel so much stronger now and I wanted to thank you, Zach. I thought love was the last thing I needed. I was wrong. You're the start to my finish. I'm the A to your Z. We're like pieces of a jigsaw puzzle and I cannot wait to see what the future holds for us. To an alphabet's worth of love!'

'A to Z,' I say, clinking her glass and curling my arm around her waist. We share a lingering kiss before sitting back down and digging into the zucchini pasta.

'This is so good,' Alice says. 'You know, I've been waiting a long time for this dish.'

'Was it worth the wait?'

'Let's just say that this is by far our best date yet. But Zach, now that the alphabet is up, what will we do?'

I look deep into her sea green eyes.

'Exactly this,' I say simply. 'The letters may have run out but my love for you never will.'

Acknowledgements

Firstly I'd like to thank Katie Seaman at HQ for offering me such fantastic encouragement, not to mention unparalleled editorial judgement, when it came to writing this. You have been a joy to work with and together we have crafted a book that I am super proud of.

Thank you to all at Harper Collins for welcoming me on board and to my superb agent Amanda Preston, plus all the team at LBA, for your continued support.

To my husband, who whisked our twins off on multiple adventures while I was on a deadline, to my parents, who have been pillars of strength, and to my best friends, who are such rays of sunshine. Thank you.

Thank you to the book bloggers who spread so much bookish love and the authors who have continued to write fabulous tomes through these challenging times. What a great big bunch of champs you are.

And finally, thank YOU for reading this book all the way through to the thanks-fest that is the acknowledgments section . . . That's commitment! I really hope this book has made you smile. I do love a chat so please come and say hello, you can find me on Instagram, Twitter and Facebook @byhannahdoyle.

H x

Dear Reader,

We hope you enjoyed reading this book. If you did, we'd be so appreciative if you left a review. It really helps us and the author to bring more books like this to you.

Here at HQ Digital we are dedicated to publishing fiction that will keep you turning the pages into the early hours. Don't want to miss a thing? To find out more about our books, promotions, discover exclusive content and enter competitions you can keep in touch in the following ways:

JOIN OUR COMMUNITY:
Sign up to our new email newsletter:
http://smarturl.it/SignUpHQ
Read our new blog www.hqstories.co.uk
🐦 : https://twitter.com/HQStories
f : www.facebook.com/HQStories

BUDDING WRITER?
We're also looking for authors to join the HQ Digital family!
Find out more here:
https://www.hqstories.co.uk/want-to-write-for-us/
Thanks for reading, from the HQ Digital team

ONE PLACE. MANY STORIES

If you enjoyed *The A to Z of Us*, then why not try another delightfully uplifting romance from HQ Digital?